Praise for

J.S. MONROE

'The most ingenious thriller you will read this year. I couldn't put it down'

MJ ARLIDGE

'A book that will send chills down your spine'

SUNDAY EXPRESS

'Clever, convincing...
Highly recommended'

MICK HERRON

'Original and brilliantly plotted... Amazing'

ROSAMUND LUPTON

'Pacy and propulsive'

DAILY TELEGRAPH

'An intelligent and inventive thriller'

JP DELANEY

'Brilliantly original...
Kept me guessing to the very end'

PETER JAMES

Also by J.S. Monroe

Find Me
Forget My Name
The Other You
The Man on Hackpen Hill
No Place to Hide

HIS FINAL PATIENT

J.S. MONROE

HEAD of ZEUS

An Aries Book

First published in the UK in 2026 by Head of Zeus,
part of Bloomsbury Publishing Plc

9 7 5 3 1 2 4 6 8

A catalogue record for this book is available from the British Library.

ISBN (PB): 9781801109437
ISBN (eBook): 9781801109390

Cover design: Gemma Gorton | Head of Zeus

Printed and bound in Great Britain by Clays Ltd, Elcograf S.p.A.

MIX
Paper | Supporting responsible forestry
FSC® C018072

Bloomsbury Publishing Plc
50 Bedford Square, London, WC1B 3DP, UK
Bloomsbury Publishing Ireland Limited,
29 Earlsfort Terrace, Dublin 2, D02 AY28, Ireland

HEAD OF ZEUS LTD
5–8 Hardwick Street
London, EC1R 4RG

To find out more about our authors and books
visit www.headofzeus.com
For product safety related questions contact productsafety@bloomsbury.com

HIS FINAL PATIENT

For Hilary

"She philosophically noted dates as they came past in the revolution of the year. Her own birthday, and every other day individualised by incidents in which she had taken some share. She suddenly thought, one afternoon, that there was another date, of greater importance than all those; that of her own death; a day which lay sly and unseen among all the other days of the year, giving no sign or sound when she annually passed over it; but not the less surely there. When was it?"

—Thomas Hardy, *Tess of the D'Urbervilles*

1

You didn't believe me at first.

"If it's real, why isn't it happening to me?" you used to cry.

To be fair, I'm not sure I believed it either in the early days. Or maybe I just didn't think it was anything special. I can't have been more than five, the first time it happened. We'd recently moved down from Edinburgh to Wiltshire – Dad had a new job – and I remember walking into the sitting room, which was full of packing boxes. I jumped with fright, as if I'd heard something, and then – a second later, that was the strange thing, it was a second afterwards – the clock on the mantelpiece started to chime.

I kept quiet about it for a while. I wasn't scared, but I just didn't think anyone would be particularly interested. In the same way that children are unaware of skin colour, I was "time blind", untroubled by small discrepancies in chronology. One day, after I heard the phone start to ring,

I knew that it was Uncle Dougal, Dad's brother, before anyone answered. Dougal hadn't rung for months and there had been no recent mention of him. So how did I know it was him on the phone? I just did. I decided to tell Dad and remembered this slow smile creep across his face like a melting glacier, as if he'd been waiting for the day when I would tell him. He didn't say I was being silly, or that I was imagining things; he just disappeared into his study and emerged with a pack of hand-drawn cards.

You and I had often played pairs with Dad in front of a roaring fire on cold winter afternoons, but this was different. Someone, Dad I presume, had drawn coloured images of planes, bottles and sailing boats on little square pieces of cardboard. They were well worn and kept in a red cigarette tin with "Benson & Hedges, British European Airways" printed on the lid.

To begin with, he laid them out like playing cards, face down on the kitchen table. He would point at a card and ask me what the image was on the other side. Each time, he would carefully note down the results in a notebook. He was a very precise man – think bicycle clips, pencil-thin moustache, immaculate fingernails – and his writing was neat and small. Unusual, I realise now, for a doctor. Variations soon followed. He'd place a card in the tin, close it and ask me to guess the image. And then he'd ask one of us to hold the card and the other one to say what it was. It was all about getting different "senders".

He was always keen to include you – maybe as the control for his experiments – and sometimes you'd guess the card correctly. Sometimes. Dad was encouraging – "keep going, you're doing well" – but it was clear that your successes were down to nothing more than chance. I don't remember ever getting any of them wrong, even when he placed the card in the tin. I could always see the images so clearly, particularly if Dad was concentrating on the card. The connection seemed to drop when he was distracted or had turned away. We had to stop the tests because of your tantrums.

"It's not real if it's not happening to me!" you'd wail, over and over. "It's not real!"

Later that night, I saw you practising with the cards in your room, as if you were performing a magic trick. Again and again, you dealt out the cards, spreading them out across your bed. But it was never about sleight of hand. Never about chance.

Dad was very patient with both of us, our different needs. When he was home in time, he loved to read us tales from Greek and Roman mythology. I would sit and listen, you would bounce around the bedroom, unable to concentrate. So he'd close the book and tell the stories – Theseus and the Minotaur, the twelve labours of Hercules, Jason and the Argonauts – in his own words, involving us whenever he could. That got your attention, particularly when he was Medusa and we were both turned to stone. You would get bored in the end, though, and walk off, unable to sit still. And that's when he would bring out the cards and test me again, almost as if he were making absolutely sure. Sometimes, he would send me from the room and hide an old coin. I always knew where to find it.

"It's a gift, truly remarkable," he used to say to me. "Use it wisely."

2

Present day

DI Silas Hart knows he should be happy. It's his birthday, for God's sake. Mel, his wife, gave him a special present this morning. Even Conor, their son, called on his way to work without asking to borrow money. And his colleagues have bought a cake – sitting on his desk now, a solitary candle guttering into the cheap icing as they sing "Happy Birthday". But he's not happy. He's scared. A profound, lingering fear sits in his stomach like a malignant tumour, growing bigger by the day.

"We didn't know how old you were, sir," DS Strover, his colleague, whispers, nodding at the candle. He's glad Strover's here today. A mind and demeanour as tidy as her desk, she couldn't be more different from him, but she's his only real ally in the office. They look out for each other, have done for the ten years they've worked together. She's got a first-class degree in forensic science; he has intuition – at least, that's what he tells himself. Whatever it is they don't teach at university.

Strover's also the one person who's aware of how much he hates office celebrations, and that they've only remembered because HR has started to circulate birthday reminders to everyone in a misguided attempt to foster "workplace wellbeing". HR probably bought the cake too. At least it's not Colin the Caterpillar.

Hart waits for the singing to stop before he leans forward and obliges with a puff. A short stab of pain in his chest triggers the usual cascade of health worries. A few weeks back, his doctor had written "SoBoE?" in his medical record. The NHS app will be the end of him, sending him running to Dr Google with all its acronyms. Shortness of breath on exertion? He's an athlete, his body a temple; he hasn't smoked for years.

"Thirty-five and looking good," some wag in uniform calls out.

Hart looks up from the corner of the Parade Room that he and his plainclothes colleagues in Swindon CID have tried to colonise as their own. The Parade Room is meant to be open plan – another HR initiative intended to break down departmental barriers – but police officers are tribal animals and always will be.

"Very funny," Hart says. He's under no illusion that his years are showing: greying hair, throat like a bearded dragon.

"Not retiring then, guv?" someone else calls out.

"You wish."

He could have retired long ago if he'd wanted to, with twenty-five years' service under his ever-expanding belt, but he's still here. Should he tell them how old he is? Tell himself? He needs to hear it.

"Fifty-seven," he says, like a criminal confessing in the dock. "I'm fifty-seven." Louder now. The number sounds worse when spoken, more final than he feared. There's no going back. He's officially the same age his mother was when her life was cut cruelly short.

"You haven't opened all your cards, sir," Strover says. He can hear his mother saying the very same thing. Except for the "sir", of course. It was "Silas" when she was cross; "Sile" when she kissed him goodnight. Mel had called him "Sile" in bed this morning too. Strover still won't address him by his preferred "boss" or "guv". But she's right. There's one card that he hasn't read.

He examines the typed writing: "DI Hart" and "by hand". Another sharp jab in his chest. His GP has told him there's nothing to worry about. Psychogenic pain, driven by the usual fifty-something anxieties. "Sniper Alley" – that's what his doctor calls the fifties. Just got to keep ducking and diving. He pulls out the card from the envelope and looks at the picture: the Grim Reaper, sickle in hand. His stomach tightens.

"You alright, sir?" Strover asks.

"Some office clown," he says, showing her the picture.

"Charming," she says, smiling. "At least it's not the Four Horsemen of the Apocalypse." Strover's Bristol accent becomes broader when she's being mischievous.

He looks away, trying to see the funny side. He needs to stop all this superstitious stuff. It doesn't suit him. Not his style. He glances at the card again. "See you soon!" the caption jokes, but right now there's nothing remotely amusing about it. What's happened to him? It's just the sort of card he would have sent to others once.

He flips it open but there's no writing inside. A colleague pulling his leg, unaware that, in recent years, he's become a fully paid-up member of Hypochondriacs Anonymous, convinced that he'll die the same age as his mother. Too many shared genes; too many relatives saying he's got his mother's mannerisms, her nose. Her high cholesterol and blood pressure as well, which did for her in the end, triggering a coronary occlusion. But only a few people know that. He and his GP, the one he's visited twice already this month.

A uniform calls out, cutting through his thoughts. "Guv, front desk on the line," he says, holding up the Parade Room phone.

"For me?" Hart asks, surprised. He stands, grateful for an excuse to escape the tawdry celebrations.

"Who paid for the strippergram?" someone asks.

Please, God, no. He's never been one of the lads, even when he was young and single. A pint after work, for sure, but he would slip away when his colleagues moved on to the gentlemen's clubs on Swindon's notorious Victoria Road.

"What about the cake?" someone else says.

"Tuck in," Hart replies, gesturing at Strover as he walks away to take the call. He's not meant to eat cake and hopes it will have gone by the time he returns.

"DI Hart," he says into the phone, watching his colleagues gather like vultures around his desk. No one eats breakfast anymore, that's the problem. Not him, of course. Porridge every day, topped with a spoonful of flax to curb the cholesterol.

"Sorry to bother you on your birthday, guv, but there's a man here who insists on seeing you."

"Me? Who is he?"

Walk-ins are rare, particularly in weather like this. It's snowing hard outside, blizzardlike.

"Won't say. Just that it's important: 'A matter of life or death.' Tried passing him off on someone else but he's not having it. Wants to speak to you and no one else."

"I'll be right down," Hart says. Who could it be? Swindon's old central police station used to be in the middle of town. Colourful characters turned up day and night at the 1960s building, but there are fewer visitors out here at Gablecross, on the eastern edges of town.

Hart senses the tension as soon as he arrives at the station front desk. It's like the air before a thunderstorm: heavy, imminent. Reception was once run by a wise old desk sergeant who'd seen it all before, knew all the local criminals by name, asking after their families as he processed their paperwork, but not anymore.

"How can I help?" Hart says, acknowledging the man and the young receptionist. She's clearly nervous and needs reassurance from a senior colleague. One of the few advantages of having some years on the clock.

"Do you think it's true?" the man says, as Hart makes a rapid assessment of him: early thirties, unshaven, eyes wild with fear. Not obviously homeless, but you never know these days. He's got a head tic too, but it's his pattern of speech that worries him more: fast, random, simultaneously coherent and incoherent. The last person Hart heard talking like this was Conor, during a psychotic episode. He's been healthy for a few years now, but the threat of a relapse is always there, hanging over the family like a fog that won't clear.

"Do you think we can?" the man asks, turning from Hart to the receptionist and back again. His trouser legs are wet from the snow outside and he's shaking with cold despite the station's central heating, which has been turned up high today. Too high. "He says you don't believe it. Is it true?"

Hart's starting to sweat. Who's "he"?

"Is what true?" he asks. The police have to deal with mental health issues all the time these days, picking up the pieces of a broken system.

"He says we all have a 'death day'. Just like a birthday. No cake or candles." The man laughs nervously. "That would be weird – *Happy death day to you*. And when we know the date, there's nothing we can do about it. Nothing we can do to avoid our death. Except that he says you don't believe it, that we can just ignore our death day."

"Who says?" Hart interrupts, keen to know more. But the seemingly deranged words are already sounding familiar. "Who says I don't believe it?"

The man's eyes have turned glassy, fear replaced with resignation. Hart can feel his own pulse drumming at his temples. This is somebody's son. The paramedics had once saved Conor, talked him down from the roof of the Brunel West multi-storey car park, something he'll be eternally grateful for. Now it's up to him alone to help this man. He's young, but what if he's a father too? Hart has come to identify the different tastes of danger. And right now it's sour, metallic. Has he got a knife?

"But you're wrong," the man continues. "You're wrong, Detective Inspector Silas Hart, head of Swindon CID."

How the hell does he know my name? The man's voice has dialled up a notch, in volume and speed. He's starting to shake uncontrollably, his head tic more violent.

"Once you know your death day, he's right: there's nothing – absolutely fuck-all nothing – you can do about it. It's your destiny, written in the stars, your fate. Call it what you like. But there's no escaping it." The man's started to sob now. "I've tried. Jesus, how I've tried. But once you know, you can't do anything to stop it. I wish you were right, DI Hart. God, how I wish, but you're wrong."

He pauses, his gaze rolling around the room before settling back on Hart.

"Mel isn't it? Your wife. Does she know? Spoiler alert. She's going to die too. You as well. We all are. Just best not to know when, eh? Unfortunately, I know my death day. And there's nothing" – he's shouting now – "nothing anyone can do about it."

Before Hart can move, the man has pulled out a handgun and pushed the barrel deep into his mouth. The taste of metal.

"Wait!" Hart shouts, as the receptionist screams. Thinking of Mel – how does he know *her* name? – Conor, his parents, Hart lunges towards the man, hoping to disarm him. But he's right: there's nothing anyone can do. A moment later, a bullet passes at 1,000 feet per second through the roof of the young man's mouth and deep into the dense white tissue of his amygdala, extinguishing in an instant the trillions of neural connections that once made him who he was.

3

Hart stares at the crumpled body. Blood – so much blood – pools around the top of his head like an oil spill. Brain matter too, little florets of white cauliflower. He swallows hard as the receptionist rushes out of the front door to vomit. Already he can hear people coming down the stairs behind him from the Parade Room. A more senior member of the front desk team has appeared too.

"Call an ambulance," Hart says to him. The man's body will need to be taken away as soon as possible. Nobody, least of all the public, should see the scene before them. "And get this place sealed off," he adds, as two more staff arrive.

"You alright, sir?" Strover asks, coming up to stand beside him, a hand on his arm. Hart continues to stare at the body. Could he have done more to stop him? Somebody locks the station's glass doors.

"He knew Mel's name," Hart says, realising that it's blood,

not sweat, on his own face. He pulls out a handkerchief and wipes his forehead. "Asked specifically to see me."

"Did you recognise him?" Strover asks, ushering Hart into a side room.

Hart shakes his head, still stunned. "How did he know Mel's name, Strover?" he asks, nodding for her to close the door. He shuts his eyes and breathes in deeply. Hart's been in the *Gazette and Herald* enough times over the years for someone to recognise him, but not Mel. He's worked hard to keep his family life private. "How did he know my wife's bloody name?"

"Any idea who he was?" Strover asks.

Hart doesn't answer.

"What did he want to talk to you about?" Strover asks.

"He told me that he knew his 'death day' was today and that there was nothing anyone could do about it."

"His death day?"

Hart glances up at Strover, a chill running through him as he hears her repeat the words. "Sound familiar?"

She nods, a distant look in her eyes. They both know the significance – that they've been here before.

"I want you to find out all you can about him."

Hart pauses, trying to ignore the flash flood of dread, the visceral anger. Is this really happening to him all over again? His phone is buzzing. It's Mel. She knows not to call him unless it's urgent. Is she OK? Is it Conor? The man has put him on edge.

"Enjoying your birthday?" she asks.

"Had better," he says, pushing the door ajar to look out onto the front desk. A blanket is being placed over the dead man's body.

"What's happened?" She knows him too well, recognises the suppressed shock in his voice. He explains the scene he's just witnessed. Hart doesn't add that the man had specifically asked to see him, knew her name too. He'll tell her later.

"Sile, that's awful. I'm so sorry," she says, her voice faltering.

"Your day going any better?" Hart asks.

"You sure you don't want to talk more about yours?"

"I'm fine." He's never liked talking. "How are things over there?"

"Weird, actually," she says, still clearly thrown by his own news.

Mel had stepped back from nursing after the pandemic, begun a new career as a florist, but she missed the camaraderie of the ward, if not the long hours, and has returned to working at the Great Western Hospital in Swindon, four miles down the road from Gablecross. She still does flowers, but as a side hustle for friends.

"What's up?" Hart asks.

"Can you come over? Now?"

"To the hospital? What's happened?" His fingers tighten around the phone, sensing her anxiety.

"I realise it's not great timing, but there's a patient here who's behaving really strangely. Admitted to the Emergency Department earlier."

Not Conor then. "What do you want me to do about it?" He doesn't mean to sound so unhelpful.

"Remember my friend Beth? In the mental health liaison team? She rang me a few minutes ago, asked me to go over there and see the patient."

"Not really your area, is it?"

Mel had returned to working in the maternity unit. She'd wanted more children after Conor but nature had different plans. Other people's babies helped to fill the void.

"That's the thing. When I got there, I realised why Beth had asked for me. And why I'm ringing you now. The patient was violent, ranting and raving, but before they sedated him, he was demanding to speak to someone."

"Who?" Hart asks, realising with mounting dread where this is heading.

"He wanted to speak with you." Mel pauses. "And then he…"

"What is it, Mel?" He can hear the tremor in her voice.

"He knew my name too. How does he know us, Sile?"

Hart gives an initial statement to a colleague about the suicide and checks in on the young receptionist before heading over to the Great Western Hospital. It's a place he is more familiar with than he would like. When things were really bad, Conor was admitted here almost every week. Hart used to be incensed by the sight of people on drips smoking outside the main entrance. Now, they're only allowed to vape, which for some reason bothers him even more. As he walks past, he wants to shake their shoulders and tell them to do the maths, acknowledge that they are shortening their odds. Life at his age has enough health hazards already. They might as well enter Sniper Alley with a big, fat target on their back.

"Where is he?" Hart asks Mel as soon as he arrives at the Emergency Department.

"Thanks for coming over," she says, squeezing his arm.

"I came as quickly as I could," he says, turning away. Mel looked beautiful this morning when they left the house together: short-cropped hair tinged with stylish silver (never grey), eyes luminous, alive. She looks tired now, her broad, swimmer's shoulders slumped with fear.

"You OK?" he asks, knowing that she's not. He's experienced guilt often enough in his working life – the long hours, working late into the night – but it's raw regret he's feeling now. Mel's always supported his career as a detective, as long as it never leaches into their family life.

"We've got him in one of our new majors' cubicles," she says, ignoring him. The hospital's Emergency and Urgent Care Department recently received a £30 million makeover. Give it a couple of years and it will start to feel knackered and old like Gablecross. Like him.

"How did he know my name, Sile?" Mel asks, as they walk through a glass door into a small private room with Beth. A patient is lying on a bed. He's only been lightly sedated and is already beginning to stir.

"I'm not sure, but I'll find out. I promise," Hart says, turning to Beth. "Do we know anything about him?" He glances across at the patient: middle aged, overweight, unkempt.

Beth shakes her head. "No ID on him at all. Brought in earlier by ambulance from the town centre. He was clearly having a psychotic episode."

"And what exactly did he say?"

"He said he needed help," Beth says, glancing at Mel. "That he was about to die. We get a lot of that here. Delusional behaviour, existential angst. We didn't take it too seriously. Technical name 'thanatophobia' – death anxiety to you and me."

Hart feels his face reddening. He's told Mel about his own health worries, that turning fifty-seven feels like a milestone, one he'll be pleased to have passed. But he hasn't told her how serious his anxiety has become in recent months: getting up at 3 a.m. to pace around the garden, his head full of "thanatophobic" thoughts, as he now knows to call them.

"And then he—" Beth says.

"Name-checked us both," Hart says, glancing at Mel, who starts to well up.

"I'm OK," Mel says, as Beth puts an arm around her. Hart wants to comfort his wife too, but he needs to keep things professional.

"Sorry, it just really freaked me out," Mel says, composing herself.

"It's OK," Hart says, looking at the man, who has sat up now.

"Did he say anything else?"

Beth pauses before answering. "That only you can help him. Only you can stop him from dying today."

4

"He's come round quickly," Hart says. The patient is fully conscious now, his eyes scanning the room, arms clasped around his knees.

"Unfortunately," Beth says, watching a male nurse take up position beside the bed. "It wasn't pretty earlier – a serious threat to himself and others. We'll transfer him to Applewood once he's stable."

Applewood. A psychiatric ward. Conor was in there once.

"Thanks for coming over," Beth adds, as Mel slips out of the room. "She was really upset."

"I'm not surprised," he says, eyes still on the patient. Hart's upset too.

"Here comes the big boss," Beth says under her breath, as Mel walks back in with another doctor. "Anya Baydon."

Dr Baydon – purposeful, tied-back hair – introduces

herself in a confident Geordie accent as the emergency physician in charge. She talks to Beth, who briefs her in a low voice about the patient. He's shuffled down to the end of the bed now, watched carefully by the male nurse. Hart watches him too. Who is this man? And then he looks up and stares at the assembled medics in their light blue scrubs, moving his blank gaze from one to the next. His eyes land on Hart and begin to widen in apparent recognition.

"How are you feeling?" Dr Baydon asks, glancing from the patient to Hart.

The patient remains silent but his body starts to tremble, a faint oscillation that rises up through his limbs like a Mexican wave.

"You're not a doctor, are you?" the patient asks Hart, ignoring Dr Baydon. Hart's seen fear like this before.

"I'm not a doctor, no."

"DI Silas Hart? Please help me," he whispers.

"What's wrong?" Hart asks, trying not to be unnerved by the man knowing his name. He glances across at Dr Baydon, aware that he's the least qualified person in the room to offer medical advice. She nods her approval.

"Is it still Wednesday?" the patient asks, his voice now so quiet that Hart strains to hear him.

"Still Wednesday," Hart says. "1 December." A date that's resonated throughout his life, celebrated at first, now best forgotten. "And I know that for a fact because it's my birthday today."

Good to keep him talking. Hart manages a thin smile in Mel's direction, hoping to diffuse the tension, but the room is heavy with expectation, like the stillness in court before a sentencing. If only he could rewind the day, be back where it started, curled up in bed with Mel. Warm and safe – the opposite of where he finds himself now. He'd read once about the strange aura someone feels in the moments leading up to a fit, an existential terror. It feels like that in this airless, brightly lit cubicle, as if something hideous is hiding a few seconds up the track.

"Your birthday?" the patient asks, breaking into a smile that's anything but happy.

"And I had a cake. But with only one candle."

He smiles, but the man hasn't really heard Hart. "Well today is my death day."

"How do you *know* that?" Hart asks, suddenly impatient, angry. He's not just going to stand here again, listening to all this talk of death days, and watch someone else die in front of him.

"You're not a believer, are you? He said you weren't. 'Find DI Silas Hart if you want to side with the deniers.' That's what he said to me. 'He'll keep you company in the darkness.' I tried not to believe, but he knows. He just does. I don't understand how. But once you've seen the future, you can't change it. Which bit of that don't you understand, bud?"

"Who told you this?" Hart asks, but he already knows. If only he didn't, but he does.

"He said that if we have a death day, it follows we have a death hour," the patient says, ignoring the question. "A death minute. *Beautiful baby Jane arrived in the world at 6.49 a.m. this morning.* But when's she going to leave? That's what we really want to know. When's she going to depart this world?" He pauses. "What's the time, please?"

Hart glances at his watch, wrong-footed by the man's

sudden politeness. It's almost midday. His steel Omega was a present from Mel.

"11.58," he says.

"Two minutes," the patient says, clutching his legs closer to him as he begins to rock backwards and forwards, faster now. And then a burst of anger. "I don't remember his fucking name."

Another doctor appears in the doorway of the cubicle.

"Everything OK in here?" he asks. "Duty psychiatrist, mental health liaison."

"We may need you in a minute," Dr Baydon says, looking across at Beth.

"I'm around," he says, glancing at the patient and then at his watch before walking on down the row of cubicles.

"Haven't seen him before," Beth says, which strikes Hart as odd, given she's in the mental health liaison team too. "Must be a locum."

"We're just going to give you some more medicine to make you feel comfortable," Dr Baydon says, moving closer to the patient. The male nurse steps forward too. "But it would really help if you could tell us who you are first."

"Don't touch me," he shouts, lifting his head a fraction, eyes not engaged. "Do. Not. Touch. Me."

"OK," Dr Baydon says calmly, turning to Beth. "You better get that duty psychiatrist back."

But before Beth can move, the patient has raised his head again, staring at them with visceral, unambiguous terror in his eyes. "Time?" he asks in Hart's direction, less polite now.

Dr Baydon signals for Hart to remain silent, shaking her head slowly.

"Tell me the fucking time!" he screams. The male nurse moves in close.

Hart glances at his watch and then at Dr Baydon, who nods at him.

"11.59," Hart says.

The patient is rocking uncontrollably now, banging his head against his knees, in danger of falling off the bed.

"We're going to need some backup," the nurse says to Beth, stepping forward to restrain the patient. At first he resists, trying to shrug off the nurse's firm embrace, grunting and shouting and swearing. And then he stops, as if he's suddenly been switched off at the mains. The patient looks up at them all, glancing disdainfully at the nurse's restraining hand on his arm. The nurse releases his grip. The patient's wide-eyed fear has been replaced with something else, a look of acceptance, perhaps, as he begins to slump to one side. Instinctively, Hart rushes forward, but the nurse has already stopped him from falling to the floor. He steps back as the nurse and Beth lay the man down on the bed, where he lies motionless. Beth searches for a pulse at his neck and leans in closely to his face, checking for breathing.

"Nothing," she says, shocked. "No pulse."

Hart can't take his eyes off the man, can't believe this is happening again.

"Put out a double two, double two call for adult resus," Dr Baydon says, pressing an alarm button above the bed as Beth runs out of the cubicle. Dr Baydon checks the pulse and breathing again and starts compressions on the patient's chest. Mel comes over to help as the alarm cuts through the air. Hart flinches at the sound, which echoes somewhere in his distant past.

"You're going to take over CPR for me, Mel," Dr Baydon says, "OK? I'm going to count you in." Mel nods. "Five, four, three, two, one."

Hart watches as Mel tries to revive the stranger who knew their names. Steady, strong compressions. He's so proud of her, how impressive she is in these situations. Calm and strong. And then he's back at home, thirty-seven years ago in the sitting room, where he'd tried in vain to pump life back into his mother's fragile chest, the phone receiver cupped under his sweaty chin as he struggled to hear what the operator was saying.

"Please hurry," he'd said, after twenty minutes of trying. He didn't know how long his mother had been lying there before he found her, whether her frail body could take much more. His own arms felt like lead.

"You must keep going," the operator, a young woman, had said, even more nervous than he was. "The ambulance is on its way."

Dr Baydon switches a valve behind the bed.

"Connect to oxygen now please – 15 litres," she says, placing a mask over the patient's face. "And we need IV access – use femoral if needed."

Moments later, the resuscitation team rush into the room with a trolley. The team leader introduces herself to Dr Baydon, who briefs her on the patient as defibrillator pads are attached to his chest.

"Pause CPR," the leader says, glancing at the computer monitor on the trolley. "Shockable rhythm, carry on CPR."

Another member of the team starts to charge the defibrillator, which hums in a rising tone until it begins a forceful, two-tone beep. But all Hart hears is the dreadful noise of the old defibrillator they'd used on her mother: the high-pitched mechanical whine, the soulless automated voice.

"Oxygen away, carry on with CPR," the leader says, gesturing for everyone else to move back except Mel. "OK, stand clear everyone, bed clear, one metre please, shocking now."

Hart watches Mel step away from the bed. Would his mother be alive now if she'd had this sort of modern medical attention? The patient's chest heaves upwards. Another electric shock after two further minutes of CPR, followed by an injection of adrenaline. More shocks and CPR, but with no effect.

After twenty minutes, the team finally falls quiet. The air stills, just as it had in the sitting room, when the paramedics had finally stopped trying to revive his mother. Mel wipes at an eye with the back of her hand. She's physically exhausted, emotionally spent. Hart desperately wants to go over and hug her, tell her she tried her best.

"No return of spontaneous circulation," the leader says.

Dr Baydon shakes her head in disbelief. Hart catches Mel's eye. The stranger who knew their names is dead.

5

You were too young to feel blame – a complex, wine-dark emotion – but I could sense your anger with me. Dad had just come home early from London. He'd had a troubling few days with a particularly sad patient, he said, but didn't go into details. He never did. We knew he worked as a "psychiatrist", but neither of us really understood what the word meant, let alone how to pronounce it. (You teased me when I called him a "cycliatrist".)

"What do you actually do all day, Dad?" you asked, as we sat around the kitchen table eating chocolate digestives. (I knew something was up: he'd told Mum he had stopped snacking between meals.) He tried to explain as I shuffled up next to him on the kitchen bench and lent into his warm suit.

"If you break your leg, someone called an orthopaedic surgeon will fix it for you," he said, putting an arm around me.

"And if something's not quite right with the thoughts and feelings inside here" – he tapped my temple – "a psychiatrist will try to make you feel better."

When you asked if that meant I needed to see a psychiatrist, because of my funny feelings about cards and clocks and telephones, Dad laughed out loud.

"On the contrary. I think your brother here would make a very good psychiatrist because he has what we call empathy."

"What's that?" you asked, jealousy flickering in your young eyes.

Dad paused before answering and had to stop himself from becoming emotional. "Sometimes, when I come home from work feeling sad because I have not been able to sort a patient's thoughts, your mother, who has bucketloads of empathy, will ask what's wrong, even if she's not feeling great herself."

I leaned in closer to him. He had a strange falter in his voice. You were standing on your chair, already bored by the story, restless. "When I explain to her what happened at work," Dad continued, "Mum can feel how I feel, not just because she's a doctor herself, but because she can see things from my point of view and imagine how I must be feeling. It's almost as if she becomes me. Empathy is a wonderful thing to have."

It was telling that you had to ask what it was.

I wanted to play cards with Dad, guess some more shapes and images, as I thought it might cheer him up, but he said he was too tired and had to do some work at the kitchen table. Mum came in a bit later from the village surgery, chatted with Dad – being empathetic, I'm sure – and then said we were going to find some mushrooms for Dad's tea. So the three of us spent a happy afternoon foraging in the Savernake Forest. She was obsessed with finding porcini, Dad's favourite (he preferred to call them penny buns). We liked to help too because it put her in such a good mood. Dad never spelt it out, but you and I both knew she was not like other mothers. She was always so tired.

The walk in the Savernake started well. You found the first porcini, a discovery that earned you an awkward hug from Mum. You never liked being cuddled or kissed by her. Never really liked being touched. And then I found Chicken of the Woods, growing in waney-edged shelves on a mighty fallen oak. I even knew its Latin name, Laetiporus sulphureus *– I was precocious back then, before I learnt to disguise what I knew. Mum was so pleased for me, gave me a hug too, without any awkwardness. But I went and spoilt it by wandering off on my own and coming back with a mushroom that drained the blood from her face when she saw it in my hand.*

"Put it down," she barked, in a tone of voice that we'd grown used to in recent months. Her pain often manifested itself as anger.

"What is it?" I asked. I was curious as well as precocious.

"Put it down!" She was shouting now, short of breath. I was scared and dropped the mushroom immediately, watching it roll into a bed of beech leaves at my feet. It had looked so innocuous, an archetypal mushroom – just like the one on Dad's cards, in fact.

"What's wrong?" I asked.

Mum walked us both away from the offending mushroom, an arm on our shoulders.

"It's called a death cap," she said. "It can kill you if you eat it."

I thought she was just trying to scare us, but she worked as a GP and wasn't going to stop the medical lesson now.

"It gives you terrible stomach pains, diarrhoea and vomiting," she said, as we trudged back through the leaves to the car. "But then you think you're fine. You feel better for a few days. Right as rain, in fact. But inside, the mushroom's poison has been hard at work, killing little cells in your kidneys and liver. And you die."

It was then that it came to me, an overwhelming feeling of certainty. I knew Mum was going to die too. Very soon. Maybe it wasn't rocket science. It was obvious to anyone that she wasn't a well woman. But the number three had also popped into my head: as golden as the sun.

"Three days."

I said the words out loud as we were getting into the car, in the hope that it might flush the idea from my head. But it didn't work. It was still there, like one of those number balloons at birthday parties, bobbing around in my peripheral vision, big and glowing and golden.

"What, love?" Mum said, turning to check we had fastened our seatbelts. She could see I was upset. "I'm sorry, I didn't mean to be cross back there," she added, a hand on my knee. "It's just that they're very dangerous mushrooms." She paused. "And I lost someone once, a patient..."

"Can we go home now?" you asked, kicking your legs in frustration.

"Please," Mum said.

"Please," you repeated.

"I love you, Mummy," I whispered to myself.

Back home, Mum fried the porcini in butter and served them on toast for us and Dad, who was never normally home in time for our tea. We laughed a lot and managed to cheer Dad up. He pushed his work papers to one side and started to tell us jokes. Always a good sign.

"So this man walks in to see his psychiatrist," Dad began.

"Is it you, Dad?" you asked.

"Why not. Let's say it's me. This man comes into my consulting room in London one day and says he thinks he's become a dog. 'I bark at cats whenever I see them. I like it when I'm tickled behind my ears, chase squirrels in the park and prefer my food served in a bowl on the floor.'"

We both laughed at that. Even Mum, who despaired at Dad's jokes, allowed herself a little smile.

"'No problem,' I say to him," Dad continued. "'Just hop up onto my couch and we'll talk properly about it.' And the man turns, crestfallen, and says, 'Ooh no, I'm not allowed up on couches.'"

There was a moment of silence. You looked at me and I looked at Dad and then we all laughed.

"Dogs aren't usually allowed up on sofas or chairs, you see," Dad said, sensing we hadn't quite got the joke.

In moments like that, a scene of family happiness, Mum seemed to free herself from the shackles of the pain that made life so intolerable for her. And for a few minutes, I forgot about my golden feeling in the woods.

"Can we have a dog?" I asked.

"One day, perhaps," Mum said.

Later that night, it was Dad who came to tuck us both up in bed. You were already asleep but I was wide awake, fixated with the thought of Monday.

"Mum's going to die, isn't she?" I asked, as he turned off my bedside light.

For a long time, Dad sat there on the edge of my bed in silence.

"She's not well," he said eventually. I could feel he was upset, which made me start to cry. I didn't want him to be sad again.

"It's OK," he said, resting a hand in mine on the blanket.

"What day is it today?" I knew the answer; I just needed to hear Dad say it.

"Today? Friday."

An orange day. Saturday, Sunday, Monday... a golden day.

"When do you go to work again?" I asked him.

"Monday."

"Please don't go."

After Dad had gone, I turned to look at you, envied the peace of your sleep, your empathy-free, uncomplicated ways, but then, suddenly, you were awake and staring at me. Was it fear in your eyes? Perhaps you had been dreaming. Or was it loathing?

6

The past (three years earlier)

Hart unclips his seatbelt and opens the passenger door, taking in the scented summer air: honeysuckle, meadowsweet, maybe musk mallow too. He must remember to tell Mel, who's always on the lookout for wildflowers for weddings. Strover sits quietly beside him in the driver's seat. Was he as together – so self-contained – when he was her age? They've never discussed it, but she does all the driving these days, much like Mel does. Cars just don't interest him, never have. Strover can get excited about a numberplate, knows every make of car, logo, engine size. More importantly, she's learnt when her boss wants to talk and when he prefers to sit in silence.

"Have you ever noticed how some of the worst crimes are committed in the most beautiful places?" Hart asks.

"One of the many perks of working in Wiltshire," Strover says.

"Says the Bristolian."

They have parked up in a lay-by opposite Wilton Windmill, a few miles southeast of Marlborough. Across the quiet lane, a hedgerow teems with house sparrows; behind them, the cool glades of the Brail. In truth, they don't even know if a crime has been committed here, but the uniform first on the scene was sufficiently concerned to refer it to CID. A young man has been found dead in a field.

"I think we're wanted," Strover says, gesturing at a uniform who has appeared from a track that runs up from the windmill.

Hart can tell at once that the young officer is troubled by what he is about to show them.

"Were you the one who called it in?" he asks, as they follow him through a five-bar gate and down the path.

"A dog walker found him," the officer says, avoiding eye contact. "Knows the family, recognised the deceased. She's giving a statement now at her home, just down the road." He points at a house in the distance. "There's no sign of a struggle, of violence, but…"

"But what…?"

"It's best you see for yourself, sir," he says, as they pass the windmill, its white sails bright against the blue sky. Hart stops to glance up at the mill's fantail as it creaks in the wind, turning the turret. Somewhere in the distance a cockerel cries. A small CCTV camera is perched on top of a nearby shepherd's hut, pointing at the windmill.

They enter a field used as an overflow car park, sending up a startled pheasant. Hart takes a deep breath, savours the smell of newly mown grass. An old windmill sail lies beside the wooden fence like a felled bough. In the far corner of the field, crime scene tape flickers in the warm breeze rolling across from Wexcombe Down. Beyond it, fields of sunburnt corn and barley shimmer in the July heat. No one else is around apart from another uniform, standing guard by the tape. At least the deceased's last view was a breathtaking one: Wiltshire at its finest.

"There was a crop circle in this field back in 2010," Strover says as they approach. "When it was rapeseed. A geometric depiction of Euler's identity, one of the most beautiful equations in mathematics. Links the big five fundamental mathematical constants: zero, one, Pi—"

"Not now, Strover," Hart says, but he knows it's just a sign of her "neurospicy" brain – her word, not his. She often comes up with random mathematical facts when she's feeling stressed: two is the only even prime number; the Romans didn't have a symbol for zero; in a room of just twenty-three people, there's a fifty per cent chance of a shared birthday. She'd led the way on the crop-circle investigation a few years back, when three bodies had been found in the middle of complex encoded patterns. There are no crop circles here today, just a bucolic summer morning and a dead body.

"It's his expression I can't get out of my head," the young officer says, as they walk up to the deceased. Hart wonders if it's his first corpse. The other officer stands back.

"And no one's moved him?" Hart asks both uniforms, who shake their heads. At least that's something.

Hart takes in the scene. The young man is propped up against a fencepost at the edge of the field, leaning slightly to one side. Cream chinos, petrol-blue collarless cotton shirt, navy deck shoes. No sign of a struggle, but his head is turned away. Hart moves around and squats to look at his face. The officer is right: the young man's eyes are wide open, his expression one of abject terror – gaping mouth, fear burned into his pupils.

"Jesus," he says, conscious of Strover, who has bent down to take a closer look too.

"Suicide?" she asks.

"Probably."

It's the most likely explanation, but there are no signs of self-harm or vomiting, which might suggest poisoning – no pill powder around the lips. They'll have to wait until the autopsy. It's the expression, though, that's preoccupying Hart. He knows what the pathologists say: the emotional state of a person doesn't persist beyond the moment of death. Facial muscles relax, causing the mouth to fall open and the eyes to widen. But in this case, the death is recent, the body still warm when the dog walker found him. And the expression is extreme: he looks petrified.

Hart stands up. "Next of kin?" he asks one of the uniforms.

"Two victim support officers are with his parents now. House near the pub down in the village. He'd been back living with them for a few months. Acting career in London didn't work out, apparently. The father came up here earlier to identify him."

Hart knows the Swan well, one of his favourite pubs. Ceilings draped with dry hops, homemade pheasant pie, local beer served from barrels behind the bar and a landlord always pleased to see him. What not to like? He's about to turn away when something catches his eye, half-concealed beneath the man's outstretched left hand. He bends down again and looks more closely.

"What is it?" Strover asks.

"An hourglass," Hart says. "*Memento mori*. A reminder of our mortality."

This one is small and wooden, with fine grains of carmine-coloured sand. It can't take longer than a few minutes to empty.

"Freemasons are presented with one when they join the Brotherhood," he says to no one in particular. "A reminder that life is finite. Time's running out."

A twinge in his chest. He tries to ignore it, his own fears of dying. Distracting himself, he looks out across the fields, towards Marten, Tidcombe and beyond, where the downs have gathered themselves into a mighty wave that will never break. Somewhere over there, he once visited Fosbury Camp, an Iron Age hillfort, with Mel. He likes his history, feels it's his duty to educate the youth about the force, remind them that Wiltshire Police is the oldest constabulary in the country.

"You lot are probably too young to remember," he says, turning to Strover and the two uniforms, "but in the bad old days of the eighties, criminals and Met officers were often members of the same Masonic lodge."

The uniforms shift awkwardly. Maybe they're not too young.

"You've never been tempted to sign up yourself, sir?" Strover asks, squinting in the sunshine.

"I'd rather toast my eyeballs on a fork. Call me old-fashioned, Strover, but public-service policing and membership of a secret society with a dodgy handshake don't really mix in my book. I know one or two colleagues who are 'on the square', though."

"Ward?" Strover asks.

Everyone at Gablecross knows that there is no love lost between Hart and his boss, Detective Chief Superintendent Tarquin Ward.

"Wouldn't put it past him," Hart says. "You know new members are asked to roll up one trouser leg to prove that they are unshackled – a free man? And expose their left breast to prove that they're not female?"

"You're joking me," Strover says.

"I wish I was."

Hart leaves Strover to ponder gender bias and Freemasonry as he bends down again, looking at the hourglass more closely, searching in vain for any marks or writing. He pulls out his phone and takes a photo.

"I want a full CSI report," he says. "And make sure they check the CCTV footage from the shepherd's hut over by the windmill," he adds.

He'll be given nothing but grief, of course. Ward will demand to know why he's deploying expensive forensic resources for what appears to be a tragic suicide. And not for the first time, Hart will explain that it's just a hunch, as it always is with him. A gut feeling, which has served him well over the years, that the scene didn't present in the way it should. Too many anomalies, like the man's expression. There's also been an uptick in local suicides in recent months, which is making him twitchy.

And the hourglass bears all the signs of a signature.

7

A female uniform lets them into the parents' house, a large, thatched property surrounded by thick gravel. Staddle stones stand sentinel by the entrance. Behind the property, a small farmyard with a battered Land Rover Defender and rusting machinery in a modern barn. They follow the officer across the flagstone floor to the farmhouse kitchen, where the couple is sitting at an old wooden table, hands cupped around brightly patterned mugs. The house feels cool and dark, the windows shuttered. Are they trying to keep out the grief?

Hart introduces himself and Strover, signals to the uniforms to leave them on their own. The mother, Anne, is wearing leggings and a dark-blue fleece. When she gets up to make them tea, Hart clocks the name of a local racing stable printed on the back of her fleece. In other circumstances, he would ask for tips for Newbury on

Saturday. Her long, dyed-blonde hair is tied up, her eyes raw with crying. The father, Crispin, is older, with sandy hair and crimson trousers. His farmer's hands are large and rough, his face ashen.

"Have you brought him off the hill yet?" Anne asks, dabbing at her eyes with a tissue. "He'll be getting cold."

Hart glances at Strover. They've come to a good arrangement in these circumstances. Her tone is more reassuring than his.

"I'm afraid we need to carry out a few further investigations at the site before your son is moved," Strover says.

"Isn't it bloody obvious what happened?" Crispin says, struggling to curb his emotions. Hart's been there himself, knows that anger is so much easier than grief, at least in the beginning. His early twenties were fuelled by rage after his mother died. Arrested for drunk and disorderly behaviour, before being quietly let go when it became clear he was the son of a serving police officer.

"We just need to be sure of the cause of death," Strover continues, looking across at Hart. "Once the site has been checked, there'll be an autopsy. After that, you'll be able—"

"To bury him. Thank you for that."

Hart breathes in deeply as Anne pours them tea. These encounters never get easier. The moment they do, he'll retire.

"I'm sorry to ask, but was your son particularly depressed in recent weeks?" Hart asks. "Shown any suicidal ideation?" There might well be nothing to see here, just another tragic suicide.

"Our son's name is Milo," Crispin says. "No thirty-year-old should be back living with their parents. Even a resting actor. Of course, he wasn't happy about that."

"We didn't mind so much though, did we?" Anne says, looking up at her husband, who turns away. "Nice to have him around again."

Hart knows how she feels. It was good to have Conor back living at home – good for a while. He's recently moved in with Jess, his new girlfriend.

"I think he felt safe with us," Crispin adds.

"Was there anything that made him feel particularly unsafe?"

He can feel Strover flinch at his insensitivity, but he needs to know why their son looked like he'd just seen the gates of hell.

"Milo was frightened of many things in life, always was, from an early age," Crispin says.

Hart glances at Strover. "Slept with the landing light on when he came back," Anne says, her voice barely a whisper. "Scared of his own company."

"But never suffered from stage fright," Crispin says defiantly, clinging onto the fact for comfort. "He loved the theatre. His happy place, he called it."

"Was he taking any medication?" Strover asks.

Another exchange of glances between the couple.

"He'd recently started on antidepressants again," Anne says. "At the suggestion of Dr Rory Garstan, his psychiatrist."

"Selective serotonin reuptake inhibitors," Crispin says, spitting out the sibilant words. "SSRIs."

"You're not a fan?" Hart asks. He'd read up on SSRIs after Conor went on them briefly. Lifesavers for some people, the cause of suicidal ideation in others.

"We tried to talk him out of it," Anne says. "It didn't go so well the last time he was on them."

"May I ask what happened?" Hart says, cursing again his own emotional clumsiness.

"He tried to kill himself. It's how we found out he was on them."

"He's an adult, thirty years old," Crispin says. "We couldn't tell him what he should or shouldn't be taking. He didn't want us to know he was on any medication at all – he was ashamed."

"And also relieved, I think, when we found out," Anne adds.

"But his psychiatrist, this Dr Garstan – he clearly thought it was OK for him to go back on them again?" Hart asks.

"I should never have offered to pay for that man," Crispin says.

"Dr Garstan's one of the best in the country; he practises in Harley Street," Anne says.

"And Wiltshire, unfortunately," Crispin adds.

"It sounds like you almost blame him for your son's death?" Hart asks.

"We blame ourselves," Anne whispers, putting a hand on her husband's forearm.

"We'll need to talk to Dr Garstan, as a matter of course," Hart says.

"He lives over at Pewsey," Crispin says. "When he's not gadding about in London."

"He's been very helpful in the past." Anne pauses. "Helped me through a bit of a wobble."

A pause. Hart glances across at Strover.

"We found an hourglass beside his body," she says, taking her cue.

"A symbol often associated with Freemasonry," Hart adds, wondering if he can flush out a connection.

Crispin looks at his wife. Hart detects the faintest shake of her head.

"There is something you should know about Milo," Crispin says.

"Darling," Anne says, clearly trying to stop him talking.

"They need to hear it. Might be important."

Anne doesn't reply. An uneasy stillness descends on the cool kitchen, a sanctuary from the heat of high summer. It must be a sanctuary in here at the height of summer. Hart's often fantasised about running a small farm like this: Mel feeding a baby lamb on her lap while he's out checking the flock, loyal sheepdog at his side.

"What might be important?" Hart prompts. Maybe Milo was a Freemason after all?

Crispin glances at his wife again before turning to the detectives.

"In some ways, what's happened is not such a surprise." He pauses. "Milo had many strange ideas, too many unhelpful thoughts in that young head of his. The craziest conspiracy theories. In recent weeks, he became fixated on his own death. We've no idea why. He was just obsessed with the idea that he knew…"

Crispin wells up, trying to stifle his tears, head in his hands, but they are coming in waves now, his strong farmer's shoulders heaving up and down. Anne tries to comfort her husband and then she looks up at Hart.

"Milo knew he was going to die today."

8

"It's a clinical skill I've had for as long as I can remember," Dr Garstan says, sitting back in his consulting room. "A strong sense of where someone is going in life, which can help my patients visualise a better future for themselves and disrupt unhelpful patterns of thought."

Hart has only been listening to Garstan for a few minutes, but the psychiatrist is already irritating the hell out of him. Is it the toned physique or medical arrogance? Maybe it's just the evidence of wealth – in his voice, his house, his appearance. He's dressed in a Patagonia gilet and T-shirt, crisp chinos and expensive trainers; more tech bro than shrink.

"Of course I take extensive patient histories, but someone's future can hold as many clues as their past," he continues. "I'm utterly devastated to hear about Milo – we were making good progress, identified so much he was looking forward to in life."

Hart had called Garstan an hour earlier to break the news and explain that they wanted a chat. The psychiatrist was working at home today, rather than up in Harley Street, and could see them after he was finished with a local patient. Contemporary, abstract paintings and vast geometric mirrors had set a surprisingly modern tone on their arrival at the main house, a Queen Anne pile in a hamlet outside Pewsey. And the bright-white space they are in now, a stable block to the side of the property, feels more like a start-up office than a shrink's consulting room: carbon-fibre road bike propped up in the corner; sideboard with Nespresso coffee machine; SMEG fridge below. The moulded-plastic chairs and desk are bright and modern too – not a Freudian sofa in sight.

"How are his poor parents?" Garstan asks. "Are they bearing up?"

"Not great, to be honest," Hart says, thinking back to the sobbing figure of Crispin, the look on his wife's face as she showed them to the door. Nobody should see their children die before themselves. "As you'd expect."

"Of course."

Hart studies Garstan as he shakes his head in reflection. Forty-five going on thirty, the bastard. Like a well-preened bird of prey: tall and slim, Roman nose, slicked-back hair, porcelain-blue eyes. And his head seems permanently tilted upwards, adding to his air of superiority.

"I appreciate you've come here for some answers," Garstan says, "and I will do all I can to assist you in your inquiries, but I need to respect Milo's patient confidentiality. Even in death. Until I can talk to his parents. Ask how much they are happy for me to share with you."

"They are the ones who gave us your contact details," Strover says.

"I understand," Garstan says. "But I can't talk about an individual patient. Against the rules. Sorry."

A pinched smile. Hart manages not to roll his eyes. It wouldn't surprise him if Garstan high-fives his patients. He couldn't be more different from Jonathan, the young psychiatrist who weaned Conor off his medication and got him out into the world again.

"Did Milo ever talk about his own death?" Hart asks.

"I'm so sorry," Garstan says, holding up his hands as if in surrender.

"His parents said Milo knew he was going to die today," Hart continues. He's used to people not answering his questions. "I reckon it's something I might just confide in my psychiatrist, if I were convinced I was going to fall off my perch on a certain day."

This time Garstan doesn't say anything.

"He never mentioned that to you?" Hart asks.

Again, Garstan doesn't reply, almost as if he hasn't heard. He doesn't look guilty or awkward, like a lot of people Hart's sat opposite over the years. He decides to let the psychiatrist wallow in silence, if that's his game. Strover knows what he's up to, learnt not to fill the "no comment" void. Garstan shuffles some papers confidently on his desk.

"Nice place you've got here," Hart eventually says. Maybe Garstan is used to long silences – par for the course with his patients.

"It was my father's."

Of course it was.

"He was also a psychiatrist. Tends to run in families, you know."

"Like undertakers," Strover says.

Garstan looks up.

"And police officers," Hart says.

"Was your father...?"

"Wiltshire Police," Hart says.

"And yours?" Garstan says, turning to Strover. Hart needs to get the interview back on track. It's in danger of becoming a group therapy session.

"Forensic scientist," Strover says.

"Interesting."

Strover looks away. She rarely talks about her family. All Hart knows is that her father died when she was a teenager.

"This is pretty interesting too," Hart says, calling up an image of the hourglass on his phone. "We found it beside Milo's body."

Hart leans forward across the psychiatrist's glass-and-steel desk and shows him the photo. Garstan offers a quick smile.

"It should really have wings," he says, without missing a beat. "*Tempus fugit.*"

Garstan is annoyingly unruffled. Hart sits back again, glancing around his consulting room to look for something – anything – that might trip him up.

"Why do you think Milo had it with him?" he asks.

"A meditation aid, perhaps? A reminder to live life to the full? Time flies."

"I know my Latin," Hart says, bluffing.

"I really have no idea why he had it."

Hart decides to change tack, try to throw him off balance. "Are you a Freemason, Dr Garstan?"

"A Freemason?" The psychiatrist seems genuinely surprised, begins to laugh. "And even if I were, DI Hart, I'm not sure I'd tell you. Isn't that rather the point? Your lot used to be riddled with them, I gather. Why on earth do you ask?"

Hart explains about the symbolism of hourglasses in Freemasonry, sensing that he's flogging a dead horse. But there's still something about Garstan that troubles him. On the drive over, he had researched online what he could about him – his smooth career progression from Cambridge Medical School to Harley Street, via St Thomas'. Turns out Garstan's something of a celebrity psychiatrist, or at least he boasts a scattering of celebrities on his client list. (Unlike his older brother, another psychiatrist, who seems to have ploughed a humbler furrow.) And it's all to do with his "clinical intuition", as he likes to describe it in media interviews: "a unique ability to help clients visualise their futures and savour forthcoming positive events." More manifesting life coach than Freudian shrink, but what does Hart know?

"Did Milo ever visit you at your Harley Street practice?" he asks.

"He became a patient of mine when he moved back in with his parents. It made more sense for everyone if I saw him here."

"Are all your patients private?"

"They are in Harley Street. I see some NHS referrals here – through the Avon and Wiltshire Mental Health Partnership."

A partnership Hart knows all too well. "And Milo was a private patient?"

Garstan remains quiet.

"His parents said they paid, so we'll assume he was. Do you offer your Harley Street patients anything different?"

Strover must be wondering where he's going with this.

"How do you mean? All private psychiatrists are regulated by the Care Quality Commission."

"I'm not suggesting otherwise. But would it be fair to say that, with your private patients, you place greater emphasis on their future? Rather than their past. Help them understand where they are going in life?"

"And how to get there, yes. It's easier to unlock someone's potential when you can see it."

"And you do this… how? A lot of people, some of them quite famous, seem very keen on your services, particularly your life coaching."

Garstan smiles for the first time in a while.

"I was lucky enough to be born with an unusual gift, DI Hart. Let's call it—"

"Clinical intuition?" Hart interrupts.

"Exactly," Garstan says, seeming to process the fact that Hart has done his homework.

"Not unlike being a detective," Hart says.

"We clearly share a talent."

"And your clinical intuition gives you a special insight into your patients?" Hart asks, keen to shift the focus back onto Garstan.

"I help them to connect with different versions of themselves, who they were in the past, who they are now, and, more importantly, who they will become. Visions of the future are often the preserve of the psychotic, so I prefer not to use such terms as 'second sight', 'precognition', 'clairvoyance', or 'remote viewing'. It puts people off. Let's just say I'm able to gain a very refined insight into their lives and leave it at that."

"You can see into the future?" Hart asks, unable to conceal his scepticism.

"I'm not the first psychiatrist to possess such skills, and I won't be the last."

"And you know that for certain, of course," Hart says. "That you won't be the last."

Hart can't help smiling. He glances at Strover, who suppresses a smile too.

"This isn't a joke, DI Hart. It's a gift I was born with and I have a duty to use it responsibly to help others. And I've clearly failed Milo. He had a bright future ahead of him."

"And you saw that?"

Garstan nods.

"But he didn't have a bright future, did he?" Hart says. "That's the point. He died this morning."

"I saw that too."

"Of course you did." Hart can barely disguise his disdain now.

"When you rang earlier, the news didn't come as a complete surprise," Garstan says.

For the first time, the psychiatrist looks less together, genuinely emotional.

"This morning, while I was still asleep, or at least in that strange hypnagogic state between sleeping and waking, I dreamt of his body, lying in a field. I woke up and turned to my sketchbook, which I always keep beside my bed, and drew a windmill."

He leans forward and passes them his sketchbook.

Hart looks at the drawing. Not bad and clearly a windmill. In the right-hand corner, Garstan has written the time: 6.06 a.m. He shows the drawing to Strover, who studies it for a moment and then looks up at him. Is she thinking the same? When he rang Garstan earlier, from the car on speakerphone, he hadn't told the psychiatrist where Milo had been found, just that he had died.

"Did you speak to anyone after I called you?" Hart asks.

"Only to Katya, my PA, why?"

"And she hasn't spoken to anyone else? The dog walker who found the body?"

"Not that I'm aware of. Katya is from Ukraine, commutes from Shrivenham. She doesn't know anyone around here, let alone a dogwalker in Wilton."

So how the hell did Garstan know that Milo was found lying dead near a windmill?

9

"I was told in my police training not to let personal emotions influence procedural decisions," Strover says to Hart, as they drive away from Garstan's house. "Just because you don't like someone, sir, it doesn't mean that they're guilty."

"Listen to you," Hart says in the passenger seat, glancing across at Strover. "As if you've never been tempted to press charges that little bit harder if they're a total arse."

"Tempted, but never succumbed."

Hart smiles. Strover's hair seems shorter than usual today, almost spiked, accentuating her gamine features: a pinched nose and natural eyebrows. She's what Hart's mother used to call a tomboy, but he can't say that these days. Not that Strover would mind. She cuts her boss some slack, has so far resisted calling him out for the occasional slip-up. Maybe it's because she knows he never means to cause offence.

He hopes so. His motto has always been to live and let live. Just not in the case of Garstan.

"He's definitely hiding something," Hart says as they head back towards Wilton. The plan is to check in on the CSI team who have already set up shop at the windmill and then have a quick pie at the Swan down the hill.

"He seemed genuinely upset by the death of Milo," Strover says.

"You think so? Didn't seem very surprised."

"That's because he saw it coming."

"Strover, please. You can tell me anything – that you believe the world is flat, that spaghetti grows on trees, the moon landings never happened and that 'they' is a single pronoun – but don't ever – ever – tell me you seriously think someone can see into the future."

They drive on in silence for a while, through Milton Lilbourne and East Grafton.

"As it happens, sir, I'm identifying as non-binary these days," Strover says, as they reach Burbage. "I'd prefer it if you called me 'they'."

Hart glances at Strover and looks ahead. Why the hell did he include gender pronouns in his list of unlikely beliefs? Mel would have killed him if she'd been here.

"Mind if I just stick with Strover?" he asks, trying to sound casual. Strover shakes her head in mock despair. "I mean, if it's OK with you?" he adds.

At least the gender-neutral name now makes more sense. He'd only ever known his colleague as Strover. That's how Strover had arrived in the force and very few people seem to know of a first name. HR presumably does. He doesn't. Never thought to ask.

"And, for the record, it's all completely fine by me," he continues, trying not to be unsettled by the silence, the yawning generational chasm that's opened up between them. "You know, your choice. Hundred per cent." He pauses, wondering whether he's about to step on a landmine. "I can't say it comes as a complete surprise."

Strover smiles. Hart turns to look out the window and smiles too, feeling weirdly lighter. Maybe they both knew that they ought to talk about it at some point. Not for his benefit but for Strover's – all he's ever been bothered about is whether his young colleague is happy and Strover seems to be in a better place than ever. An increasing number of tattoos, just like Conor, but all still below the waterline. Out of sight, out of mind. Hart can cope with that.

"And I knew, by the way, because I'm a sensitive, enlightened soul who is in touch with my fellow human beings, rather than being a clairvoyant," he adds.

"Sensitive?" Strover says, laughing.

"All part of my intuition," he says.

He's relieved that he appears not to have ruined their relationship. Or been cancelled. In truth, it was Mel who'd first tipped him off about Strover's gender, but he'll take the credit. He's about to ask if Strover's told other colleagues (he's usually the last to hear station gossip) when his phone rings.

"DI Hart?" the caller says on the car speakerphone.

"Speaking."

"This is Crispin, Milo's father."

Hart raises his eyebrows at Strover.

"How can I help you?"

"Did you manage to see Dr Garstan?"

"We've just left him, why?"

"Are you still in the area?"

"We're on our way back to Wilton. To the windmill." No need to mention the pub. "Forensics will be there by now."

"I need to speak to you about Garstan. Somewhere private. Away from the house. Park up on the road below the windmill and head into the Brail behind you. There's a bench, near some carved totem poles. I'll be there in half an hour, maybe sooner."

Hart's about to suggest they meet after lunch, at a place easier to find – totem poles? This isn't the Wild West – when Crispin hangs up. Two seconds later, a text comes through from him with a What3Words location. Hart turns to Strover and reads it out: "Trudges. Denoted. And, er... Pronouns."

10

Strover pulls into the lay-by opposite the windmill and they walk back down the path to the field beside it. CSI have only just arrived, but a tent has already been erected in the far corner. Hart suddenly feels overwhelmed by grief for Milo, a young man still lying where he died. He'll call Conor later, arrange to meet for a pint, tell him how proud he and his mother both are, the way he's turned his life around.

Hart has a quick chat with the crime scene manager, who has come across to meet him.

"You've got the hourglass?" Hart asks.

"I took it home to boil an egg," he says. "Of course I've bloody got it."

Hart likes the CSM, despite his sarcasm. Or maybe because of it.

"We're about to check his room at the parents' house," he adds.

"Go gently with them," Hart says.

"We always do."

And bulls never cause carnage in china shops. CSI make Hart seem positively sensitive.

After explaining that he'll be back shortly, Hart heads over to their car with Strover. They drive down the hill 500 yards, away from the windmill, and pull over. According to What3Words, it's a ten-minute walk from here to the totem poles. They head up a track into the Brail beyond at a brisk pace, inspired by the blur of a hare as it cuts across the path ahead.

The Brail was once part of the ancient Savernake estate and is rich in ash, oak, beech, sweet chestnut and a rare black poplar. There's a Roman villa too. Hart's become increasingly interested in trees as he grows older. Not just identifying them by their appearance, but by their sound as well, how the poplar mimics a rushing stream and beeches roar.

He spots the totem poles before they notice Crispin. It's only as they approach the wooden carvings that he sees Milo's father on a bench, looking down a vista in the trees towards Hotspur House in the distance. He turns as they draw close to him.

"Thanks for coming," he says.

"No problem," Hart says. "How can we help?"

"Do you mind if we walk?"

"Of course," Hart says.

Crispin seems to have aged in the few hours since they first met. He rises stiffly from the bench, rubbing a hip as they set off slowly past the totem poles. One features a carved owl, the other an Easter Island face. There's a joke in there somewhere: what's with the long face? If Mel were here, she might humour him with a smile. It's why he loves her.

"How did you find him?" Crispin asks.

"Dr Garstan?" Hart says. "He seemed upset by Milo's death."

Crispin fails to conceal a smirk. "But not surprised?"

Hart glances at Strover. "Not entirely."

"I don't know what happened between them, but Milo went downhill fast after he began to see him. As far as I'm concerned, he's got Milo's blood on his hands," Crispin says, looking ahead.

"In what way?" Hart asks. "That's quite an accusation."

"There's a fine line between encouraging someone to make the most of life and telling them they are mortal. The notion of his own death, however distant, would have terrified Milo. He was fragile when he came down from London – work had completely dried up – but he was doing OK, coping. Until he started seeing Garstan. It was my wife's idea – I don't blame her – but we should have sent him to see someone else."

They walk on in silence, the path opening up into a bright clearing.

"Reminding someone of their mortality might be a bit harsh, but it isn't a crime," Hart says, suspecting – hoping – that Crispin has more light to shed on Garstan.

"If I tell you something about him, can you guarantee my anonymity? I don't want it coming back to bite my backside."

"Of course," Hart says, feeling his chest tighten.

"I run a shoot on my land. Pheasant, a few partridge.

Garstan shoots too, but not around here. I know the owner of the land near Pewsey where he shoots. Good friend. Garstan's a flash bastard, fond of double gunning."

"Double gunning?" Game shooting isn't really Hart's thing. Always preferred the races.

"You have two guns and someone – a loader – to load them for you," Strover says, before Crispin has a chance to explain.

Hart looks at Strover in surprise.

"Exactly," Crispin says, unfazed by Strover's knowledge. "Garstan prefers big shoots with a large bag. Horrific, if you ask me. Dead pheasants raining down all around, only to be bulldozed later into pits. It's disgraceful, all about the money. We like to shoot for the pot around here."

"Game shooting isn't illegal yet in this country," Hart says. He's got nothing against it but agrees with Crispin about the commercial shoots. At this time of year, the countryside is crawling with hundreds of overfed pheasants too fat to lift off the ground. Where's the sport in that?

"It won't be long before it is illegal," Crispin says. "Anyway, my friend, he knows Garstan quite well. More of a business arrangement than true friendship. Garstan brings a lot of wealthy pals down from London."

"Fellow psychiatrists?"

"Plastic surgeons, actually."

Always nice to see new faces, but Hart checks himself.

"Garstan's got a lot of guns," Crispin continues. "Buys them from Purdey's on South Audley Street. Loves his Damascus over-and-unders. All licensed, of course. Bit of a fetish thing going on, if you ask me."

Where's Crispin going with this?

"My friend says Garstan's also got some other guns," he continues. "Ones that are definitely not licensed. He showed them to him once."

"What sort of guns?" Hart asks, glancing at Strover. This is more like it.

"A whole range, apparently, given to him over the years by patients who didn't trust themselves with them. And he's never quite got around to handing them over to you boys. That's his story anyway. One of them's a sawn-off shotgun. Lethal little shorty. Why in God's name would you own something like that?"

"And they're kept at his house in Pewsey?" Hart asks, unable to hide his interest. Owning any gun without a police licence is a serious offence, but a sawn-off shotgun is in a different league. It's a prohibited weapon. Full stop. And if someone's found in possession of one with a barrel cut shorter than twenty-four inches, or the overall length is under forty inches – *kaboom*: a mandatory five-year minimum prison sentence under Section 5 of the Firearms Act 1968.

"As far as I know," Crispin says, "in an outbuilding. Don't suppose he keeps them in Harley Street."

They come to a halt in the opening. "This might be useful," Crispin says, handing over a Moleskine notebook. "I didn't want your colleagues to get their purple-gloved forensic mitts on it."

CSI had searched Milo's bedroom earlier. Sounds like their visit hadn't been a tactful one, as Hart had feared.

"It's Milo's journal," Crispin continues. "I'd like it back, please, when you've finished with it. And I'd rather you didn't let it out of your sight. I can't bring myself to read it, not yet. There might be something in there."

Hart takes the journal and passes it to Strover. "Thank you. We'll take good care of it."

Crispin stops to look at Hart.

"Nail that bastard Garstan for me, will you?" he says. "For Milo."

11

Dad said later that I didn't leave Mum's side all weekend. I hadn't told you that she was going to die on Monday and you carried on obliviously, tearing around the garden on your new bike.

I don't know whether Dad told my morbid prophecy to Mum – it's hard for a seven-year-old to judge a marriage, what information is shared – but she showed me more love that weekend than usual. Perhaps she knew too. Several times she cried out in pain, but it wasn't until Sunday afternoon that she really began to deteriorate.

You and I sat on the bottom of the stairs when the ambulance came. Dad had sent us to our bedrooms, but we'd crept down, drawn by the sight of strangers in green uniforms in our house, the eerie spill of flashing blue lights on the kitchen wall. A neighbour came round to sit with us when she was taken away. Dad went along too, said he would be back as soon as he could. I wanted to go as well, be with Mum, but I wasn't allowed. Instead, Dad had told us both we could kiss her before she was wheeled into the ambulance. You ran off – you didn't know it would be the last time you'd see her alive – but I kissed Mum goodbye, sobbing my heart out as Dad gently prised my arms away from her listless body.

I don't know how I got to sleep that night. Maybe the neighbour, a kind woman with a bright blue streak in her hair, slipped something into the hot chocolate she made us both before bedtime. The phone had rung in the late afternoon – I knew it was Dad – and I had stood at the top of the stairs, trying to listen, but I couldn't work out what the neighbour was saying. Later, she said she was popping next door to collect some things and would be staying the night on the sofa. That in itself was so strange, a sign that the world as I knew it had stopped spinning. Dad would be back very late, she said, when I came down that night and talked to her in the darkness. I didn't want to see that our neighbour was actually lying on our sofa, where my mother had lain so often in recent months. Was she going to marry Dad too?

Monday began early. Dad must have returned sometime in the night because I could hear him talking in the kitchen. You were still asleep. All that cycling round the garden yesterday had tired you out. I think it was your way of coping. It was the neighbour who saw me first, standing at the kitchen doorway. She nodded at Dad, who turned. His eyes were red, hair a mess. He didn't speak for a few moments, just pressed his lips tightly together. And then he knelt down and hugged me.

"She's dead, isn't she?" I said, strangely unable to cry. It was Dad who was sobbing.

"I'm so sorry," he managed to say. "It was very peaceful."

"What is it?" you said, standing at the door, looking at us hugging each other. "What's wrong?"

"Come here," Dad said, gathering us up into a group hug, but I could feel you pulling away as he tried to explain what had happened.

It was much later in the day when Dad found me in the garden, sitting on the wooden swing he'd roped up for us under an apple tree.

"You were right," he said, pushing me gently back and forth.

"What time did she die?"

"Early this morning," he said.

"Was she scared?"

"Not scared, no. The doctors had given her some medicine to make her feel better. She said she was feeling sleepy and then…"

"Went to sleep."

"That's right."

He pushed me some more in silence. I often asked him to play with me on the swing, but he was always too busy. Would he have more time now?

"How did I know?" I asked.

"I'm not sure," he said. "How did it feel?"

"Golden."

"How long ago did you know?"

"When I picked the bad mushroom. I just suddenly knew."

"She loved you very much." That strange wobble in Dad's voice again.

"Even when she was cross?"

"Even when she was cross." He paused. "Best not to tell anyone that you knew. Our secret, eh?"

"OK." Back and forth I swung, no longer kicking my legs. "What happens if I get a funny feeling again? That somebody else is going to die?"

"You come and tell me."

"Even if it's about you?"

"Particularly if it's about me."

We got a dog soon after Mum died – a terrier-cross puppy. Dad called her Barka and let her sit on our sofa. She was a great comfort to me, but I'm not sure you ever bonded with her. We had a connection, another thing that made you jealous. I understood her. It started when I realised Barka knew when Dad was coming home from work. Ten minutes before he arrived, she would get up from her bed in the kitchen and sit at the window in the front room. Dad's office hours were never the same. And he used to cycle up from the railway station, so it's not like Barka heard Dad's car in the drive or anything like that. Sometimes he even came home by taxi. And on each occasion, Barka would be waiting for him at the window, tail wagging. I would wait for him too, stand beside Barka and watch for Dad's tall, stooped figure in the road. Everyone seemed to have a gift except you.

At school, whenever I mentioned Barka's behaviour, you tried to dismiss it as nothing. Just like you did when I mentioned how I always seemed to wake up a few minutes before our morning alarm, even when we were going away on holiday and it was set for an earlier time than usual. Or when I insisted that I could sense if someone was staring at me from behind. (Dad said it was called scopaesthesia.)

And later, you thought I was insane when I told you of a German parrot in the Second World War that used to warn of bombing raids in Leipzig two hours before the sirens; or how the animals in Belgrade Zoo had behaved strangely in the hours leading up to NATO bombing raids – just like the elephants in Sri Lanka had moved to higher ground before the tsunami struck in 2004.

You didn't like it either when we went over to the church to put flowers on Mum's grave. You would only stay for a few minutes, urging me to come home with you. But I liked to sit on the grass beside the grave and talk to Mum, Barka at my side.

"She can't hear you," you'd say. "She's dead." But I could hear Mum and she could hear me. "Freak," you'd mutter under your breath as you walked away, just loud enough to be heard, but I knew you were envious, wanted to listen to Mum's voice too.

One day your jealousy turned into something darker. You'd got back from school early, before Wendy, our au pair, had arrived to cook us our dinner. (Dad hired Wendy, from Dublin, after Mum died.) I'd stayed on for the school reading club. Barka would know when we were coming home too but she wouldn't wait at the window if it was just you, which made you so mad. (You thought I'd trained her not to go to the window, but I hadn't.)

That day, when I walked up the road, half an hour after you, Barka wasn't waiting for me at the window either. I sensed straight away that something had happened to her. Barka would always wait for me. And when you seemed upset, shut away in your room, I feared the worst. The carpet was wet outside your door.

Dad found her bedraggled body two days later, down by the river that runs through the bottom of the village. We buried her at the back of the lawn. The ground was hard and Dad got blisters on his hands. He said Barka must have escaped from the garden and drowned. I never told him about the wet carpet, but I think he knew.

12

Present day

Mel leans forward and cups her hands around Hart's. They're sitting in a corner of the café by the entrance to the hospital, trying to make sense of what had happened earlier in the Emergency Department.

"Give me a break," he says, as Mel frowns at the pain aux raisins in front of him. "It's my birthday. And the worst on record, no question. I think I'm allowed 300 calories of butter and dough."

"I'm sorry," Mel says, tearing a piece off and eating it. She usually steals the gooey centre, so he can't complain.

"And our day started so well," Mel says, licking her fingers.

It's the eight hours since that's been such a shitshow. For her as well as him. Mel had battled so hard to save the patient, just as he'd done with his mum. He had been with his dad when he'd died too, but that had been different.

It was 2 a.m. in Prospect Hospice and he'd slipped away in his sleep. Dad probably hadn't heard, but he'd told him that he would soon be with Mum.

"Are you OK?" Hart asks. It had all been so physical, Mel pumping away as if her own life had depended on it too.

"Shattered. Haven't had to do that for a while," Mel says. "Beth said they've never seen anything like it either." She pauses. "I'm also relieved, which I know isn't a great thing to be feeling right now. Shameful, in fact."

"How do you mean?"

"It really upset me that such a troubled man knew my name, had asked for you. But now? He's dead and, well, you know, it's no longer such a big deal. That's terrible of me, isn't it? A patient died."

Hart squeezes her hand, knowing he hasn't told Mel everything yet, that he will have to explain all sooner or later.

"It isn't terrible," he says. "Do they know why he died?"

"Some venepuncture blood tests were taken during resus. To try and work out what was going on."

"And?"

"They were just checking for red and white blood cells, kidney function, electrolyte balance, that sort of thing. You'll have to wait for the autopsy. The only surprise was his epinephrine levels – adrenaline to you and me. Off the chart, apparently."

"He was given a shot, wasn't he?"

"Even so."

"He was terrified, Mel. Terrified of dying."

"Not the only one around here," she says, raising her eyebrows.

"That isn't funny."

"You're doing fine, Sile," she says. "You've reached fifty-seven with no serious medical complications. You're bloody lucky. Lighten up a bit, will you? Everything still works – with a bit of encouragement." She smiles, stroking the back of his hand with her thumb.

"It's hard when someone asks to see you in person and then blows their brains out," Hart says, pulling away, welling up. "And then, less than an hour later, another man claims to know you before having a cardiac arrest."

"I know, I'm sorry." She pauses. "Any idea how they knew your name? How this guy knew mine?"

Hart shakes his head. He hasn't told her that the man at the front desk knew her name too. Earlier, Mel had persuaded him not to return to Gablecross straight away, despite pressure from colleagues to be back in the office. She knew he needed to talk through everything that's happened today, try to make sense of the traumatic events. They had gone for a walk around the hospital car park, before heading here to the café. Hart had remained largely silent. Mel's late mother was always urging him to articulate his emotions more, to see a therapist. He's got nothing against confiding in total strangers. It helped when he and Mel were going through a rocky patch. But opening up doesn't come naturally to him, even with Mel, and it was walking the Camino de Santiago with her that got them laughing again.

"I was sent a birthday card in the office this morning," Hart says, making a determined effort to communicate.

"One card? More popular than I thought."

"A few more than that, actually," he says. "And a cake. With a candle."

"Good old HR."

"And no, I didn't eat it all. Not even a slice."

"You'll waste away if you're not careful." They both know that's never going to happen.

"This card," he says, "it was unsigned, had a picture of the Grim Reaper."

"Someone else with your sense of humour."

"It wasn't funny, Mel."

"Quite funny."

Mel's got her own sense of humour back since returning to nursing. A requirement of the job. Same for policing, except that he seems to have mislaid his today. He looks around the café and takes a deep breath. The moment can't be put off any longer. He leans forward, ready to tell her who sent the card, how he thinks the two men who died knew both their names. And then Beth appears.

"You guys OK?" she says, glancing at them both.

Hart looks up, relieved. "Can I get you a coffee?"

"I'm good." She pauses, puffing out her cheeks. "That was quite something, wasn't it?"

Hart and Mel nod. No one knows what to say. "Tragic," Mel offers.

"You got a moment?" Beth asks Hart, sitting down at their table.

"Sure."

"Pathology's pulling its finger out. Dr Baydon's upstairs now, talking to an old bloke who keeps going on about cricket. Once he heard you were involved, he said he'd fast-track the autopsy."

"Malcolm Strangeways," Hart says, smiling. One of the few advantages of getting older. Contacts are made over the years, people remember, return favours. Hart couldn't wish for anyone better to carry out the autopsy. Malcolm did one for him three years ago, on a young actor found dead by Wilton Windmill. "Used to be at the Home Office. One of the best forensic pathologists in the business."

"There's something else," Beth says, retrieving an object from a side pocket of her scrubs. "The patient had nothing on him when he was brought into A&E. No wallet or phone. At least we thought not. But I just found this, in his jeans."

Beth holds up a small hourglass. "I thought it might be of interest."

13

Hart knows that he is wanted back at Gablecross – his phone is showing a string of missed calls from Strover – but he needs to drive over to Wanborough first. The village is only five minutes away and he will be back at the station feeling better for the detour. Stronger. He's not religious but St Andrew's Church, on the southern edge of the village, is his go-to place in times of crisis. And today is already turning into a crisis of clusterfuckery proportions. His parents had retired to Wanborough and both are buried in the graveyard.

He pulls up in the church car park, the hourglass that Beth gave him in a plastic evidence bag on the passenger seat. He should ring Strover back, hear what she's got to say, tell her what happened at the hospital, but he needs to get his own head around it first. He's still haunted by the patient's manic last words.

"'Beautiful baby Jane arrived in the world at 6.49 a.m. this morning.' But when's she going to leave? That's what we really want to know. When's she going to depart this world?"

Hart steps out of the warm car into the cold afternoon air. The churchyard is carpeted in thick snow. One day he will bring Strover here, bore his colleague rigid with the history of the church, just like he's bored his family. St Andrew's is one of only three in England with a western tower and a central spire.

He sets off past the headstones, listing like stranded ships in the whiteness, down the path to the far end of the graveyard. He'll show Strover the family grave too. His dad, always looking for ways to save money, had inscribed his own name on Hart's mum's headstone when she died, including the date of his birth, but kept his date of death clear.

"The stonemason can fill it in when I'm gone," he'd said. "Save me a fortune."

Much to Hart's annoyance, he'd also got the mason to add his own name too, once again including his date of birth but leaving a space for Hart's death to be added later. Never mind that Hart fancies his own headstone, to be shared with Mel, and wasn't consulted. It was such a *Dad* thing to do: practical, planning ahead, thrifty.

"Buy one, get two free, I say," he'd joked.

Despite the unwarranted namecheck, Hart feels nothing but love for his parents as he heads towards their grave. Snow starts to fall heavily again, thick flakes swirling around him. He pulls up his collar to shield himself from the cold. His parents are buried in the far corner of the graveyard, beside a drystone wall. It's early afternoon and peaceful, the noise of the day absorbed by the snow, except for the distant hum of the M4, which he finds faintly reassuring. It's only when the motorway falls quiet that one needs to worry.

He used to come to this spot when Conor was running him and Mel ragged. Sometimes Mel accompanied him. The sight of his parents' names always seems to lift his spirits and, if he is honest, a part of him likes seeing his own name with theirs, set in stone. But today, as he approaches the grave, he almost loses his footing with shock.

"Oh no," he whispers. "No, no, no…"

A wind chime tinkles from a nearby grave. High up in the pine trees a solitary crow calls out, cutting through the chill stillness of the air. If the headstone had been defaced with graffiti, he could pretend it's impersonal, a wanton act of vandalism. But the writing in black paint is neat, intentional, and inscribed in the space after Hart's date of birth. There is nothing random about the date of death either: *4 December.* Three days from now.

Hart sinks to his knees and stares at the snow-capped headstone. Three days. The chest pain begins again, thoughts start to churn. He needs to get a grip, see this for what it is: targeted psychological harassment by someone with a grudge. Nothing more, nothing less. He's fit and healthy, taking Sniper Alley by storm, here for the long haul.

"It's me," he says, calling Mel on his mobile, his hand shaking in the cold.

"Where are you? I can hear birds." Hart looks around the graveyard, listens to a brave wren punching above its weight. A fireburst of song from a bird no bigger than a ping pong ball.

"I'm down at Mum and Dad's."

He hadn't told Mel he was coming here when he left the hospital. It was an impulse decision.

"Oh Sile," she says, knowing that he only visits when he's in trouble. "You OK?"

"Not exactly," he says. "Someone's defaced the headstone."

"What? How?"

He tries to describe the sight in front of him, glancing around the graveyard again. There are still no CCTV cameras here, even though lead was stolen from the church roof a few years back. The burglars had been disturbed, leaving a chunk of lead behind in the graveyard. Another piece turned up in Bath. The lead was replaced with Welsh slate, burglars never caught.

"It's official, written in stone," he says, wishing he were being funny. "I'm going to die in three days."

"Sile, you're not about to die. You're fifty-seven and doing just great."

That's what his mother thought. And look what happened to her.

"And your mum had an underlying medical condition," she adds, reading his mind. "You don't. You see your GP more often than you see me. He's given you a clean bill of health. Many times."

"Physical health."

Most recently, his GP had reassured him that a mouth ulcer was not oral cancer, that his red urine was due to beetroot rather than a kidney infection, and that one pupil wasn't smaller than the other and he didn't have a brain tumour.

"We've been here before, Sile. If your head's not straight, you need to see someone. Otherwise..."

"Otherwise what?"

"You're fine."

He knows she's right. His GP has suggested as much. But if he lets someone else poke about inside his head, he's worried what they might find. Looking around the graveyard one more time, he heads back up the path to the car. He knows he needs to tell Mel who's responsible, who did this to his parents' grave, sent him the card and told the two men they were going to die, but he can't bring himself to confide in her, not yet. It will worry her senseless. Him too. Because he knows that the moment he does, the death threat becomes real, something he can no longer deny. And the countdown will begin.

14

"I've been trying to call you," Strover says, as Hart sits down at a desk in the corner of the Parade Room. The Wanborough church diversion took longer than he thought – one road was closed because of the snow – and the day is almost done.

"I saw," Hart says, knowing that Strover deserves an apology. He had meant to call on the drive back from Wanborough, but he was too preoccupied with the grave and its desecration. The sight had shocked him to the core and then saddened him, but now all he feels is anger. He's already phoned the stonemason to get the writing removed. Seems like it will cost a lot more than his dad saved on the three-for-one job lot.

At least he's able to work at his preferred desk. Sometimes new recruits try to sit at it, unaware of the Parade Room's unspoken hierarchy, until they are quietly moved on by

Strover. Hart doesn't like to pull rank. But he does like a corner desk, with his back to the wall. A place where he can see what's going on, who's coming and going. No surprises. That's how he prefers life. And if Ward walks in, he's got time to jump out the window.

"How was the hospital?" Strover asks. "Is your wife OK?"

Hart talks Strover through what happened in the Emergency Department, the mention, once again, of "death days", the shock of seeing another stranger who knew his name die in front of him. And the hourglass that Beth had found in the patient's jeans, now with Forensics.

"That's why I was trying to call you, sir," Strover says.

Hart looks up. "When the ambulance crew came out to Gablecross, to take the body away from the front desk, they found this."

Strover holds up another hourglass in a plastic specimen bag. It's just like the one found with the patient in the hospital.

"I'll take it over to Forensics, see what they can find."

"Make sure they don't lose it this time," he says, peering more closely at the hourglass.

Three years ago, CSI had lost the one found beside Milo's body in Wilton. That's what happens when the bean-counters cut budgets. Hart leans back in his chair, hands behind his head. He's trying to look relaxed, but he's feeling sick inside. After failing to tell Mel what's going on, he needs to talk to Strover. It's time to front up.

"I don't think we can pretend any more, deny who's behind all this," he says. "My parents' headstone – in Wanborough – has also been defaced. That's why I was late getting back. Long story, but my name's on there too – just my birth. Dad got a job lot when Mum died. Someone's added my death date: 4 December."

"What?" Strover asks, as Hart shows a photo he'd taken on his phone. For a few seconds, Strover is speechless, staring at the image. "That's awful. I'm so sorry."

"It has to be linked to Garstan," Hart says. "Dr Rory Garstan. We both know this whole shitshow's got his fingerprints all over it. I hoped to God it wasn't him, but it can't be anyone else. There's no other explanation. We need to find out where he is. When he's due to be released."

It feels such a relief to be finally dealing with the psychiatrist, confronting head on what happened in the past.

"That's the other reason I was calling you," Strover says. "Garstan's out already."

Hart looks up, shocked. "What?"

He's been in denial about the psychiatrist ever since he put him away three years ago. Buried his head in the sand. Out of sight, out of mind. Hoping in vain that sending him to jail would be the end of the matter. As if.

"When?" he asks.

"Seven days ago."

Just in time for Hart's fifty-seventh birthday. And for the 4th of December. He slumps down in his chair, closes his eyes. It all makes hideous sense now, as he knew it would. When the psychiatrist was first sent down, three years ago, he'd made a note to keep track of him, follow his progress inside, wait for the inevitable news that he would only serve half his sentence or less because of prison overcrowding, but life moves on. After the first few months, he'd been too busy on other cases to check. Or maybe, deep down, he just didn't want to know.

"He was due to be let out six months ago, but there were concerns."

"Tell me about them."

"According to prisoner location," Strover adds, "he was moved from Bristol to Barontrent last year."

HMP Barontrent, a Category C male prison east of Upavon, one of Wiltshire's two prisons. Hart knows it well, provided it with plenty of inmates over the years, including a few lifers. Once among the worst prisons in the country, it has improved recently, focussing on training and resettlement.

"Do we know where he is now?" Hart asks. Garstan would have liked it at Barontrent, where most of the senior staff are rumoured to be Freemasons, promoted for their dodgy handshakes rather than their talent or experience.

"I've been trying to speak to his PO, but the Probation Service is currently on strike."

Of course it is. Hart can't blame the staff. Britain's prisons are screwed, their overworked employees facing daily safety concerns. Reduced supervision of former offenders in the community – people like Garstan – is the least of their worries.

"But we do know Garstan was picked up at the gates by a black Mercedes," Strover says. "All-electric CLA. Sport edition, by the looks of it. I got some photos sent over."

Strover has a contact who works at Barontrent.

"Numberplate?" Hart asks.

Strover shoots him a look.

"Registered to Garstan's Pewsey address."

Strover passes a photo over to Hart, who squints at the grainy image. "Who's driving?" It could be anyone.

"This one's clearer," Strover says, handing him another

photo. "It looks like Garstan's old PA. Katya? It was the company car."

Hart studies the second image. It's definitely Katya.

"ANPR?" Hart asks.

"Last seen heading eastbound on the M4, leaving at Junction 12. An hour later, it heads back westbound on the M4, before dropping down towards Pewsey. Home, presumably."

"We need to check Garstan's house, see if he's moved back in, what sort of state it's in. And find out from the General Medical Council if he's applied to practise again."

"Is that really likely?" Strover asks.

"The NHS is crying out for more psychiatrists. Wouldn't surprise me if the GMC overlooks the small problem of a prison sentence."

"A criminal record's not an automatic dealbreaker, then?" Strover asks.

"Apparently not." Hart says, pulling out his phone. He's had an idea. "I took a photo of the patient who died at the Great Western," he says.

Dr Baydon wasn't happy when he'd taken it, until he reminded her that the patient had appeared to know his name and a member of her staff. His death was not only a police matter, but a potentially personal one too. Strover's phone pings as the photo arrives.

"Send it over to your friend at Barontrent," Hart adds. "See if someone recognises him."

"You think he might have met Garstan there?" Strover asks.

"It's possible."

A long shot, but there has to be a connection between

Garstan and the men who died today. Neither had struck Hart as upstanding citizens. Prison is an obvious place for them to have met the psychiatrist.

"And the man at the front desk?" Strover asks.

Hart blanks out an image of him.

"Oddly I didn't take his mugshot. But the CSI snapper did. Get a copy from him and send over the least shocking image to Barontrent too. But warn them first, eh?"

For some reason, Strover has an unusually high tolerance when it comes to gore – even for a police officer – and seems genuinely surprised when others are upset.

Hart looks again at the hourglass on his desk, turns it over in the bag, watches the granules fall. If both men were inmates at Barontrent, Garstan could have spent time with them. He and Strover need to ask around, find out what sort of reputation Garstan had inside, who he mixed with.

He thinks of his parents' defaced gravestone and bunches his fists. 4 December. Three days from now.

15

It wasn't the first time that Gaby had disappeared. She would often go off on her own into the woods after school and not come back until late. But on this occasion, she didn't come back at all. I knew why she liked to vanish. She lived with her Dad on the canal, which sounded fun, but he was a bit of a boozer and a narrowboat could suddenly feel very small when the only other person on board was off their head. She was in Year Six when she vanished and was one of my closest friends. We were all at the same village primary school and promised to stick together when we went to the Academy in September, but your lack of interest in Gaby's whereabouts shocked me.

Our primary was big on the outdoors – forest school learning – so it was hardly surprising that Gaby was so at home in the woods. But this time it felt different. Her dad called the police at 1 a.m. He'd been at the pub until midnight, too drunk to notice she hadn't come in from school. The police and an Emergency Duty Team from Social Services, who knew Gaby well, were on the scene by 2 a.m., and rang round Gaby's friends, including me, because she'd left her phone on the boat. Most people didn't pick up. Their parents didn't let them have phones until Year Seven, let alone keep them in their bedrooms, but Dad had given us mobiles after Mum had died. (I think it made him feel more connected to us.) I answered in a sleepy voice and looked under my bed – where Gaby liked to stay on sleepovers – before confirming to the female officer that she definitely wasn't with me.

The next morning I told Dad what had happened in the night and he, rather than Wendy, dropped us off at school. He'd usually left for work before the school run. We were met at the school gates by a number of police officers, who were talking to parents. Search teams, they said, were already scouring the nearby woodland for Gaby, using drones and heat-seeking cameras, and parents were signing up to help look for her during the day. Gaby's dad was there too, in a baggy sweater, jeans and ruffled hair. He looked guilty and like he hadn't slept all night.

Our Year Six teacher explained in the first lesson what had happened and two other pupils said that they'd had voicemail messages from the police left on their phones in the night – a new experience, as we all tended to text each other. The teacher tried to reassure us, but she was clearly shaken by Gaby's disappearance. She then announced that the whole school had been asked to draw pictures of Gaby, which would be put up in the assembly hall.

One girl started to cry because she suddenly couldn't

remember what Gaby looked like, but then the teacher found some photographs of her and passed them around. I sat there for a long while before I started to draw, thinking how I might depict my friend. Gaby was a wild, feral child with bird's nest hair, always climbing trees and eating things – blackberries, hedgerow apples – that she had found. Her dad was a bit of a forager. Should I draw her with juice smeared around her mouth? Up a tree? We'd bonded when we both agreed that trees could talk to each other, their roots entwined like holding hands.

At one point friendly female police officer came into the classroom and asked if any of us knew where Gaby might be. I think we would have told her already if we knew. She walked around the classroom, admiring our drawings, and said they were so good the police might have to use us in future missing-person cases. When she got to me, she noticed that I hadn't started to draw anything yet.

"Did you know Gaby well?" she asked.

I didn't like her past tense.

"She's my best friend," I said.

"And you don't know where she might have gone?"

"I'm thinking," I said, chewing the end of my pencil.

"Well, let us know if you have any ideas."

And then it came to me. Once the police officer had moved on to the next desk, I started to draw. I knew exactly where Gaby was. High up in a tree canopy, that's all I knew, all I could feel, but that meant only one thing. I started with a large oak, and then the long ladder that went up to the observation platform. It was once used by gamekeepers when they were culling deer, but it had fallen into disrepair. I drew Gaby next. I knew she wasn't injured or distressed.

Trees were her happy place. We'd seen the platform on a mushroom hunt with Mum, who had told us not to climb up because the ladder's rungs were rotten and it was dangerous. Neither of us had been back since. Gaby must have been feeling brave.

Dad had arranged for Wendy to pick us up from school. He was sorry that he hadn't been able to join the other parents in the search during the day and was keen to know that we were safe. We all handed in our pictures at the end of the day, but I hadn't told anyone where I thought Gaby was. I wanted to go there and find her myself, reassure her that it was OK to come down, that she wouldn't be in trouble.

"Can we join the search for Gaby?" I asked, as we both walked home from school. Wendy was ahead of us, talking to a parent. "I think I know where she is."

"You do?" you asked, surprised, perking up. You'd drawn a silly missing poster, depicting her as a stick figure, which had upset me. You weren't taking her disappearance seriously. "Shouldn't you tell the police?"

"She doesn't like them," I said. "They took away her dad once."

"And you really think you know where she might be?"

"I know exactly where she is."

"How?" you asked, looking at me. For the first time you seemed interested in Gaby.

"I just do," I said, not wanting to make you jealous again.

"Like you knew when Mum was going to die?" you asked. I had his proper attention now. "And what card Dad had put in the tin?"

I nodded. "I can see a ladder," I said.

After dropping our school bags at home, we set off from the village with Wendy and headed up into the woods. Some parents were coming back, crestfallen and upset. Others, like us, were just starting to search for Gaby. It took us half an hour to reach the clearing near the oak tree. I suddenly panicked, worried that we were in the wrong place. No one was around, the scenery started to look unfamiliar, overgrown, and I couldn't see a ladder anywhere.

"Does she feel close?" you asked. I thought you were taking the piss, but you were serious. "I think I can feel her presence," you said.

I looked up and your eyes were scrunched shut, as if you were trying hard to imagine something.

"Are you OK?" Wendy asked, glancing at me in case I knew what you were doing. I knew exactly what you were pretending *to do.*

Opening your eyes, you breathed in slowly, as if you were meditating, looking around at all the trees. And then you started to sprint.

I couldn't keep up with you, but I followed as fast as I could and soon saw the ladder in the far corner of the clearing. You were fifty yards ahead now and shouting. "It's OK, Gaby, I'm here," you yelled. "I've found you." You turned to the forest and shouted even louder: "It's OK everyone, I've found her! I've found Gaby!"

When Wendy and I caught up with you at the foot of the tree, you were already on your phone, about to dial 999.

"Let me call them," Wendy said, taking the phone from you. "I've got the missing person number."

"...Gaby, the missing schoolgirl... Yes, we're with her

now," Wendy was soon saying, checking a police leaflet she'd picked up at school.

"Do they want my name?" you asked Wendy. "Tell them my name. Do they know how to spell it?"

As Wendy gestured for you to let her speak to the police, I looked up into the tree and there was Gaby's frightened face staring down. When she saw me, she seemed angry, as if I'd betrayed her. I hadn't wanted it to be like this. I was hoping to find her quietly, reassure her, coax her down without any fuss.

You were in the papers the next day. "'Psychic' boy finds missing schoolgirl". You talked of a sixth sense, how you had pictured a ladder first and then a tree canopy. Gaby's dad gave Dad a bottle of champagne, the only way he could think to thank us. Did I mind what had happened? What you had done? Gaby knew the truth and I have never forgotten.

16

The past

"We've got two choices," Hart says to Strover, opening the car door to cool down. They are parked in the lay-by across from Wilton Windmill. The summer air is hot and still, a mist of dandelion seeds drifting listlessly in the slanting sunshine. "Either we go in hard with a magistrate's warrant to search Garstan's House. Or..."

"We go back and ask him politely if he's got any unlicensed guns."

"And you know which one I prefer."

"I know you don't like magistrates."

Never has, never will.

"Garstan might just show us his licensed guns, like his..." Hart pauses, trying to remember the name. He'd checked the police records earlier and Garstan has valid licences for three shotguns.

"Damascus over-and-under," Strover says.

"How do you know all that stuff anyway?" Hart asks.

"My partner shoots."

"And does he have a Damascus under-and-over?"

"Over-and-under. She doesn't, no. Nothing quite so flash. But she used to work in PR for Purdey's."

Ouch. There'd been a male partner in the past – Sean, an Irish screenwriter and pub quiz expert – but still, he shouldn't make assumptions. Why Strover still wants to work with him is anyone's guess. He's too old, too unreconstructed. Actually, that's not true. Too old, perhaps, with some baked-in generational prejudices that he's working on, but he hopes he's not unreconstructed. Last week he heard a uniform say that he had two pronouns if he was ever asked: "fuck" and "off". That was unreconstructed, offensively so, as well as grammatically incorrect, and he would hate to be put in the same camp as that person.

"So let's drive back there and explain we want another quick chat," Hart says. "Give him a chance to show off his armoury. If he doesn't get out the shorty and hand it in, we can ask him directly, turn up the heat and see how he responds."

Hart steps out of the car. "First, though, we need to check in on CSI," he says, as he slams the door shut and heads off towards the windmill.

Two minutes later, he's talking to the CSM. "There's nothing here, guv," he said. "I said the same to DCS Ward too."

"You what?" Hart asks.

"The boss was here earlier. Said he was passing by."

What the hell was Ward doing here? Checking up on him, seeing for himself whether a rural suicide warranted the full CSI treatment? Ward still hasn't forgiven him for the crop-circle investigation five years earlier. Hart had dragged Porton Down's name through the mud at a time when Ward was trying to mend fences with the government's secretive military research centre. The Novichok attack on the Skripals in Salisbury a few years earlier had led to some serious bad blood between the force and Porton.

Hart looks out across the shimmering fields and back at the white tent, which is already being dismantled. Milo's body has been taken away for an autopsy. He will read his journal when he returns to the office.

"Don't forget the security camera on the shepherd's hut, over by the windmill," Hart says, looking across the field at the white sails.

"We're on it," the CSM says.

"Anyone else's prints on the hourglass?"

Had Ward asked the same question?

"You mean apart from yours and Strover's?" The CSM is only half joking.

"Give us a break," Hart says, irritated. "We didn't touch it."

"Nothing. Just the deceased's. But the granules inside are interesting. We've taken the hourglass apart, run some initial tests on them. They're animal rather than mineral."

"Animal? What sort?"

"Maybe a pig? Wild boar? It looks like powdered bone."

Twenty minutes later, they are back at Garstan's house again outside Pewsey. Hart asks Strover to pull over while he finishes his coronation chicken sandwich, bought from a farm shop. There was no time for a pie at the pub in Wilton, which pained him. Strover bought a spelt salad. The pillared entrance to Garstan's house is 300 yards up the road, gate open.

"You can take the lead," Hart says, wiping his mouth. "Go in with some serious shooting talk, drop in that your partner likes a loader."

"For the record, she doesn't."

"Whatever. Just get Garstan relaxed. Talk the talk. I suspect we'll have to wait for a gap between patients. He'll be nervous, wondering why we're back so soon, but it's better he's—"

"Sir," Strover says, interrupting. She nods as a car pulls out of Garstan's drive and onto the road, turning away from them. "I know that car. BMW X5."

Hart watches as Strover whips out her phone and takes a photo.

"Not really in the mood for Top Trumps," Hart says.

"I mean, I know that car as in I know who owns it," Strover says, expanding the image so that they can see the numberplate. Hart leans over. The photo is blurred, but just clear enough.

"That's DCS Ward's new whip," she says, turning to Hart. "Saw it in the car park yesterday."

"What the—"

A second later, Hart's phone rings. It's Ward.

17

"Should I answer it?" Hart asks Strover, holding up his phone. "Do you think he saw us?"

"Not from this distance," Strover says, looking down the lane at Garstan's entrance. They are parked in a small lay-by, 300 yards up the road. "Lucky he didn't turn our way."

"I better take it," Hart says, answering his phone. "DI Hart."

"Silas, how are things?" Ward asks. "Mel still enjoying life as a florist?"

Hart hates it when Ward asks about Mel, as if he's interested in the family lives of his staff. Having said that, he did seem genuinely concerned when Conor was unwell.

"All good, sir," he says. "Mel's got two weddings this Saturday. Kitchen's like a greenhouse. *Agave amica* a-go-go."

That should shut him up. Mel's taught him all the Latin names for flowers, including tuberoses. In truth, she's missing the nursing, talking about a return to the Great Western Hospital, but no need to share that with Ward.

"Excellent, excellent. My wife's a big fan of *Verbena bonariensis*. The garden's full of it."

Ward has never made any effort to disguise his private education and academic bent, particularly when he's talking to someone like Hart. After Westminster School, Ward went up to Oxford, where he read theology. Only God knows why he chose to pivot into policing.

"I have an interesting proposition for you," he says. "Do you have a moment?"

Hart looks at Strover. They both know Ward only makes suggestions if a) they might further his own career, or b) they'll hold back someone else's. He's the most ambitious man Hart knows.

"I'm all ears, sir," he says, wondering whether it's just Ward or if arrogant people the world over have no idea how they sound.

"You might have heard we've been having an internal review of cold cases."

Ward lets the phrase hang in the air: "cold cases". What detectives are given when they're put out to pasture, or brought out of retirement, usually in a department dressed up as the Major Incident Review Team to make them feel better.

"Cold cases," Hart repeats, trying to own the phrase, take the sting out of it.

"Murdered mispers where we've never found the body – they're the ones that really stick in the craw," Ward continues. "The cases the media give us a hard time about. And here's the thing. I think we might have someone who can move the dial for us."

Hart looks across at Strover and then back down the lane at Garstan's house. They both know who Ward has in mind.

"And who might that be?" Hart asks, bracing himself for the answer.

"A rather brilliant psychiatrist – Dr Rory Garstan. I gather you saw him earlier today about that sad suicide case in Wilton." Hart closes his eyes. This isn't happening. "I was passing and dropped in on CSI, by the way. I think you might have been at the pub. It's clearly suicide, not quite sure why you called in the cavalry, but there we go. Your call."

It is his call and Ward should back off. And no, he wasn't at the Swan, much as he wanted to be, but Hart bites his tongue, waiting to hear what Ward has to say about Garstan.

"Anyway, Rory has a practice in Harley Street, as I'm sure you know, and does a lot of good work down here too, with the Avon and Wiltshire Mental Health Partnership."

"Rory" now, is it? Maybe if Hart punches himself in the face, this will all be a bad dream. But Ward is still talking about Garstan.

"The remarkable thing is, he's no ordinary psychiatrist. I've actually known him for a while – we go shooting together."

Hart looks across at Strover again. Crispin's allegation is becoming more credible by the second. Increasingly complicated too.

"But he's only recently – today, in fact – explained exactly what it is he can do," Ward continues. "You're going to think I've been on the sauce, but he's got a talent. A truly exceptional talent."

"And what sort of talent is that, sir?" Hart asks, shaking his head in disbelief.

"For perceiving something, a person, a place or an object, that isn't there. We're not talking about seeing someone's future, which I know he claims to do with his celebrity clients in London. This is something else, related but different."

"It's called remote viewing, sir," Hart says.

"You're familiar with it, then?"

Only in as much as Hart's seen *The Men Who Stare at Goats*, read how the Pentagon once invested in psychic research to give American troops an edge on the battlefield. And he knew a so-called "psychic cop" at the Met who used clairvoyance to help him track down villains, including Lord Lucan. Apparently, the fugitive aristo is buried under a housing estate in Uckfield. Colleagues dubbed him the "Psychic Flop", so low was his success rate.

"I wouldn't say familiar," Hart says. "I'm not exactly the biggest believer in extrasensory perception."

"Me neither," Ward says. "Absolutely not. Don't get me wrong. But Rory's offering – off the clock – to try his hand at finding a few mispers. And I thought we'd start with the suspected murder cases. Nothing to lose except our reputation, so the plan is not to mention Dr Garstan's involvement. We've come into some 'credible new evidence' – that's all anyone needs to know at this stage. He wishes to remain anonymous too. I want you and Strover to liaise with him, be our sole point of contact. If nothing comes of it, nobody's the wiser. But at least we can say to the families – to the media – that we tried."

Hart knows what's happened. Garstan panicked after

their visit to his house this morning, sensed Hart was onto him. So he's played his joker, maybe something he's had up his sleeve for a while now, for when things get sticky. He rang his old shooting pal Ward and offered his "psychic" services. Maybe pulled in a Freemasonry favour too.

"Are you still there?" Ward asks.

"I'm here," Hart says, wishing he wasn't.

"The thing is – and I know I can tell you this in confidence, trust you with it – he gave a small demonstration when I saw him today."

"What sort of demonstration?" Hart can't believe Ward has bought into Garstan so completely.

"With some cards. Different images. I held the cards, he had to guess what they were. Got them all right."

Of course he did. For someone who might have gone into academia, Ward is displaying alarmingly little evidence of critical thinking. Hart's about to challenge him when he sees Ward's car up ahead, coming down the lane towards them. He must have doubled back.

"Get down," Hart whispers to Strover. They both put their heads below the dashboard as the car draws near and passes their lay-by. Hart and Strover's usual car is being fixed in the garage, so there's a good chance Ward won't recognise their temporary vehicle.

"A plane, a bottle, a sailing boat, a mushroom… I forget what the others were," Ward is saying on the phone, as Hart and Strover stay bent double, heads almost touching beneath the dashboard. "But here's the thing: he got them all right. And yes, I checked for mirrors. Of course I did. I'm a bloody detective, after all."

A detective who's always been more interested in climbing

the greasy pole than solving cases. Hart waits until he's sure the car has disappeared before he sits up again. He indicates to Strover, now also upright, to drive off in the other direction. He can't risk another flypast by Ward.

"That's extraordinary, sir," Hart manages to say.

"Isn't it? Anyway, drop by when you're next in the office. We're going to try Garstan out on the Sophie Mills case. I've outlined the basic details to him. And I want you to be the SIO. You'll work well together, I know. And you're more familiar than anyone with the case. Give him a call now if you're still in the area. I'm sure he'll be pleased to see you again."

Hart had worked briefly on the investigation, soon after he'd become head of Swindon CID, but he had been finding his feet. It had been a high-profile case and Wiltshire Police were heavily criticised for not solving it. Sophie, nineteen, had last been seen on CCTV leaving Angelo's nightclub on Fleet Street in Swindon in the early hours of a cold February night two years ago. She had been living with her grandmother in Cleverton Court, a tower block on the Penhill estate, and had a history of mental illness, suffering from anxiety and alcohol dependency. Occasionally on the game too, working first on Manchester Road and then moving over to Gorse Hill.

After calling for an Uber outside Angelo's, she had been seen on CCTV getting into the car on her own. The Uber driver, in a subsequent interview, said that he'd dropped her off outside Cleverton Court at 3 a.m., which was confirmed later by Uber's data. He had driven away before seeing her enter the property. A friend later came forward, saying that she had received a voice message from Sophie at 3.05 a.m., asking if she could stay at her place – ten minutes' walk away, on the other side of the Cricklade Road – as she'd lost her keys and was unable to wake her grandmother.

Sophie had also spoken of having met a man at the nightclub who had frightened her with his talk of dark sexual fantasies. She had left the club in the Uber soon afterwards. The male suspect had never been identified, despite multiple interviews with men who had been at the nightclub that evening. (Hart remembers having to conduct a dozen of them himself.) Her friend, who had gone to the nightclub with Sophie but left an hour before her, was also unable to identify the suspect, as she had not seen Sophie talk with any men. In a second message, left two minutes later, Sophie had said she was walking over to her place anyway. The friend had only picked up the voicemail messages the next morning. Sophie had never turned up.

18

Hart doesn't like it when he's been wrong-footed. Particularly if Ward's involved. But as Strover steers the car through the gates of Garstan's house in Pewsey for the second time in a day, he knows he's got no option but to talk to the psychiatrist. And instead of asking him about the illegal possession of a sawn-off shotgun, he'll have to feign interest in his batshit claims to see around corners.

"Do we not mention the guns at all then, sir?" Strover asks.

"Not until we know how close he really is to Ward. Whether people who shoot together, stay together. Not my world, but I'm guessing they're as thick as thieves."

"Freemasons?"

"That too."

"And Milo? Should we mention him again?"

To his shame, Hart had briefly forgotten about the young man who had taken his own life in a field this morning,

Garstan's drawing of him. Ward had thrown him off his stride.

"Not unless he does," Hart says.

After his boss had called him in the car earlier, Hart had gritted his teeth and rung Garstan, explained how much he was looking forward to working on a cold case with him. He couldn't believe he'd managed to get the words out. Garstan had said that he had a busy afternoon with patients, but he could see Hart and Strover in the early evening. Meanwhile, could they possibly arrange to bring along something that Sophie Mills – the misper – had owned? It would help him to locate her. *Dear God.* Should he bring along the Shroud of Turin too?

Katya, Garstan's PA, greets them at the front of the house.

"We've come to see Dr Garstan," Hart says.

"He's not here," she says in a strong Ukrainian accent.

"No?" Hart asks, surprised.

"I mean, he's here, but not in the house. He's outside. Shooting clay."

Strover throws Hart a knowing look.

"He told me to take you to him," Katya continues. "It's a bit of a way. We can go in the buggy?"

She points at a golf cart in the corner of the courtyard.

"OK," Hart says, as they walk over to the vehicle. "So he's expecting us."

"Of course," she says.

"Saw us coming." Hart glances at Strover and winks.

The irony of interrupting Garstan's clay pigeon shooting is not lost on Hart, given that their original plan was to talk to him about his guns. Instead, they had driven back to the office to collect some possessions, as requested, from the

Sophie Mills case, which Strover has brought along with them.

"Dr Rory thought you might be interested in the shooting," Katya says. "Having a go yourself."

As if on cue, two cracks of distant gunfire carry through the warm evening air, echoing around the woods behind the house. Katya flinches at the sound. Hart knows how she feels. Whatever extrasensory powers Garstan might possess have clearly deserted him: Hart would rather sort his sock drawer than "have a go" with a shotgun.

Hart and Strover climb into the back of the buggy as Katya steps into the driver's seat and they accelerate away.

Two minutes later, the buggy pulls up at the end of a track beside a fenced paddock. They have left behind the formal gardens that surround the main house and are now in a wilder part of the estate. The only sign of civilization, apart from the paddock, is a dark green gazebo. To their right, Garstan is standing with his back to them, a shotgun broken over his forearm, waiting, headphones on.

They are all about to climb out of the buggy when Katya glances across at Garstan, who has yet to see them, and then turns round in her seat.

"I told Milo never to come back," she says. Hart looks at Strover and then at Katya, who seems upset. "After his first session with Dr Rory."

Hart signals for Strover to take up the conversation. He wasn't expecting Garstan's PA to talk about Milo.

"Why shouldn't he have continued to see Garstan?" Strover asks, resting a hand on Katya's arm.

A stifled sob and then Katya shakes her head, climbs out. "Already I have said too much. Milo – he was a sweet boy."

They watch her walk off to arrange some chairs and a table in the gazebo. She won't say anything else, not today. They need to speak to her again, though. It could be crucial. *Damn Ward. Damn his shooting buddy.* Hart needs to stick to the facts. One of Garstan's patients took his life in a field this morning, convinced that he was destined to die today. And Garstan enjoys a lucrative trade in London as a psychiatrist who encourages people to live life to the full because it is finite and often short. That's all he knows, all he can say for the moment. Dots, not yet joined.

He watches Katya open a cool box, check inside and close it again. Is it picnic time? Hart would rather be at home, having a beer with Mel. Maybe a barbecue. He could do with blackening a fat sausage or two. He looks around, tries to clear his thoughts, get his bearings. In the distance, Milk Hill and the nearby white horse, branded onto the flank of the hill like a giant livestock mark. Garstan has still to acknowledge their arrival. Maybe he hasn't heard them. Either way, Hart's not interested in playing power games.

A moment later, Garstan snaps shut the gun and puts it to his shoulder. Two clays spin up into the low evening sky. Garstan hits them both, each one exploding in a puff of red powder. He breaks the gun, hangs it over his shoulder like slain quarry and walks over to them.

19

"Sorry about that," Garstan says, removing his headphones. "Last pair."

"Is that Italian?" Strover asks, nodding at the gun. "Perazzi?"

Strover's going in hard with her gun talk, breaking the ice. They need Garstan to relax.

"You shoot?" Garstan says, eyes lighting up. "Fancy a go?"

"My partner shoots," Strover says.

"MX 2005," he says, admiring his gun. "If it was good enough for Peter Wilson, it's good enough for me."

"He won gold, didn't he?" Strover asks. "Double trap, London, 2012." Hart's impressed. Strover's a walking Wikipedia.

"Despite dropping two birds in the last ten. You sure you don't want a go?"

Strover declines with a tight smile.

"DI Hart? Or may I call you Silas, now that we're going to be work colleagues?"

"Guns make me nervous," Hart says. Particularly ones without a licence, but that will have to wait. *Colleagues? Give me a break.*

"Shall we?" Garstan says, ushering them towards the gazebo. "Cold beer? Something soft?"

"Soft for both of us," Hart says.

"Of course, here on business rather than pleasure," Garstan says, smiling at Strover. Is he flirting? Good luck with that. "On duty."

They sit down at the table. Katya passes cans of sparkling water to Hart and Strover, an Asahi beer for Garstan.

"I've been reading up on the missing person case that Tarquin Ward wants me to help you good people with. Printed out a photo of Sophie Mills."

Hart doesn't need reminding of the grim details. Without a body, no option can be ruled out, but it's most likely she was unlawfully killed.

"It's a tragic story," Garstan says. "But maybe we can provide closure for her family."

"The grandmother's dead," Hart says. "Her mother's still around, but they've been estranged for years."

Hart reminds himself that he's dealing with one of Ward's friends, needs to be more cooperative. Or at least appear so.

"We've brought along Sophie's small handbag," he says, turning to Strover.

"A sequin clutch bag," Strover says. "Found near the entrance to Cleverton Court."

Strover pulls out the bag, labelled and wrapped in plastic, and passes it over to Garstan.

"OK to hold it?" he asks.

"All good," Strover says. "The lab's tested it multiple times. Only her fingerprints and DNA were ever found on it."

Hart wonders what Garstan is going to do next. Lay the clutch bag on the ground, surround it with scented candles and sacrifice a small she-goat? What was Ward thinking when he got this muppet on board?

But Garston places the bag carefully on the table in front of them, still in its wrapping.

"May I keep this overnight?" he asks.

Strover glances at Hart.

"Of course," Hart says.

"There were a few items in there when it was found," Strover says, getting out the bag. "Lipstick, a five-pound note, no bank card, a condom, some chewing gum, paracetamol. We've brought them along too, if you're interested."

"The more the better," Garstan says, as Strover passes them across to him. Each item is labelled and in a separate plastic bag.

"So how exactly does it work?" Hart asks, trying to bury his scepticism. "This remote viewing business?"

"I'm not entirely certain myself," Garstan says, smiling. "But I know that if I tried to explain, talk to you about psychometry" – he rests a hand on the bag – "how it feels as if I can tune into something that others can't, I'm not sure you'd believe me anyway. Most people don't. You're lucky to have such an enlightened Detective Chief Superintendent."

Enlightened? Hart keeps a straight face, avoids looking at Strover.

"I don't need to be psychic to sense your cynicism, Silas," Garstan says, moving his hands over the collection of

Sophie's possessions with the reverence of a priest. "Do you ever hear voices? In your head?"

Despite himself, Hart feels his stomach tightening. Conor suffered from auditory hallucinations and for a while Hart wondered if he did too. He had heard voices in his early twenties. Just for a few months. Argumentative, discussing his mother's recent death, blaming him. The voices quietened, but the thought of them still terrifies him: if they are inside his head, there is no place to hide, no way to block them out.

"Does the idea frighten you?" Garstan continues. Hart needs to work on masking his feelings.

"Not really thought about it," he says. *If only.*

"It used to frighten me," Garstan says. "Until I realised we all have internal conversations and debates – at times mine are like rowing siblings. One gradually learns to tune into the most helpful voices and close down the unhelpful ones. The same is true for what I'll be doing here." He gestures at Sophie's personal effects. "It's about shutting out the mental noise and listening with your subconscious mind."

"Listening to what?" Hart asks.

"The signal."

"If you say so." Hart hopes Ward's not paying for this.

"Let me give you an example of how it works," he says. "If you've got a moment?"

"Sure," Hart says, glancing at Strover, wondering if he's about to perform the same card trick that he impressed Ward with.

"I spend a lot of my time listening to patients," Garstan continues. "Hearing about their anxieties and fears, hopes and dreams." He pauses. "May I ask, are your parents still alive?"

"No," Hart says, feeling uncomfortable again.

"It's OK, we can stop. I just wanted to show you how these things might work." He glances at Sophie's possessions on the table. "I'm sorry, that was a very personal question, none of my business."

"It's OK," Hart says, thinking that Mel would tell him not to be so closed. "My Dad died a couple of years ago," he says briskly. "And I lost my Mum when I was twenty."

"I'm so sorry. Your mother must have been quite young."

"Fifty-seven. She died of a heart attack. Coronary occlusion. Furred-up arteries."

He tries to shut out an image of her lying at an awkward angle on the sitting room floor.

"And may I ask how old you are now?"

"Me? Fifty-four."

"And do you ever worry about your own health? You look in great shape, I should add, but the detective's lifestyle, all those late-night stakeouts – it can't be the healthiest existence."

"I take care of myself, what I eat," he says, trying not to dwell on the chips he had on the way home yesterday. "I know these things can be hereditary."

"And let me guess, you have a caring wife who nags – sorry – who gently reminds you about your diet, how much you need to exercise."

Maybe this man really does have a gift? He could be describing Mel to a tee.

"I'm lucky, yes. Mel, she takes good…" He stops himself. He doesn't need to be sharing this sort of private information with a stranger. But Garstan is annoyingly persuasive, has a knack of getting him to open up. And a part of him knows he should seek help for his burgeoning illness anxiety disorder, as Dr Google calls it. Mel's always urging him to talk to someone. Why not take some free advice now? "Let's just say we look out for each other."

"Mel sounds like a very caring partner." He pauses. "May I ask, does the prospect of turning fifty-seven yourself ever scare you? Given what happened to your mother?"

Hart swallows. "Again, I haven't really given it much thought," he says, lying for the second time. His fifty-seventh birthday has appeared on the horizon like a looming iceberg.

It's a while before Garstan speaks again. "So, as I sit here, listening to you, I try to tune into what you're really saying. On the surface, but also below, the micro-tremors in the voice, as well as what's not being said. I'm sure you do the same as a detective. And if I'm honest, I'm tuning into some serious anxieties around your health, whether you'll outlive your mother. Just as I'm picking up something already about Sophie from these."

Garstan gestures at the bags on the table.

"But the difference is her possessions aren't talking," Hart says, keen to restore some scepticism, remind himself that this man's a charlatan. But Garstan's observations have unnerved him with their accuracy.

The psychiatrist smiles, choosing not to answer.

"I'll spend some time on my own with these tonight," he says, "but I can confirm already that Sophie has passed. A long time ago. It's now up to me to find her."

20

I still remember the first time I was frightened of you, scared of what you might physically do to me. I was always weaker, the sickly sibling, but we were meant to be equals. I don't think you ever saw it that way, always delighted in reminding me that I was your "baby brother". Mum and Dad tried to treat us the same – they were scrupulous about that – but you didn't make it easy for them. Or for me.

We weren't allowed to watch TV when we were very young. I didn't think we even had one in the house until I found Dad laughing at repeats of The Two Ronnies *on a set hidden in a cupboard in his study. It didn't matter – we used to watch TV at friends' houses – but it still felt like a betrayal of sorts.*

So instead of Blue Peter, *we were encouraged to go out into the Wiltshire countryside after school and not return until dinnertime, which could be as late as 8 p.m. in the long summer months. Endless hours of happiness, except that they weren't for you. I loved to wander in the forest, collecting leaves and beetles and sheep's wool that had snagged on barbed-wire fencing, or climb beech trees and listen to the blackbirds, wondering what they were saying to each other – the trees and the birds. But you were bored. And you took out your boredom on me.*

I had what Wendy called my "imaginary friends", addressing them aloud long after most "ordinary" children had grown out of them. To you, they were always just stupid. And you were mad at me, complaining to Wendy that I was constantly talking to myself.

To me, of course, they weren't imaginary, but that's another story. To you they were a source of constant irritation and one day, when Wendy was off sick, you flipped. Dad was meant to be back early, but you spoke to him on the phone (I knew it was him before you answered). You said that his train had been cancelled, and you saw your window.

I was almost twelve and still struggling to get over Barka's death, but taking great comfort from talking to her. I could sense her presence everywhere that afternoon and, thinking you were outside, I asked Barka if you had drowned her in the river, as I suspected. I didn't realise you were outside my bedroom door, listening to every word.

"I am so sorry he did that," I said, sobbing.

The door burst open and you stood there with a roll of brown packing tape in your hand, looking around the room.

"Who are you talking to?" you asked.

"No one."

I knew you didn't like my imaginary friends, so I made sure not to talk to them in front of you. I'd learnt very quickly to stop talking to them in front of anyone as soon as I started at the Academy (although mobile phones were a good cover, particularly with headphones).

"I heard you talking."

"I was chatting to Barka," I said, sensing her presence again and feeling a sudden wave of defiance. "I miss her every day."

"Barka's dead," you shouted. "Why are you talking to a stupid dead dog? Why are you always talking to invisible people? Where are they? All these friends of yours? You've got no real friends because you're a weirdo. A fucking weirdo."

I was shocked by your language. Scared too. It's not that I didn't swear myself – our first year at the Academy was turning into a swearfest – but I'd never heard you do it with such venom. And then you ran at me. I tried to jump out the way, but you were too strong and pinned me down on the bed. For a moment, I didn't know what you were doing as you spun me onto my front, until I felt cold metal on my wrists and realised you'd handcuffed me behind my back. You'd come home with the cuffs from school one day. Dad told you to return them, said that they were too realistic, but he never checked, expecting you to be honest.

You had wrestled me to the floor by now and I was screaming.

"Let go of me, let fucking go!"

It was then that you covered my mouth in the parcel tape, binding it round and round my head. All I could think of was how much it was going to hurt when I pulled the tape off, how much of my long hair I might lose.

"Try talking to them now, you stupid prick," you shouted.

I was crying and making strange, muted grunting noises,

but none of it seemed to affect you in any way. You stopped at the door and turned.

"If your friends are so real, they can rescue you. Dad's not coming home tonight."

You slammed the door and were gone.

Later, much later, you returned, bent down and unlocked the handcuffs in silence, avoiding all eye contact. Were you ashamed? It was hard to tell. I doubt it. You just didn't want to get into trouble with Dad.

You must have smelt the urine, but you didn't say anything as you stood up. Strange, given how much you used to tease me if I'd wet my bed. You didn't do anything about the tape either, which was beginning to dissolve around my mouth. Thanks Mum, *I said to myself. (She had insisted on bulk-buying recycled paper tape, not the plastic sort, which would have hurt much more.) I'm not sure you'd thought it through, how I might be able to suck and chew it. Instead, you just stood at the door and stared at me as I yanked the sodden tape down below my mouth with my freed hands. I could already feel it pulling painfully against my hair, but I'd decided I would have a shower and let the tape soak before I tried to remove it.*

My other plan, formed over several hours of captivity, had been to scream the moment I could open my mouth. The neighbours would hear and come rushing. I would explain what had happened, they would call the police and you would be taken away. Instead, now that I was finally free, I just sat there on my bedroom floor, smelling of piss, and cast my eyes downward in shame. This was all my fault. I had brought it upon myself. I knew you had always been jealous of my imaginary friends – how I could hear Mum at her grave, talk to Barka – and I'd rubbed your nose in it, gone on and on about it until you could, quite reasonably, take no more.

I heard you move to leave and looked up. We stared at each other in silence, not as siblings anymore but as strangers. Finally, we were being honest with each other. Despite our shared genes, we had no common interests, except, perhaps, in what Dad did at work. Even then, we came at it from different directions. I liked Dad's description of inhabiting someone else's feelings in order to understand them better; you liked to fix things, always had done. It was usually your bike, or a broken radio, but someone's brain (never their mind) would do.

"Don't tell Dad or it will be worse next time," you said, slamming the door. "And never, ever talk to your imaginary friends again," you added, from the landing. "You are not a fucking child anymore."

I stared at the door for several minutes, trying to understand what had happened, what you had done to me. I would have to tell Dad. I no longer felt safe in the house alone with you. And then the door was open again and you were standing there, tears streaming down your face. It was a long time since I'd seen you cry.

"I'm sorry," you said. "I just want to hear Mum. Like you do. I'm so sorry."

You didn't deserve my sympathy, but I stood up, walked over and gave you a hug. For a few seconds, you didn't respond. Instead, you just stood there, arms at your side, sobbing. And then, very slowly, you wrapped your arms around me, like someone feeling love for the first time.

"Please don't kill me," I whispered.

21

Present day

Hart sits in his car on the driveway of their house in Marlborough. Home, sweet home. One of his ears is ringing, a constant, accusatory tone, as if someone's just hung up on him, and his legs are heavy with adrenaline. Too much fighting with the tiger. He checks his racing pulse – twenty-four beats in fifteen seconds: ninety-six beats a minute – and thinks again about the two men who died in front of him, his parents' desecrated grave. Did Garstan know he would go there today?

He glances up at their semi-detached house, trying to distract himself, restore some calm. Built in the Arts and Crafts style, it was part of the town's first social housing project and designed according to Garden City principles, as he's always trying to tell Conor. Does any of it ever go in? He should head inside. Jess, Conor's girlfriend, has come over for his birthday dinner.

"You OK, honey?" Mel whispers, as she greets him with a hug in the hall.

"Shit-shower of a day," he says, blinking back the tears. "But that's fifty-seventh birthdays for you. How's Conor?"

He can hear him in the kitchen, talking and laughing with Jess. A primary school teacher and a "keeper", last time he talked to Conor about her. He knows their son's been in a good place for a while now, but Hart worries every day about a relapse.

"He's great," Mel says, kissing him on the lips. "Relax. Something's changed in him recently. He's better than we could ever have dreamed."

Hart pulls back from Mel's hug to look at her. For a while Conor had driven the two of them apart, when he got caught up in County Lines, but that's all in the past. Mel's in a good place too, eyes alive and luminous.

"You did all you could today," he says, thinking back to the CPR Mel had administered.

"He just seemed so determined to die," she says.

He said that if we have a death day, it follows we have a death hour. A death minute.

Hart shudders at the memory, pushes it away.

"But let's try to forget all that, shall we?" Mel adds. "At least for tonight."

Hart follows Mel into the kitchen, surprised to find it's been decked out with balloons and streamers.

"Here's the birthday boy," Mel says, as Conor and Jess break into the day's second rendition of "Happy Birthday". This time, he's not complaining as he walks over to hug them both.

"You alright Da?" Conor says. Hart's not quite sure why

his son has started to call him "Da" in a mock Irish accent, but he likes it better than the Thames Estuary twang he used to favour.

"A beer?" he asks.

"A Pride, thanks," Hart says.

"Roads OK?" Conor asks, passing him a bottle and glass. They're like a pair of middle-aged men now, discussing their journeys in front of the fireplace. Conor's come a long way since being sectioned.

"Not great," he says, pouring his beer. They drink and chat before sitting around the kitchen table for bangers and mash. Jess is vegetarian and Mel's cooked her some meat-free Richmond sausages. The two of them get on well, Mel conscious of how indebted they are to her for Conor's continuing recovery. And Mel's right: he is on top form tonight, full of confidence and banter. Looking stacked too – powerlifting five nights a week at the gym – and working with a local pest control firm. Not exactly what either of them had in mind for him when he left school, but that was before the skunk did its worst. And it's a far cry from being curled up in the corner of a psychiatric ward. Just don't ask Conor about rats, not unless you've got three hours to spare.

"They're so frickin' intelligent they can be taught to recognise their own names," Conor is saying, as Jess smiles at Hart from across the kitchen table. "They can play video games, memorise mazes, even recognise pain in other rats."

"They must love you," Hart says.

"Who, the rats?"

"Your colleagues. I thought your job was to kill them."

"Cockroaches in Calne tomorrow," Conor adds. "Then it's over to Corsham for cluster flies."

Hart is glad they've moved here. Mel's commute to the hospital is longer than when they lived in Swindon, but she loves the communal allotments. And he's within a stone's throw of the parkrun on the common. No excuse not to run five kilometres at least once a week, particularly as Jess is an alarmingly keen runner. She's made a plan for the four of them – Mel and Hart, Conor and her – to do the Marlborough parkrun together on Saturday. They're even sharing their times on a running app. Sweaty photos too.

Later, over the washing up, party hat askew, a little pissed if he's honest, he talks to Jess about Conor.

"Thanks, you know, for all you've done for him," he says. "He seems in a good place right now."

Hart glances at his son in the other room, chatting and laughing with Mel. Aswad's "Don't Turn Around" is playing on the sound system. He and Mel had gone on one of their first dates to see the reggae group play at the Albert Hall, when he was a sergeant in New Cross Gate and she was a student nurse in Lewisham.

"I'm not sure I can take any credit," Jess says, drying a plate. Conor glances across at them. "This new therapist is helping, even though he's only seen him the once."

"Not talking about me, I hope?" Conor says, dancing to the music as he comes through to the kitchen. "Why you doing the washing up anyway? On your birthday?"

Because you never do, but Hart bites his tongue.

"Just telling your dad about the new therapist," Jess says.

"More of a life coach," Conor says. "Absolute bloody gamechanger. 'Live each day as if it's your last – because one day it will be.'" He laughs. "That's about the gist of it. We all could be run over by a bus tomorrow. Life can be short so *live* it."

Hart stops washing the glass he's holding in the foaming sink, his back still to Conor.

"What's his name?" he asks, trying to remain calm. *No cake or candles... That would be weird.*

"Not sure he's quite your type, Da," Conor adds.

"A bit too delulu for you," Jess adds, smiling as she nudges Hart.

"What's this guy's name?" he repeats, starting to wash the glass again, slowly tracing the rim. *He says we all have a "death day". Just like a birthday.*

"Greg," Conor says. "Don't know his surname. Never thought to ask."

Greg... Gregory... Rory. It could be Garstan. *And when we know the date, there's nothing we can do about it.*

"When did you see him?" Hart asks, his stomach tightening like a vice. Maybe it was before Garstan was released from Barontrent?

"Last week? Or was it the week before? Can't remember. Work's been mad. Full tonto."

"Two weeks ago, maybe, babe?" Jess says. Hart realises everyone's quite drunk, including him.

"Was it?" Conor asks. "Anyway, booked in again to see him this week."

"And where do you meet him?" Hart asks.

"Down at the centre on Fleming Way. Greg was meant to spend the day working with the homeless boys, fixing their heads while they try to find a place to live. No one bothered to turn up in the afternoon, so I asked if I could have a chat."

Hart closes his eyes, trying to work out why he's so worried, why old anxieties are stirring like sleeping monsters from the deep. Conor regularly goes over to the homeless centre to volunteer. It's where he had ended up himself when things went seriously Pete Tong, as he likes to describe his breakdown. Hart's always been impressed by his loyalty to the place, his desire to help others. He gets it from Mel.

"Did this man give you a card?" Hart asks.

"A card? Everything alright, Da?" Conor says, looking at Jess for an explanation.

Hart takes the tea towel from Jess, dries his hands and turns to face Conor. The music has stopped.

"Maybe a telephone number?" Hart asks. "An email?"

"Nothing like that, no," Conor says, staring at his dad in the tense silence that ensues. "But he did give me this," he adds, placing a small hourglass on the shelf above the sink. "*Tempus fugit*. Time flies, to you and me."

Hart stares at the object, watching the red grains of sand as they slip through the narrow neck. *Tell me the fucking time!*

"Is something wrong, Da?" Conor asks.

Mel walks into the kitchen.

"All good in here?" she asks.

"Dad wants my life coach's number, that's all," Conor says.

Mel turns to Hart and smiles quizzically.

"Thought it might be helpful," Hart says, trying to ignore the hourglass. It could be a common prop, used by self-respecting life coaches everywhere. "Given what wonders he's worked for Conor here. Might make me less of a grumpy old sod."

"Nothing old about you, birthday boy," Mel says, kissing him.

"Oi-yoi, not in front of the children," Conor says.

"Maybe a bit grumpy at times," she says, kissing him again. "But nothing that an early night can't sort."

Hart closes his eyes. If only it were so simple. Targeting him is one thing, but not his son. Conor is still very fragile, despite the bluster. The music starts up again.

"Out of interest, does this Greg bloke ever talk about your future?" Hart asks, as Mel tries to get him to dance. He knows he should leave it, but he can't. "As well as your past?"

"That's the lit thing about him," Conor says. "He's got this gift. Once he gets to know someone properly. I told him one of my big fears in life is dying. You know, after all that happened. Next time he's going to tell me when I'm going to die. Bit dark – can't lie, I'll be cacking it – but how frickin' cool is that? I might not have long, apparently, cos of the skunk, but hey, bring it on, I say. I'd rather know. Life. Is. For. Living."

22

Hart knows the parkrun shouldn't be about times. It's to do with community participation, pensioners and prams, families and dogs. But today it's about one thing: twenty-five minutes, his goal for the past six months. OK, so it's also about beating Conor, who's standing beside him in the snow on Marlborough Common, and impressing Jess, who he won't be seeing again unless she laps him (she regularly runs sub-twenty). When he was younger, Hart could run 10K in forty-five minutes, but as Ward so kindly reminded him, he's not young anymore. He's fifty-seven. But if he can run 5K in twenty-five minutes, he'll be happy. He'll also be in considerable pain. His PB in recent years is 25:30, a while back now. For the past few months, he's been regularly north of twenty-seven minutes and struggling to walk the day afterwards.

"Don't overdo it, Sile," Mel says, standing beside him in her running gear and bobble hat.

"I won't," Hart says, lying. It's do-or-die today. Destiny day.

"Three, two, one," a volunteer says on the mic. And then the runners set off with a loud cheer. At least there's no starter gun. He's not sure he could cope with that. The man at the front desk had pushed the barrel so hard into the roof of his mouth, determined to destroy every last inch of his brain.

It's at the 1 km mark that the pain in his chest begins, growing worse as he slogs up the slow hill at the far side of the common. The long, snow-wet grass doesn't help, nor does the sight of Conor in front of him, pulling further ahead. He can't be sure, but it looks like he's caught up with a couple of the homeless who stay at the hostel on Fleming Way. Who knew they were so fit? His head is also hurting, the result of too much beer last night, but it's his chest that's worrying him. A pain like he's never felt before, jolting through his heart like bolt lightning.

"I tried to tell you that you'd die today," a familiar voice says close to him. "But would you listen?"

Hart shoots a look at his fellow runners. *What the hell's Garstan doing here?* He's a cyclist not a runner. But it was his voice, no question. A fit father and his annoyingly young son overtake Hart. Eight, maybe even seven years old?

"Alright?" the dad says to him.

"Saving myself for the second lap," Hart says, trying to remain calm.

"Second lap?" the voice says. It's definitely Garstan's. "Aren't you forgetting something?"

Hart looks around him again. Still no sign of the psychiatrist. Is he suffering from auditory hallucinations? He picks up the pace, determined to keep Conor in sight.

Not because he doesn't want to be beaten by him, but because he suddenly feels very vulnerable. He should stop, pull over. The pain is now unbearable, Garstan's voice in his head louder.

"Some people die happy, doing something they love at the point of death, but I'm not sure they'll be saying that about you," Garstan continues. "I mean, it's not as if you actually like running. You just do it in a vain attempt to keep off the belly fat. Not sure it's working too well."

Hart looks down at his own stomach, which has become so swollen that he can no longer see his feet. He's heard voices before, but not this deafening. And they've never been identified so clearly with a particular person. Maybe Garstan's communicating with him using telepathy? This must be what it sounds like. Garstan's the sender, he's the receiver.

"Conor's doing well," Garstan says. "Must be all that coaching I gave him at the hostel last week. 'Run each race as if it's your last.' But you? You're fifty-seven, DI Silas Hart. You shouldn't be trying to run a PB with a hangover and no training. You should be back at home, tucked up in bed with your lovely wife Mel. What the hell are you doing?"

Hart puts his hands over his ears. He should never have told him her name.

"You OK?" a man asks, running alongside him.

"Stitch," Hart says, sliding his hands from his ears to the back of his head, a standard cure.

"This too will pass," the runner says.

"Hope so," Hart says.

"Looks like she's got more than a stitch," the runner adds, nodding with a smile at a woman lying in the grass beside the course. Hart's eyes widen. Mel has broken off from the runners and is giving CPR to someone, pumping her chest harder and harder. And then the woman turns and screams, her face contorted in agony. *Mum!* Mel stops. Her hands have crushed his mother's fragile ribcage and are embedded in her chest cavity. Mel lifts them up, appalled at what she's done, the blood dripping from her fingers.

"Mum!" Hart cries out. "Mel!"

"Sile, Sile," Mel says.

"It's not your fault," Hart shouts, running on, his own chest thumping so loudly that it feels like it's about to implode too. "You tried your best," he calls back to her. And then he puts a hand to his torso, which is no longer there, and he can feel his heart, touch it, grasp its soft, marmoreal flesh between his fingers. And it's no longer beating.

"Sile," Mel says, louder now. "Sile!"

Hart opens his eyes, staring at the ceiling, breathing hard. He touches his bare chest, wet with sweat. And then he turns to Mel, propped up beside him on an elbow, her face radiant in the warm glow of her bedside light.

"You OK?" she says, running a hand through his hair.

"Jesus," he whispers and closes his eyes again.

"What's going on, Sile?"

"I think I'm going to die on Saturday."

23

Hart's up early, before Mel and definitely before Conor and Jess. The lovebirds had stayed up late last night, long after Mel had removed his birthday hat and taken him to bed. His head hurts as he makes himself some porridge. He'd drunk too much beer and couldn't sleep after Conor's revelation about the hostel. And then, when he had finally drifted off, the parkrun nightmare had started. He hasn't had a dream like that since he was a teenager. He's not sure he can face running at the weekend.

Why, though, had Garstan's apparent connection to the hostel so troubled him? It wouldn't be the first time the psychiatrist had been linked to the homeless. And there's no evidence that Conor had actually seen him. Just like he'd found no hard evidence that Sophie had met him all those years ago. Besides, Conor said that the man he spoke with was called Greg. And with luck it was before Garstan's release. But then he looks at the hourglass, still there on the shelf above the sink.

Hart feels Mel's hands on his shoulders before he hears her. He turns round to see her sleepy face.

"Morning, honey," she says, kissing him.

"Tea?" he asks, walking over to fill the kettle at the sink.

"You're not telling me something, Sile," she says, watching him from across the kitchen. "Last night – you were shouting like a man possessed."

"I'm late for work," he says, but he knows he should talk about the nightmare. He hadn't been able to when she woke him last night. Instead, he'd closed his eyes and let Mel hold him like a baby until he'd fallen back to sleep.

"Late? It's only 7 a.m."

"There's a lot on."

"You need to tell me, Sile. Is it the patient who died yesterday? Who knew our names?"

Hart switches the kettle on. "That was unnerving, I can't pretend it wasn't. Not exactly great for you either."

"It's my job to try and save lives."

"Mine too."

"And the man at the station front desk?"

"That was pretty upsetting too."

She comes over and gives Hart a long hug from behind. "How did they both know your name?" she asks.

He still hasn't told her that the man at the station knew her name as well. It's time he came clean, explained what's bothering him, what caused the nightmare. He's told Strover, after all. Mel knows him better than anyone, but what will she say? Will she use it to call time on his own mental health, tell him he needs to see someone?

"The apparently funny birthday card I was sent – the Grim Reaper," he says, turning his attention to the kettle. "I think it was from Dr Rory Garstan. That Harley Street psychiatrist? The one who claimed he could see the future?"

"Garstan? Who you put away? I thought that was all behind you."

"So did I."

"I seem to remember it got very personal."

Hart doesn't want to admit it, but Mel's right. Garstan nearly destroyed him.

"Is he out?" she asks.

"Eight days ago."

"Where is he now?"

"Back home, we assume. Big house outside Pewsey. We're paying him a visit today." Hart drops his teabag into the bin. "I think he's trying to mess with my head again."

"Well don't let him."

"And maybe Conor's too."

"Conor's?" Even Mel, always a picture of calm, can't disguise her surprise. Her anger.

"This new life coach of his, at the homeless hostel. The one who told him to live each day as if it was his last. And gave him that thing." He nods at the hourglass above the sink. "I think it might be Garstan."

"Oh, no," Mel says, walking away. "Please tell me you're making this up."

"I may be wrong," he says. He hates seeing Mel upset, particularly when it's to do with his work. It throws up too many questions, why he chose to go into policing at all. Maybe it's time to retire. He'd almost resigned when they'd lived in London, appalled by the Met's institutional racism and misogyny (not to mention the Freemasonry). He'd made the mistake of taking Mel out for a drink with his colleagues after work. "Conor wasn't actually sure when he saw the life coach. It might have been before Garstan was released."

An awkward silence descends on the room as Mel busies herself with emptying the dishwasher. Hart walks over to the window and stares out onto the garden, cradling his mug of steaming tea. It always amazes him how the roses can look so forlorn at this time of year and come to such vibrant life in the spring. More snow fell overnight, turning the bird table into a miniature Alpine hut.

"I also think it was Garstan who defaced Mum and Dad's headstone," he says, turning around. "Added the date of my death. 4 December – Saturday."

Mel stops unloading the dishwasher and leans back against the sideboard, arms folded. Never a good sign.

"And I think he's planning to tell Conor his death day too," Hart adds.

Mel shakes her head in slow disbelief and walks to the kitchen door, where she turns to face Hart.

"Don't let this man destroy our family," she says, her anger rising. "Not now, not after all we've gone through. You need to get a grip. You're not going to die on Saturday. Don't be so ridiculous. So bloody selfish. We've been through this enough times. And Conor's not going anywhere soon either. He's doing well. We are too. You need to put this sick man behind bars again, Silas – where he clearly belongs."

24

When did it all start? The animus? I've asked myself that question a lot recently, as I've started to write down these thoughts. You've always resented me, not just my "gift", but, my achievements at school too, which is so strange, given how much you had going for you. OK, so you were never the sharpest pencil in the box, but you more than made up for that in other ways. You captained the school shooting team, even won competitions at Bisley for your dead-eyed accuracy with a rifle; dated the hottest girls; became head boy. I was the nerdy, quiet one in the corner, always signed off sick from sports, bullied for my "gay" hair. Except that I had the one thing you craved but could never have. And then you took your jealousy to a new level. I thought nothing could be worse than the time you left me handcuffed in my room.

It was a sunny afternoon, one of those summer days that you never want to end. The air was filled with the smell of new-mown grass – the neighbours', not ours – and butterflies were dancing from flower to flower, too giddy to settle. I was lying on a tartan rug in the orchard, underneath a gnarled old apple tree. I should have been revising for my biology GCSE, but I was on my back, staring up at the high white clouds scudding across the sky. A young collared dove landed on a low branch, close to where I was lying. I'm not sure it had seen me, but it was still looking around, checking for danger.

"It's OK little fella," I whispered. "You're safe here. No one's going to harm you."

Barka used to chase pigeons – squirrels too – but never with much conviction. She just saw it as a bit of fun.

This dove was beautiful, with its prim collar and soft, lavender plumage. No wonder doves are a symbol of peace.

"Welcome to our garden," I said, smiling up at the bird, tilting my own head to mimic the way it was now looking down at me.

And then the peace of the afternoon was shattered by the crack of gunfire. The next moment, the dove had dropped to the ground, followed by a flurry of falling feathers, a burlesque curtain call that seemed to mock the bird's sudden demise.

I knew at once what had happened and leapt up to see you standing thirty yards away, near the house, air rifle still pointing in my direction.

"Why the fuck did you do that?" I asked.

"Talking to the birds again?" you said, cracking open your rifle and reloading. You put it to your shoulder and aimed in my direction. "I suppose it's better than talking to Mum."

I didn't like your tone, or where the gun was pointing.

I glanced around in the tree above me to see if there were any other birds, but you were only interested in me now.

"Put the gun down," I said, walking towards you. "Where did you get it from anyway?"

I'd never seen him with a gun at home, only at school, when I went past the firing range once.

"Stay exactly where you are," you barked, the gun still to your shoulder.

"Easy," I said, putting my hands out in front of me. "OK."

I stood still, lowering my hands to my side.

"Now pick up an apple and put it on your head."

"What?" I asked. "You're out of your mind."

"Me?" you said, laughing that cruel laugh of yours. "I'm not the mad one around here. Trust me. Now pick up a fucking apple."

I looked at my feet, trying not to linger on the dead dove a few yards away. A small exclamation mark of blood had punctuated its neck. There were plenty of apples lying in the long grass – big, fat cookers. Instinctively, I reached for the biggest one I could see, already knowing what you were going to do next.

"Now put it on your head," you said.

"Seriously?"

I looked over at you, hoping you'd pull out of this stupid stunt, but you gestured with the barrel, flicking it upwards.

Hands trembling, I placed the apple on my head, trying to make it balance.

"Take away your hands," you said. I could see you were enjoying this. I removed my hands and the apple rolled off.

"If you stopped shitting yourself, it might stay," you said. "Now try again."

This time I pressed my feet hard into the ground, trying to stop my legs from shaking, and the apple stayed on my head.

"So tell me, Mr fortune teller, great seer of Pewsey, am I about to shoot my baby brother between the eyes or hit the apple?"

"For fucksake, this isn't funny. You're too far away."

"Too close, I think you mean," you said, glancing behind you before taking a few strides backwards.

"Now for the fun part," you continued. The barrel was rock steady, which was something, but it was still pointing directly at me. "Hit or miss?"

I closed my eyes, wondering for a second what would happen if I made a run for it. Knowing you, you wouldn't hesitate to shoot me in the leg. Or maybe in the backside, just for the fun of it. And then I saw the ripe, frangible apple explode into a million pieces.

"You're going to hit the apple," I said, opening my eyes. I was calmer now, reassured by what I'd just seen.

"And you're sure of that?" you asked.

I was about to nod when I remembered the apple. Moving my head in any direction wasn't a good idea.

"Sure as night follows day," I said, not that it always did, of course, but now wasn't the moment to enter into a discussion about the direction of time.

For what seemed like an eternity, we stood facing each other, across the grass where we had played when we were younger, grass that Mum used to mow because Dad was away in London so much. Friendly, family grass that was never meant to become a killing field.

"How about if I shut my eyes?" you said. "Fate is blind – isn't that what Dad once told us?"

My own eyes widened as yours closed. At least he'd been listening to Dad's stories. "You're fucking crazy!"

"Call me Tiresias."

Perceived the scene, and foretold the rest. *Dad loved* The Waste Land. *I wished he were here now, but he was out at work, as you said. When we were younger, he had told us all about the blind prophet Tiresias, how he could see the future, from which there was no escape. You had squirmed when he'd also explained how Tiresias had spent seven years as a woman before becoming a man again, giving him a unique insight into both genders. I'd found it intriguing, the story lingering long after the telling. Those had been happy days, when Mum was still alive and Dad had time for us.*

And then, without warning, you fired. I stood there in shock, waiting for the pain. An air rifle pellet might not kill me, but it could bruise my skull, blind me if it caught an eye. Smash a front tooth. But no pain came. All I could feel was a slight dampness on my hair. I put my hand up to touch my head and looked at my fingers, dreading the sight of blood. There were only pieces of apple.

"Maybe you can see the future after all," you said, calling back as you walked towards the house, your airgun broken over one shoulder. "Don't tell Dad I've got a gun or next time I'll put a bullet in that fucked-up head of yours."

25

The past

It's 8 a.m., too early to be in the Parade Room, but a 6 a.m. phone call from Ward has already ruined Hart's day. He'd stopped off at the Slaughtered Lamb last night after their visit to Garstan's house in Pewsey – the psychiatrist's personal questions about his health, his mum's death, had upset him more than he wants to acknowledge – and the hangover's not helping.

"There's no bloody way Garstan can know just from holding a handbag—"

"Clutch bag," Strover says, correcting Hart.

"…From holding a clutch bag where Sophie Mills is buried. I'm sorry, call me old-fashioned, but the only way he can know is if he's—"

"Morning Silas," DCS Ward says, strolling into the Parade Room. Two uniforms at the far end – the only other people in at this hour – fall quiet. Hart stops ranting too.

"Good morning, sir," Hart says.

"A word in my office?" he says. "Strover too, please."

Strover and Hart look at each other as Ward walks out again.

Hart rubs the back of his neck. Maybe if he goes home, has another shave, a second bowl of porridge and walks back in here again, Garstan might never have been born.

"Does Ward really believe Garstan's found her?" Strover asks.

"It's like he's joined a cult," Hart says, shaking his head. "Or dropped acid. Or both."

"I mean, looking at the bigger picture..."

"A missing person is found. I know. But by some shit-gibbon shrink who can 'see' where the body is buried? Please. It's total bollocks, Strover. And you know it."

Just like Garstan's impromptu diagnosis of his own health anxieties, his worries about his mum's death at fifty-seven...

"In better news, Forensics have sent over some footage from the CCTV up at the windmill," Strover says, flipping open a laptop.

"Anything interesting?" Hart asks, as he walks over to Strover.

"They've flagged 7.16 a.m.," Strover says, scrolling through the footage. Hart leans in closer. Milo appears at the foot of the windmill, looking around him in a distressed manner. It's an upsetting watch. The young man is clearly agitated, repeatedly running his hand through his hair, his movements jerky and panicked. Paranoid. Again, Hart thinks of Conor. And then Milo pulls out a phone.

"Hello?" Hart says. "I thought he'd left his mobile at home."

"He did – currently with digital Forensics." Along with his bank cards and driving licence.

"Who's he calling? And what the hell did he do with that phone?"

"Must have chucked it. I'll get onto CSI now."

The only possession they had found with Milo's body was the hourglass.

"Get them to go back there and widen their search. We need to find that phone. And see who he was talking to. Take no crap from the service providers either. Not many people were making calls on the network in that area at 7.16 a.m."

CSI won't be happy, but the CCTV footage changes everything. Who was Milo talking to so soon before he died? The call log on his other phone, the one he'd left in his bedroom, was a tragic snapshot of a man living in isolation. Nothing outgoing for weeks, just some missed calls and increasingly concerned voicemails from his parents.

Hart's own mobile rings. It's Ward's secretary.

"We're coming," Hart says and hangs up.

A minute later, Hart and Strover are in the Detective Chief Superintendent's office. No need to tell the boss that Milo's case is looking less straightforward by the minute. Certainly not a regulation suicide. They're here to talk about Garstan and the Sophie Mills case. Ward hasn't asked them to take a seat.

"It seems like we might have a result already," Ward says, sitting at his desk. Behind him, a wall of books and some old photos of him as a student, dressed in a gown and mortar board, rowing on a river in an eight, riding a bicycle. Every time Hart's here, he has the same feeling: Ward would have been happier if he'd stayed on at Oxford.

"Is Dr Garstan certain?" Hart asks.

"He wouldn't have rung me so early this morning if he wasn't completely convinced. Sorry to have disturbed your beauty sleep, Silas, but I knew you'd want to be the first to know."

"Of course, no problem," Hart says, remembering how amazed he was that Mel hadn't heard the call, didn't stir as he'd peeled himself out of her warm embrace, only to be floored by a sledgehammer of a hangover.

"The signal wasn't great," Ward says. "Apparently Rory experienced a lot of 'noise' – 'interference' – during the overnight remote viewing, but the location should become clearer once you're on site."

There'll be a lot more noise if word gets out that Wiltshire Police has gone all woo-woo. Hart has been thinking through the logistics ever since Ward called. Garstan is convinced Sophie's remains are on scrubland on the southern edge of the Groundwell Industrial Estate, north of Swindon town centre. Annoyingly, it makes sense: the location is close to the Penhill estate, on the other side of the Cricklade Road. Sophie would have passed near it, if she'd walked from Cleverton Court to her friend's house that night.

The site had also been searched by CSI, supported by police officers, during the early days of the inquiry. Hart remembers talking to the team that had fanned out through the trees, confronting a young colleague who'd suggested Sophie wasn't worth the search because she was lowlife, on the game. Had that person been typical of the team's attitude at the time? Had they missed something? Not tried hard enough?

"We'll head over there now and take a look," Hart says.

"In terms of the public, we'll need community liaison officers on site, of course. The search area will need to be screened too. And remember, the official line – with colleagues and the media – is that we've received 'credible new evidence' that has pointed us to this site as a possible area of interest. As a force, we never give up on anyone – that's the message. We do not say that a Harley Street psychiatrist has had a vision. I'm not bloody stupid: I know how it would look. The press would have a field day."

"Once we've had an initial recce…"

"We commit," Ward says. "Specialist search team, forensic archaeologists, ground-penetrating radar, dogs – I want the lot."

Hart hopes Ward knows what he's doing.

"I'm aware what you're thinking, Silas," Ward says. "Both of you. But trust me on this one. I know Rory better than you do. He wouldn't waste my time. We go back a long way." All the way back to the same Freemason lodge, no doubt, raising trouser legs together. "I just wish he'd offered his services sooner," Ward adds.

Hart's done enough biting of his tongue.

"Why do you think he didn't come forward before?" he asks. "Revealed this 'talent' of his earlier?"

Strover throws Hart a concerned look.

"I'm not sure," Ward says. "Worried what people might think? Let's be honest here: I can see the scepticism etched on your face from a hundred yards, Silas. You're more guarded, Strover, always have been. Inscrutability is a good quality to have as a detective. But I can feel your circumspection too. It's OK. You're a scientist by nature. I get that. Remote viewing is nonsense, an insult to mechanistic materialism.

But the truth is, we need to be seen to be doing something about these cold cases. They're an embarrassment to the force. If we find Sophie, that's wonderful. And who knows? We just might. And if we don't, then at least we've tried. More importantly, we've been seen to try. We never give up."

Hart lets Ward's words flow over him. Somehow, this feels even worse than believing in Garstan's nonsense. In Ward's world, it's irrelevant whether Sophie's found or not. The whole operation is nothing more than an elaborate PR exercise. Good optics is not what he'd signed up to the police for.

"Best of luck, Silas, Strover. Keep me posted. And remember, not a word about Garstan's involvement to anyone. Our secret, eh?"

26

Hart could think of better places he'd rather be than at the back of a light industrial estate in Swindon on a hot afternoon in July. Cornwall, for example, where they used to go for their family holidays. Pedn Vounder, perhaps, buying a decent pasty from the campsite shop at Treen before the steep climb down to the beach, with its warm cerulean shallows and butter-soft sand.

A burnt-out motorbike has scorched the tarmac cycle path that runs up through the scrubland from the Cricklade Road to the industrial estate. Stolen and joyridden, torched and abandoned. Crushed cans of dark fruit cider and Captain Morgan Pepsi Max litter the illicit footpaths that run through the undergrowth, along with spent cylinders of nitrous oxide and faded bags of Haribo Goldbears. Hart remembers what a colleague said to him when he came back from London to live in

Swindon: "Avoid the four Ps – Penhill, Pinehurst, Park North and Park South."

He watches a member of the Major Investigation Team move through the trees with a ground-penetrating radar unit. Word of "credible new evidence" had spread like wildfire through the station. And once it was clear that Ward was personally involved, Hart had no trouble persuading the search team to deploy to the site as a matter of urgency – and with more diligence than before. He'd been up here earlier for a recce and is keen to get the whole shoddy sham over with as soon as possible. Word had clearly spread outside the station too. The crowd now gathered at the far end of the cycle path, where it meets the Cricklade Road, all seem to know that the GPR unit is using electromagnetic waves to scan beneath the soil, looking for the remains of local woman Sophie Mills.

"Just what Ward wanted," Hart says, watching more people wander across from the Penhill estate to see what all the fuss is about. And there is a lot of fuss: three police vans and a lorry, a digger waiting for instructions, a white operations tent, a police handler with his cadaver dog, a cocker spaniel called Spencer (another dog, Frank, specialises in drugs, cash and firearms), and at least ten CSI investigators searching bushes and fallen trees in a large area cordoned off with tape.

"What do you think the chances are?" Strover asks.

"Of finding Sophie? About as much chance as I have of becoming the next Chief Constable."

"Quite high then, sir," Strover says.

Hart manages a smile. He likes Strover. Earlier, he'd rung Garstan and heard himself asking if he had "received" more specific coordinates for Sophie's body. Sadly, Garstan couldn't be any more precise about the target of his remote viewing. "I just know she's somewhere in that scrubland behind the estate," he had said. "I'm sorry, there was a lot of static."

Static? He's not the Droitwich bloody transmitter.

"Will Sophie's mother come?" Strover asks.

"I doubt it," Hart says. A family support officer had tracked her down earlier to explain about the search for Sophie, but she seemed more concerned about her next score than her estranged daughter.

Hart watches as Spencer's handler walks over to the crowd of onlookers at the far end of the cycle path. He lets several of them pet the dog and makes polite conversation. All good PR. And then the handler, now talking to a man, glances over in their direction and points at Hart. The man is with a woman, but she's keeping her distance, either because she's afraid of dogs or the police, or both.

"Here we go," Hart says.

The woman, in her early twenties, starts to argue with the man, who's now remonstrating with her. After a heated discussion, she leaves him and walks down the path towards Hart and Strover, lighting up a cigarette.

"Detective Hart?" she asks nervously, turning her face away from him, as if he's a CCTV camera.

"How can I help?" Hart says. He wasn't expecting to field questions from the public today. A community liaison team was meant to be up here two hours ago, handing out leaflets, explaining what was happening, but they must be liaising with a different community.

The woman looks shifty as hell. Familiar too, but Hart

can't quite place her. She tries to keep her face away from them as she watches the search team. The man starts to furiously gesture at her.

"You're alright," she says to Hart, starting to walk away again.

"Please, we're here to listen today," Strover calls after her. "Not to arrest anyone."

She stops and turns, draws heavily on her cigarette as she deliberates whether to walk or talk.

"I knew Sophie, that's all," she eventually says.

"Did you give a statement at the time?" Hart asks. Maybe that's why he recognises her. "When she disappeared?"

"You for real?" she says. "You'd have nicked me."

"We're not here to arrest anyone today," Strover repeats. "Do you have something to share with us now?"

The woman eyes Strover up and down.

"I'm not giving no name or statement," she says. "You probably know me anyway."

"That's fine," Strover says. Hart's happy for his colleague to take over. Where has he seen this woman before?

"Me and Sophs, we used to hang out," she says.

"Did you go clubbing together?" Strover asks.

"Not on the night she disappeared, if that's what you mean. But I saw her that day. We did a bit of shopping together."

That's one way of describing it. Freetail therapy is another. Hart's placed her now, remembers the day she walked out of Morrisons with £100 of fresh lamb stuffed up her skirt. Turned out it wasn't even for her – she'd taken pity on a group of penniless Kurdish refugees who'd recently arrived from Europe.

"How was she?" Strover asks.

"Not great. Living on the streets. Head fucked. Doing too much Special K. You know how it goes."

Ketamine – Conor took it for a while too. It was the incontinence – "ket bladder" – that got to him in the end.

"But she'd started to get help," the woman says.

"Where from?" Strover asks.

"The shelter."

Hart looks up.

"What sort of help?" he asks. Given Sophie was regularly homeless, Hart and his colleagues had visited all the shelters in Swindon when her disappearance was investigated two years ago.

"You know, with her life and that. Where she was going, which was nowhere. What she wanted – just to be off the game and the K and not have to lift her dinner every night."

"Which shelter was this?" Hart asks.

"The one on Fleming Way." Where Conor ended up. He'd paid a visit himself, partly to thank the staff for helping his son, but he can't recall any record of Sophie, or of anyone offering life-changing advice. "It's just so sad, that's all," she continues. "I think she was starting to get her shit together. Helping others too – refugees and that. I should've said something to you lot at the time, but she didn't want anyone to know she was homeless."

"Why not?"

"Embarrassed, maybe? Shame. Dunno. I can still remember what she said to me that last day. Live your life now because you might get run over by a bus tomorrow."

"Those were her exact words?" Hart asks.

The woman takes another drag on her cigarette, cocks her head and exhales into the warm air.

"Something like that," she continues. "Said some other stuff too. Had this weird feeling that she might die that day, really strong, so she was going out to have a good time at Angelo's. Just in case it might be her last ever night. Wish I could have joined her on the lash. And then she, well…" She looks across at the search team. "Then she was dead, wasn't she? Shitbaked I was, when I heard."

27

"Any news on Milo's burner phone?" Hart asks Strover, happy to be back in his favourite corner of the Parade Room. He's left CSI to it up at the industrial estate, confident that they won't be in touch any time soon. The woman who came over to talk to them is more of a worry. Milo's own conviction that he was going to die has echoes of Sophie's apparent sudden awareness of her own mortality, two years earlier. Echoes, nothing more.

Strover went straight over to the hostel on Fleming Way before coming here and spoke with the manager. As Hart had noted two years earlier, there was no record of Sophie's visits, although it was before the new manager's time. They'll need to persuade Sophie's friend to give a proper statement, but right now Hart's more concerned with Milo's death.

"Cell tower triangulation has confirmed a phone was in the approximate location of the windmill at 7.16 a.m.,"

Strover says, "but until we find the handset, and Digital Forensics get into the call log, we won't know if it was Milo's – or who he was speaking with."

The CSM hadn't been impressed when he was told to return to the windmill, but his team is currently searching the site for a burner phone. He had perked up when Hart informed him about Milo's journal. Digital Forensics are still examining his regular mobile.

Hart has the Moleskine journal open on his desk now, Crispin's instructions to not let it out of his sight ringing in his ears. But as soon as he starts to read it, he knows the journal could become crucial evidence. It's too personal, too raw, to ignore. A part of him feels guilty about reading the private diary of a young man in his twenties – it could so easily be Conor writing, a reason why, perhaps, he hasn't read it sooner – but the detective in him reads on.

My dream to speak Shakespeare's most famous soliloquy has died and with it all hopes of a meaningful life.

Hart takes a deep breath. His own dad had urged him to set his sights as high as possible, because if you fell short of your goals, you'd still end up in a better place than if you'd set your sights low. But that way, disappointment lies too, as Milo discovered. Hart skims through other pages about his life in London, the endless rounds of auditions and crushing disappointments. A more recent entry catches his eye:

G might have sorted Mum's wobble, but I really don't want to see him. I don't want to see anyone right now and I know that's not healthy. My own fix must come from within.

And then Hart comes across another entry and sits up in his chair.

Mum kept pushing me and Dad said he would pay, so

I finally decided to go and see G today, as much to please them as anything.

First impressions were good. I liked him and we got on well, discussed a shared love of road cycling. He's got a nice Bianchi. He said he wanted to find out a bit about me, my past, and asked me to describe my hopes and fears. He quickly seemed more interested in the latter, probing with questions about my childhood anxieties, which are too long to list here. Just ask Mum and Dad.

He then talked a bit about himself, how he differed from other psychiatrists in that he liked to focus as much on a patient's future as well as their past. But he didn't just mean encouraging me to make plans. He meant he could sometimes actually intuit a patient's future. And once he'd seen it, he could help a patient to get the most out of their life, knowing how long it would be.

"Strover, have a read of this," Hart says, calling his colleague over. "Milo's journal, talking about someone called 'G' who could see into the future."

Strover comes across to read over Hart's shoulder.

I'd heard a bit about G's practice in London – Dad had cut out an article in one of the Sunday magazines for me – but I didn't really believe in any of the claims. And it seemed more geared towards life coaching than psychiatry. He never got out a crystal ball, or anything wacko like that, but at one point during our session, he talked of something called "clairsentience." All good psychiatrists, he said, had empathy with their patients and this just took things to a different level: a visceral insight that allowed him to understand where patients' lives had gone wrong and how to work towards "improved outcomes"…

"What do you think?" Strover asks.

"I mean, it sounds plausible enough when Garstan puts it like that," Hart says. The marriage counsellor had talked about empathy and improved outcomes to him and Mel a few years back. And it's what the team of management consultants had discussed last month when they swarmed through Gablecross, looking for ways to cut costs.

"But buried in all the psychobabble he's still making an outlandish claim," he continues.

"That he can see into the future," Strover says.

"Why anyone pays for this so-called treatment beggars belief," Hart says, flicking through the pages. He stops at another entry.

Saw G for the second time today. He continued to probe my darkest fears. I nearly had an anxiety attack, right there in his consulting room. He told me that it was essential to understand and confront what made me frightened. We went back to when Mum and I nearly died in a head-on car crash on the way home from a friend's fifth birthday party. I was somehow unscathed, sitting in the back, but I thought Mum had died. The driver of the other car had been killed instantly. For fifteen minutes I sat there, looking at Mum's bloodied face, her head hanging limply to one side, thinking she was dead. I had tried to comfort her, but the airbag was in the way. She wasn't dead, of course, but I had attachment issues for years afterwards. And I still fear death to this day. Ever since the crash, it feels very close, just beneath the surface, like the other side of a coin. Even now, as I write this, I think I could die so easily. Death's always here, hidden but life-adjacent. G kept asking me about that, again and again, my profound fear of dying.

"When was this entry?" Hart asks, turning back the page.

"Three weeks before he died," Strover says. They look at each other for a moment.

"He seems to have written nothing after that," Hart says, flicking through the rest of the empty journal. Then, on the very last page, he spots one final entry, in small, shaky handwriting.

Tomorrow's my last day. I can hardly breathe.

And then below it:

Do but consider this small dust

Here running in the glass,

By atoms moved.

Hart's phone rings. It's the CSM, calling from the industrial estate.

"Sir, I think we might have found something."

28

Strover and Hart step inside the white forensic tent that CSI has erected around the suspected crime scene – a small clearing deep in the scrubland. They are both wearing protective overalls and covers on their shoes. Hart hadn't expected the call from the CSM or the one from Ward a few minutes later. His boss had clearly been asked to be kept personally updated on any developments and was more than a little smug when he called Hart.

"Seems like our friend Rory Garstan isn't selling snake oil after all," Ward had crowed. His friend, not Hart's.

"What have we got?" Hart asks the CSM. The digger had peeled back the topsoil like a surgeon cutting into soft flesh, before retreating to allow the ground-penetrating radar to scan the exposed earth below again. Three CSI investigators are now on their knees, trowels in hand, painstakingly digging around what appears to be a large turquoise suitcase.

Hart suddenly feels very warm. He needs to stick to the facts here, follow the evidence. Sophie Mills disappeared two years ago, body never found, most probably killed unlawfully after disappearing somewhere near the Cricklade Road. Credible new evidence… this is where it all breaks down. There's nothing credible about a psychic shrink who claims to have located Sophie's body with remote viewing. Nothing. But here he is, standing in a forensic tent as a bulging suitcase is extracted carefully from the grubby Swindon soil.

"Looks like you're going to be our next Chief Constable," Strover whispers, out of earshot from the CSI investigators.

"Drop it, Strover."

"You don't think it's Sophie?"

Hart shakes his head.

"I don't know what I think. But something's very wrong here."

He considers Garstan again, how he had described at their first meeting the "gift" that he had been born with and his "duty to use it responsibly to help others". Assisting the police to solve a cold case certainly ticks the responsible box. But if the suitcase really does contain the remains of Sophie, there's only one rational explanation for how Garstan could possibly know where she is buried. And Hart's determined to keep things rational.

He signals for Strover to step outside the tent.

"You alright, sir?" Strover asks.

"No, Strover, I'm not bloody alright. Not alright at all. We've got ourselves a big problem."

"How do you mean?"

"Why do we have a problem?" Hart can hardly believe

he needs to explain. "Because in my world, the only explanation for how Dr Rory Garstan knows the location of Sophie Mills' body is because he put her in the suitcase and buried her himself. Occam's razor. Usually right."

"It's just possible he might have some special—"

"I thought you were meant to be the scientist around here, the one who believes that two plus two equals four, not five."

"Isaac Newton had a strong religious faith," Strover says. "Not so keen on the Holy Trinity, but he believed in the Bible. Into palmistry too, apparently."

"Newton was hit on the head with an apple, Strover."

"Which prompted one of his greatest discoveries."

"What exactly are you saying here?"

"That we should keep an open mind, sir, that's all. Newton's laws of motion paved the way for modern science, but he was also obsessed with searching the Bible for prophecies. 2060 would be a significant year, he predicted – the beginning of the Apocalypse. Not such a bad shout back in the seventeenth century, given the way we're going. Maybe, just maybe, Dr Garstan does have a special gift."

Hart sighs, looks down the cycle path at the crowds beyond the crime scene tape. Mel would say the same thing if she were here: keep an open mind. He's never going to hear the end of this from Ward. There's no way that he can float his theory – the only sensible one in town – that Garstan must have killed Sophie himself. Ward won't want to hear it, will block him if he tries to prove Garstan's involvement, regardless of whether they are Freemasons or not. What matters to him is that Sophie's body has been found and can finally be laid to rest. The main suspect, he will argue, is still the mystery man in Angelo's, whose dark sexual fantasies frightened Sophie into leaving the nightclub early. Ward has always been keen on that line of inquiry. In his mind, today's discovery has only confirmed it.

"Gifted or not, Garstan should now become our prime suspect," Hart says.

"Even though there's nothing to link him to Sophie?"

"She had a history of mental health issues, including anxiety," Hart says. "So did Milo. There's still a chance that Garstan might have dropped in to volunteer at the hostel, off the books, and seen Sophie."

"But I can't believe that if I killed someone, I'd tell the police two years later where the body was buried," Strover says. "Not if I'd got away with it."

Hart has had exactly the same thought.

"But what if Garstan were responsible in some way for Milo's death and felt well and truly spooked by our visit? He calls Ward, his shooting/Freemason buddy, and helps to find a missing person's body. Cue good PR for Wiltshire Police – and brownie points for Ward. It's also the perfect distraction from Milo's death. No one interviewed Garstan after Sophie went missing two years ago. He's calculating he's still off our radar, in the clear."

"And he is. We've got nothing to link him to Sophie's death. Or Milo's."

"Not yet."

One of the CSI investigators appears outside the tent. "Guv, you might want to take a look."

Hart and Strover step back inside. The large suitcase has now been eased from the earth and placed to one side on some white plastic sheeting. The atmosphere in the tent has become reverential, like a chapel, as it often does in moments such as this. Hart watches as an investigator cuts open the side of the suitcase, running a knife all the way round the rusty zip, as if he's skinning an animal. Very slowly, he lifts off the lid and places it on the sheeting. Inside the suitcase, layers of wrapped black plastic, which he slits open. Hart holds his breath.

And beneath the plastic, covered in pale grave wax, a collection of dismembered human remains. After a few seconds, the investigator looks up and says what Hart is thinking.

"The skull's missing."

29

You managed to appear pleased for me when I was accepted to read medicine at Cambridge, but the barbs soon flowed thick and fast. Intelligence came at a cruel cost, you said, as we walked along the Backs. It wasn't worth the rub. Where were the relationships? Where was the glory? The celebrations? The famous Cambridge student life? It was all work, work, work, no time to come up for air. And it was true, I had to study so hard just to avoid being thrown off the course, day and night, terms and holidays. Most of my fellow medical students were planning on going into academia. I was one of the few who wanted to interact with patients, be at the bedside rather than in the lab.

"I'm not jealous, you know," you said, as we stopped on Magdalen Bridge to watch the punts pass below us on the Cam. "You deserve it."

I was surprised by the generosity of your tone. Suspicious too. You were reading medicine at Aston University at the time, having failed to get into Oxford. (You blew a lot of your exams at Aston, but kept resitting them until you passed.) Nothing wrong with Aston, of course, but the two medical schools were at opposite ends of the league table, something that I knew upset you far more than me.

"Thank you," I said.

"Just tell me one thing. Did you see all this? Getting into Cambridge?"

We were back to that again. "Did I see it? I suppose I always had a goal."

"That's not what I'm asking. You know what I mean. Did you know*?"*

"I knew, yes," I said, treading carefully. And it was true: I'd always seen myself here, ever since Dad had brought us both to Cambridge as teenagers to show us around his old college. "All I can say is that it's the most extraordinary sense of certainty," I added, "like slipping on a heavy winter coat that fits perfectly."

"And that made it easier, seeing it?" you asked. "Easier to achieve?"

I hesitated before speaking again. "This is about Mum, isn't it?"

"I just think, if you really can see things, you know, in the future, you're not making the most of it."

"What do you expect me to do? Hire a booth at the end of Brighton Pier and cradle a crystal ball?"

"Of course not."

"Then what? It doesn't feel like I'm wasting my life here," I said. And I wasn't lying. For the first time ever, I felt more comfortable in my skin and was finding like-minded people,

friends who had their own unique gifts. I'd recently joined the university branch of the Society for Psychical Research, set up in the late nineteenth century to investigate psychic phenomena in a scientific spirit. Its first president, Henry Sidgwick, was professor of Moral Philosophy at Trinity College, Cambridge, and had coined the word "telepathy".

"That's why you and I are so different," you said. "If I were in your position, had your… power, I would be doing so much more with it."

We set off walking again, back into town. You had a train to catch, had only come to Cambridge for the day. Not really to see me, but to attend a conference. We had drifted apart as brothers. In the years after Mum died, Dad had tried hard to keep us together as a unit, but by the time we'd left school, we'd become strangers. Given how cruel you'd been to your "baby brother", I can't say I ever missed you, but I still felt we'd failed as a family. And then Dad had been offered a post at Duke University in North Carolina and we both urged him to take it, to rent out the family home in Pewsey. He needed finally to draw a line under Mum's death and get on with his life.

Years later, having never heard from you, you sent me a card when I became one of the youngest consultant psychiatrists in the country. I didn't open the card at first. We hadn't communicated for so long. At lunch, I walked down to the Thames to clear my head and read it there, looking across to Big Ben and the Houses of Parliament.

Mum would be proud of you – but you know that already.

Nothing about your own pride in me. You couldn't find it in yourself. Jealousy had fermented into bitterness and it broke my heart. Dad was proud of me too. He was now back from a happy second career in America and had been enjoying his well-earned retirement until rheumatoid arthritis reared its ugly head.

I tried to put myself in your shoes, understand how you felt, as Dad had encouraged us to do as children. Academically, I might have been more successful, but what did that matter? We were flesh and blood. There was only one thing that separated us and that was beyond my control.

Later that year, I was shocked when you turned up at my wedding. You slipped into the Methodist church in Marylebone – Dad's favourite place of worship when he'd lived in London – just as I was pledging my love to Rob, one of the medics who had been on my course at Cambridge. He was a neurologist in Queen's Square, and we'd been dating off and on for five years.

"To have and to hold from this day forward..."

It was as traditional a service as we could make it. For Dad.

No one turned around, no one saw you when you arrived. Thankfully, I had sensed your arrival a few minutes earlier, which had given me time to prepare myself before you actually appeared. Think about why you might have decided to attend. I glanced up as you took your seat, half hidden by a pillar near the back of the church, and we stared at each other for a second, and then I turned away. I had more important things on my mind.

"For richer, for poorer, in sickness and in health..."

You didn't stay for the reception or hear Dad's speech. He told some good psychiatrist jokes. Of course he did. I cried when he talked about Mum. He suddenly struck me as a frail old man, barely able to walk, and he could have done with your support that day. It wasn't his choice. You had chosen to stop loving him, never once visited him in America. He always loved you, loved us equally. They both had.

Afterwards, I kept asking myself: what was the point of you coming to the wedding if you didn't want to talk to me, or to Rob or Dad? Your appearance had changed too. You were sporting a beard and wore ridiculous dark glasses inside the church. It was clear that you didn't want anyone to recognise you. And no one I spoke to at the reception afterwards seemed to have seen you arrive or leave. Of course, people knew we were no longer talking – everyone loves a family rift – and I'm sure someone would have mentioned it if they'd seen you. Later, I told Dad that you had turned up. I thought he would be pleased, have something to hold on to: there were still some slim strands of family that bound us together. But he was devastated.

So why were you there? It's then that I had a bad feeling, like the smell of rotting deer in a roadside ditch.

30

Present day

Strover's already in the Parade Room by the time Hart arrives. Sometimes it takes a particularly early start to secure their corner.

"Morning, sir," Strover says, sounding annoyingly perky for the time of day. "Journey in OK?"

"All good."

Hart had used the drive over from Marlborough to tell himself to stop worrying about Conor's revelation last night that he'd seen a life coach at the hostel. Before setting off for work, he'd made Conor and Jess some tea, knocked on the door and left it on a tray outside their room. Jess had emerged, bleary-eyed, and they'd had a quick chat on the landing about the parkrun on Saturday.

"Still on?" she'd asked.

"Of course," he'd replied.

He hadn't done enough training, but he couldn't pull out

now. Conor and Mel were running it too – a family outing. Jess then added that she'd checked with Conor last night and he'd definitely had his life coach session two weeks earlier – seven days *before* Garstan had been released from Barontrent. He could relax, stop having nightmares about the parkrun.

Mel was even more relieved than he was.

"Don't ever do that to me again," she'd said, kissing him goodbye on the doorstep. "You can take it – all the shit that work throws at you. At us. Conor can't. And he doesn't deserve it."

Hart glances around the Parade Room and fires up his laptop.

"Any progress with ID'ing yesterday's two fatalities?" he asks Strover.

"My friend at Barontrent thinks the patient at the hospital who died was a former inmate called Darren Eaves. Served eighteen months for domestic burglary, released two weeks ago."

"Darren Eaves," Hart says, his stomach tightening. At least there's some parity now. He knows Darren's name, just as Darren knew his.

"You're not a believer, are you? He said you weren't. 'Find DI Silas Hart if you want to side with the deniers.' That's what he said to me. 'He'll keep you company in the darkness.' I tried not to believe, but he knows."

A part of him had hoped that there would be no connection between Garstan and the awful events of yesterday. That there had been some hideous mistake. Who's he kidding? Garstan had sent these men to seek him out, to show Hart that there's no escaping your death day.

"And the man at the front desk?" he asks.

Strover pauses before answering. "Nobody could recognise him from the photo."

"You did send them a respectful one, Strover?"

"There wasn't much choice. I'm waiting to hear about a DNA match."

It's a good shout, given the police can only search against other DNA profiles taken from scenes of crime. If he was banged up at Barontrent, there should be a match.

Hart sits down at his desk and picks up an envelope addressed to him, hoping to distract himself, to forget Darren's despair. Strover collects his post every morning for him from the front desk. The envelope in his hands looks like junk mail, with a typed address. He slips it open and removes a brochure: a "coffin and cask" catalogue. His heart sinks, wondering if he should be wearing gloves, whether this could prove to be evidence, but it's been mailed directly from the manufacturers.

He flicks through it, looking at photos of the company's "natural range": mushroom, wool, bamboo, seagrass. In a normal world, he would be cracking jokes by now, reading bits out to colleagues. *Ok, so who's the joker who sent me this? A coffin's the last thing I need.* But he knows who sent it and it's not funny.

"Did you know you can even have a cardboard coffin these days?" Hart says, trying to be his old self. "'Cardboard pillow included, ensuring comfort and respect for the dearly departed.'"

Strover, seated at the opposite desk, looks across at him, and then at the brochure in his hand. "A cardboard pillow?"

"The mushroom coffin comes with a soft bed of moss

as standard," Hart continues, remembering the surreal conversation he'd had with the undertakers about choosing handles for his dad's coffin. After much discussion, they had settled on a Lincoln T-end in antique brass.

"Did he send you that?" Strover asks.

"Maybe."

Hart tosses the brochure away and glances out at the white car park. The sky is hostile, pewter grey, but at least it's no longer snowing. He glances across at Strover, who has fallen quiet.

"What's up? Coffins give you the creeps?"

But he knows it's something else.

"I've been trying to find out what Garstan was up to when he was inside," Strover says.

"Any luck?"

"He was on the lookout for potential patients."

Hart looks up. "What?"

"Keen to keep his hand in as a psychiatrist. Mental health provision at Barontrent is almost non-existent. One full-time shrink for the entire prison population, long waiting lists for therapy. Self-harm on the up, prisoners reluctant to disclose suicidal thoughts in case they're put into isolation. They were only too pleased when Garstan volunteered his services."

"I bet they were."

"It was all very unofficial, apparently. Offered to help out where he could."

Hart shakes his head. It makes sense. No doubt he was moonlighting as a life coach too, sharing his unique insights into prisoners' pasts, presents and futures. Bit of a comedown from his celebrity patients in Harley Street, but he wouldn't be the first. Jeffrey Archer and Jonathan Aitken had both helped fellow inmates with their studies and letter writing.

"Can we be certain that Garstan saw Darren Eaves?" Hart asks.

"It was all off the books. I doubt there'll be any records."

"But he must have done. It's the only explanation."

Hart stands up and looks out the window. He needs to establish exactly what happened between Garstan and his patients, how he persuaded Darren to seek him out on his release from prison, challenge him about death days.

"I tried not to believe, but he knows. He just knows. I don't understand how. But once you've seen the future, you can't change it."

Darren was sent to prove to Hart that there's no escaping fate. A wave of nausea washes through him. He's fifty-seven, with possibly only days left to live. All he wants right now is to be with Mel, hold her tight. She would reassure him that everything's going to be OK. She'd also tell him to get a grip. He swallows hard, weighing up whether the journey to the canteen is worth the appalling coffee when he gets there, but Strover spares him the decision.

"There's something else, sir. Turns out Garstan was on an ROTL."

A Release On Temporary Licence. "When?"

"Two weeks back. Wednesday 17 November. A one-day resettlement release."

"You're kidding me." Hart's whole body tenses up again. The same day that Conor saw his life coach at the hostel. Just when he thought that problem had gone away.

"Do we know what he was doing?" Hart asks. But he already knows the answer.

"Same as on the inside. Volunteering to work with people on their mental health. It ticked all the right boxes, helped him to prepare for the outside world again."

Hart doesn't even need to ask where he worked.

"The hostel on Fleming Way," he says. "That's where he was, wasn't he?"

It's Strover's turn to look surprised. Hart hangs his head.

"Conor volunteers there," he adds.

Strover has lived through all Hart's family dramas over the years, ridden their highs and lows. He gives an update on Conor's enthusiasm for the life coach, how he had signed up for a session himself when things were quiet – and had been given an hourglass.

"He must have seen Garstan," Hart says, wondering how the hell he's going to break the news to Mel. "Give me a second."

Hart dials Conor's number. No answer, so he leaves a message, turning his back to Strover. He never likes making personal calls in the office. "Con, it's Dad. About that life coach at the Fleming Way hostel. It's really important you don't see him again. I mean it. Please don't see that man again. Something's come up at work about him. Call me if you want to discuss." He pauses, wondering if he should say anything else. "Love you."

Hart puts his phone away.

"There's one other thing, sir," Strover says, watching Hart turn round.

"Go on," Hart says, knowing that Strover would have heard every word of his message to Conor.

"Apparently Garstan insisted on screening his patients when he was at Barontrent."

"How do you mean? No one-on-ones with psychopaths? I can see his point."

Strover consults a notebook, ignoring Hart.

"He put word out that he only wanted to see people with acute anxiety issues," Strover says. "Said it was his clinical specialty. People who couldn't sleep at night because they thought they might not wake up in the morning. That sort of thing."

"Thanatophobia," Hart says.

"What?"

"A fear of death. Christ, he was selecting people who were scared of dying." Hart pauses. "Just like he did with Milo three years ago."

And just like he's doing with Hart. And now with his own son.

31

An hour later, Hart and Strover arrive at the basement mortuary of the Great Western Hospital, summoned by Malcolm Strangeways, the forensic pathologist. He wanted to talk face to face, but he is preoccupied when they walk in, looking through a file. Hart glances at the two bodies on the stainless-steel tables, both covered in sheets. He assumes that one of them must be Darren, the patient who died in the hospital, and the other is the man who took his own life at the front desk.

Strover's alarmingly comfortable in the mortuary. He's OK around dead bodies, too – at least he was until recently, since he's started to imagine his own corpse on the slab. Would it be Malcolm who conducted his autopsy? Tall and old school, he is unnervingly enthusiastic about human decomposition. Last time they met, he lectured Hart on the green bottle fly and its maggots – the "gold standard" for determining time of death.

"Haven't you retired yet?" Hart asks, as Malcolm looks up.

"Too young," he says, grinning at Strover as he puts down the file to greet them. "Truth be told, once the ex took everything – including the Morgan, can you believe that? – I had no choice but to return to the crease, battered and bruised, like the redoubtable Chris Woakes with one arm in a sling, and keep batting for one's country."

Hart's not a cricket fan himself, but his spirits had risen when he'd heard that Malcolm was conducting the autopsies on both of yesterday's victims. They don't make old school forensic pathologists like him anymore.

"What do you think happened, then?" Hart says, keen to move the conversation on from cricket.

"To whom? You're keeping me busy, Silas."

"Let's start with Darren, who died here in the hospital yesterday."

"It's really rather remarkable," Malcolm says, walking over to one of the tables and gently lifting back the sheet. Hart takes in Darren's purple-bloated face, his blotchy chest. Strange to be reacquainted with a man who had died in front of him.

"In what way?" Hart asks, still looking at Darren's body. Strover leans in closer to listen. The conversation has suddenly become serious.

"I've only heard of one case like this before – Benin, West Africa, late 1970s."

"What happened?" Hart asks, nervous already about the answer.

"Someone had put a hex on the poor man and he promptly died. A Harvard physiologist named Walter B. Cannon coined the phrase 'voodoo death'. What we might now call a 'psychogenic death' – where someone dies because of their psychological state rather than any physical cause."

Hart shifts uncomfortably. "And that's really possible?"

"Medicine's only now beginning to understand the complex relationship between the mind and body. If someone is convinced that they are going to die – in Benin, because of wider cultural beliefs – then that absolute conviction can play havoc with our sympathetic nervous system, flood the body with too much adrenaline. Our visceral 'fight or flight' response."

"Kill the tiger or run away." Hart had read about hyperarousal late one night, concerned by his own surges in adrenaline.

"Exactly. Funnily enough, it was Cannon who also coined the phrase 'fight or flight' – our reaction to a perceived threat. In most cases, the adrenaline levels soon drop off as the tiger wanders away, but sometimes the adrenaline continues to surge – a sort of 'autonomic storm' – and knocks out the heart."

"So what do you think Darren felt threatened by?" Hart asks, remembering the look of abject terror on his face.

"A good question. We both know our new Dr Baydon can be pretty scary when she wants to be – a veritable Geordie tiger – but no, more seriously, the perceived threat here was quite clearly emotional rather than physical. Having read the notes, the way he was counting down to midday, his talk of a death day, even a death minute, I think Darren died of raw, unadulterated fear."

"And that's actually possible?" Hart asks, looking first at Malcolm and then at Strover.

"Oh yes. Quite possible."

"A self-fulfilling prophecy?" Strover asks, eyes lingering on Darren.

"You're absolutely right, of course. There's an element of that. We can't discount the nocebo effect either – when someone thinks that a particular treatment will have a negative outcome."

"The opposite of a placebo?" Strover asks.

"Spot on. Poor Darren here was, for whatever reason, convinced that he was going to die at midday yesterday. And his body steeled itself with so much adrenaline that it triggered a cardiac arrest."

"The anticipation killed him?" Hart asks.

"Exactly. I'm amazed it doesn't happen on Death Row in the States, where inmates are told when they're going to die. In Japan, they're given no such warning. After months, years, possibly even decades of not knowing, you're just taken away one day to die by long-drop hanging."

"Far worse, I'd have thought," Strover offers. "No time to prepare."

"But is it worse?" Malcolm asks. "Isn't that the human condition? Any of us could fall down dead tomorrow. It strikes me as quite unnatural to know what specific day, let alone what minute, will be your last on earth. No wonder Darren was terrified."

"The mounting tension would have been unbearable for him as the time drew near," Hart adds, trying not to think of his own ticking time bomb.

"Absolutely," Malcolm says, consulting his notes again. "His left ventricle is very telling. More work's been done since Cannon, of course. These days one might hazard he died of 'stress cardiomyopathy' or 'takotsubo syndrome'.

'Broken-heart syndrome' in old money. A consequence of extreme emotional stress over time that stunned his heart and prevented the left ventricle from contracting effectively."

"Did he have any underlying health conditions?" Strover asks.

"He wasn't exactly a poster boy for the British Heart Foundation," Malcolm says. "High cholesterol, occluded arteries. I did wonder if it was what we call *angor animi* – 'distress of the soul'. A sense of impending doom – a dread of dying – but it's more commonly found in patients with angina."

Hart takes a deep breath, checking for pain in his own chest. Angina is something that he's asked Dr Google about more than once recently. A symptom of coronary heart disease, it manifests as chest pain caused by reduced blood flow to the heart – exactly what his mum suffered from before she died.

"Can it make things worse – if you think you're dying? Asking for a friend."

"It's an interesting question. The literature mentions a case in the 1960s when a doctor on his morning ward round asked a very anxious, chain-smoking patient with *angina pectoris* – you could smoke in hospital in those days – if he felt he was actually going to die during one of his angina attacks. The poor fellow's eyes widened with fear and he was dead in his bed within the minute."

Hart wished he'd never asked.

"So it's definitely a thing? Dying from fear?"

"Absolutely. Rare, but a 'thing', as you put it. If you want my formal initial assessment, endogenous catecholamines – dopamine, norepinephrine and epinephrine – induced myocardial stunning and infarction. Darren was literally frightened to death."

Hart lets Malcolm's words sink in, remembering Milo's journal from three years earlier.

Even now, as I write this, I think I could die so easily. Death's always here, hidden but life-adjacent. G kept asking me about that, again and again, my profound fear of death.

There's no murder weapon when you kill someone with fear.

32

It was the brass plaque that proved one step too far for you. No doubt you came up with a justification for your own career path: private practice wasn't the reason you went into medicine. You had your NHS work, which was admirable. Initially, I only worked privately on Fridays, but I know how much it must have galled you, what it represented, me consulting in the very same rooms where Dad had practised. And the reputation that I was quietly building for a new, hybrid form of treatment, one that took clinical intuition and empathy and yes, my gift, beyond the realms of ordinary psychiatry.

And then, one day, you must have heard that I was in trouble. Dad had died two months after the wedding – he had clearly been holding on – and his death threw me, however expected it was. I was at sea, adrift, aware that I was now on my own, with no one to tether me to my family past. You were my only link, but you were refusing to see me, even when I asked to meet before Dad's funeral. You turned up at the back of the church though, just as you had with my wedding – same silly dark glasses and beard – and you disappeared again afterwards. Not staying for the wake was inexcusable. I'd had to arrange everything and I found myself consoling Dad's few friends that were still alive. Dad had tried to love you, tried so hard, but you never made it easy for him. He died not knowing if he had one son or two. I found it impossible to forgive you for that, the pain you caused him.

It wasn't long before my eight sessions a week at St Thomas' became too much, partly because I was increasingly fixated with my private work – I finally felt I was making the most of my gift, as you had urged me to do that day in Cambridge. One day a week soon became two, then three. But I was over-committing to patients, exhibiting too much empathy – one of the inherent risks of the job. (I now know why they once thought psychiatrists should be forced to retire at fifty-five: they'd go round the bend if they stayed working any longer.)

First to go was my marriage to Rob. Marrying a fellow medic works for some people, but we never saw each other and drifted apart. There was no animosity, just a grey numbness. I soon started to become shy and withdrawn, even by my own antisocial standards, and work was now untenable. So too the responsibility of Pewsey. Dad had left the family home entirely to me in his will, as you know, and I felt obliged to live there as much as I could, but the commuting was stressful.

And then, out of the blue, having not communicated for several years, you came to visit me at my flat in Borough.

You must have known that I had recently been signed off sick. Your kindness was as surprising as it was welcome. It was so good to see you. I was talking to Mum when you arrived, asking what I should do about the broken washing machine. You waited patiently, watching and listening.

"Hello Rory," I said, glancing in the mirror and then at you.

You didn't say anything for a while. Instead, your gaze just lingered on me.

"Don't let me interrupt," you eventually said, removing a stack of old newspapers from a chair to sit down. I expected a cruel aside, but it never came. You'd changed. All of a sudden you were interested in my life. "How is she?" you asked. "Mum?"

"Still knitting for Britain," I said, nodding at her in the corner. "Enjoying retirement."

"And Dad?" You glanced in Mum's direction before turning back to me with an intense, listening gaze.

"Cycled off to get us lunch from Borough Market," I said. "Took Barka too."

"How is he?"

"Oh, you know, same old Dad. Cracking bad jokes, working too hard."

"Barka's behaving?"

"Since when's Barka ever behaved?" I laughed. "I told her she wasn't allowed up on the sofa, but did she listen?"

We both looked at the sofa I was perched on, every remaining inch of it covered in towers of books and magazines. You paused for a long time before your next question, staring at the floor, twisting your hands together. And then you swallowed and fixed me in the eye.

"And how about Finn? How is he?"

I laughed, louder this time, relieved that your question was nothing more serious. You were always playing tricks on me when we were younger.

"He's fine, thanks," I said, glancing in the mirror again, shocked by the face staring back at me. And then I turned to you, wiping away a tear. "Not great, actually."

"It's OK," you said, standing up to rest a gentle hand on my shoulder. I hadn't felt your touch for years. I put my hand up to yours, to check that I wasn't imagining things. You were sweating.

"It's quite hot in here," you said, turning to push aside a dead house plant and open a window.

"Is it? I get muddled with the thermostat."

You glanced around the room again. "And a little messy."

"I tried to hire a cleaner, but Mum wasn't having it. A bit too young and pretty for Dad." We both laughed this time. "Dad always says he'll do the washing up, but he never does. Like the lawn. 'I'll mow it tonight.' And the moss on the roof. 'I'll get the ladder out at the weekend.'" I fell quiet. "Don't worry, I'll do the dishes later."

I started to cry then, shy little sobs. The chaos around me – the dirty plates, cartons of half-eaten takeaway food, piles of soiled laundry, the flies – was suddenly overwhelming. But I was also moved by the profound change in you. For the first time in years, I felt loved by my big brother.

"Would you like to live somewhere else for a while?" you asked softly. "Away from all this? A place where I can take care of you."

"I'd like that very much, I said, sniffling. "When Dad gets back from the shops."

33

The past

Ward can't disguise the look of satisfaction on his face as Hart and Strover walk into his office. This time, Ward invites them to sit.

"I don't wish to tempt fate, but that was remarkably swift and painless," Ward says. "Congratulations, both of you."

Hart wasn't expecting such warm words from Ward. It hadn't been his idea to search the scrubland south of the Groundwell Industrial Estate and he'd hardly embraced the operation with gusto. Given Ward's good mood, is now the time for Hart to state the obvious? That the discovery makes Garstan their prime suspect in what has turned into a murder inquiry?

"Have Forensics confirmed that the remains are Sophie's?" Strover asks, sensing, perhaps, that Hart is about to demolish the good mood with a wrecking ball of tactlessness.

"It's a formality," Ward says, waving away the question.

"Clothing found in the suitcase matches what she was last seen wearing in the nightclub."

"It's good news," Hart hears himself saying. "Her family can have some closure at last." He won't tell Ward about the pitiful state of Sophie's mother.

"Absolutely," Ward says.

"But we now have an unsolved murder case rather than a misper," Hart says, choosing his words carefully. "And a pretty brutal one at that. Her head was missing."

"So I understand."

"A woman came forward today, up at the crime scene. Said she was a friend of Sophie's. We hadn't interviewed her as part of our original investigation. I thought it would be good to—"

"No need to rush one's fences, Silas," Ward says, interrupting. "Sophie was missing, now she's been found, confirming our theory that she was murdered. Next we find the man who committed this egregious crime. One step at a time. Let's just enjoy the moment, shall we?"

There was nothing remotely enjoyable about the sight of Sophie's remains in the suitcase, the thought that her skull is still out there somewhere.

"Of course we'll need to open a murder inquiry," Ward says, "but we all know who is responsible."

Hart glances at Strover. Maybe he's got this wrong. Is Ward on their side and the whole thing's been an elaborate trap to catch Garstan?

"You need to find him," Ward continues. "Go through all the footage at the club again and identify the man whose 'sexual fantasies' so spooked poor Sophie that night. He'll be sweating once we've issued a statement about today's discovery and he's seen it on the *Ten O'Clock News* this evening. Someone might talk, turn him in."

No change, then. Ward's prime suspect is still a man they spent six months trying to find two years ago. Garstan remains in the clear, the psychic hero of the hour. Not that his role will be made public, because Garstan doesn't want the media attention. Funny, that.

"Of course," Hart says. He coughs, battling to control his frustration.

"You also need to visit Rory, thank him personally for his extraordinary work. I'll leave it with you," Ward continues. "I'm off on holiday tonight."

A small glimmer of hope on the horizon.

"Anywhere nice?" Hart asks.

"Sri Lanka – visiting the medieval capitals of Yapahuwa and Panduwas Nuwara with some old Oxford friends. Did you know Yapahuwa briefly housed the sacred tooth relic of the Buddha?"

Strangely not. But he and his fellow Buddha boffins can take as long as they want. Hart's got a plan.

"And when I come back, refreshed and recharged, we can talk about solving more misper cold cases. How best to utilise Rory's help. He's keen to work again with us. In a strictly private capacity, of course."

"I look forward to that," Hart says.

Hart can feel Ward's eyes scrutinising him, waiting for him to crack, finish the sentence – *...like a hole in the head* – but he holds his tongue.

"And I've been meaning to ask, I'm assuming it was just a tragic suicide?" Ward continues. "That case over in Wilton you were looking into? Rory was very upset, said he should have seen it coming, done more to help the poor young man."

Oh, the irony. How much should Hart reveal?

"We're still waiting for the autopsy," Hart says, deciding to stay silent and suck it up. "But I may have called in CSI too soon. You are right – it seems it was just a suicide."

Back in the Parade Room, Hart wastes no time in sharing his plan with Strover. While Ward is away with the tooth fairies in Sri Lanka, they have a window of opportunity in which to nail Garstan, as Milo's father, Crispin, had urged Hart to do when they'd met in the Brail.

"We arrest Garstan for the unlawful possession of dodgy guns," Hart says. *While the cat's away…*

"Arrest him? Sir, Ward will go totally mental," Strover says, in a rare expression of emotion. "And we don't actually know if Garstan's got any illegal or unlicensed firearms."

"Strover, did you trust Crispin, Milo's father, when we met him? Did you believe him?"

Strover pauses before answering, no doubt sensing that Hart is in mentoring mode. "He was upset, and blamed Garstan for his son's death, so not exactly an impartial witness."

"Your gut, Strover. What did you *feel* about Crispin?" He's beginning to sound like Garstan, but if their time working together leaves his colleague with one useful policing skill, Hart hopes it will be to listen to instinct, to trust human intuition. "He might forget to buy a ticket for the car park at Waitrose. He may drive back from the pub after one drink too many. And he might even 'accidentally' plough up the odd public footpath that crosses his land. But is Crispin really the sort to lie about his son's psychiatrist?"

"No, sir," Strover says.

"And Garstan? What words spring to mind when you think of him?"

Another pause. "Suspicious. Disingenuous. Dangerous."

"So we get a search warrant from our favourite magistrate on Prince's Street and pay Garstan another visit."

"Or we go back to plan A, thank him for his work on the Sophie Mills case, and ask him upfront about his gun collection?"

Hart gives Strover a look of disdain as his phone rings.

"Or maybe not," Strover says under her breath.

Hart listens for a few seconds, thanks the caller and hangs up.

"That was the CSM," he says. "They've found Milo's burner phone. He made one call, timed at 7.16 a.m. as we thought – to Garstan's mobile. They spoke for two minutes, twenty-five seconds."

Hart looks at Strover, weighing up the new evidence. Garstan's looking more guilty by the minute.

"What do you feel about Garstan now?" he asks.

"It still doesn't prove anything," Strover says. "Milo was suicidal, rings his psychiatrist. Very sad. End of."

"It depends what Garstan said to him," Hart says, but he's pleased Strover hasn't rolled over. He was beginning to sound like a bully, lecturing rather than discussing. Sadly, they'll never know what Garstan said to Milo. The phone log can only confirm that a call was made between the two numbers.

"Any word on Milo's autopsy?" Strover asks.

Strover's right. They should have heard back by now, found out if Milo had died of anything other than broken dreams. The arrival of Sophie's remains in the mortuary will only have slowed things down further. Homicides trump suicides, particularly when Ward's entered the game.

"I'll give Malcolm a call," Hart continues. "You jump on the magistrate search form – and make sure it doesn't sound like a fishing trip." Strover knows the score, understands the requirements of Section 8 of the Police and Criminal Evidence Act better than most. All being well, they won't have to go down to the court on Prince's Street to be issued with the search warrant. Post-Covid, video links have become the norm. "Just make sure we can get into Garstan's house before Ward returns from Sri Lanka."

Ten minutes later, Hart's phone rings. It's Malcolm Strangeways, the forensic pathologist. He can either be ebullient or terse.

"You called," he says, tersely.

"Sorry to chase, Malcolm, just wondering if there's any news on Milo, the young man—"

"In case you weren't aware, the 'Samsonite murder', as our tabloids are already calling it, is national news. I've had to drop everything, including your windmill suicide, which I'm not quite sure why was passed over to us in the first place."

"Nothing suspicious, then?"

"I've had to hand him onto a colleague, I'm afraid. As far as I know, there's no initial evidence of poisoning or an overdose. We'll need to wait for the full toxicology report, of course, but I'll bet the farm it's clean."

"So how did he die?"

"We don't know yet, but I suspect he had a pre-existing heart condition."

"Sudden cardiac death?" Hart suggests. He's been reading far too much about it. Every week in the UK, twelve apparently fit and healthy people under thirty-five drop down dead. If it can happen to under-thirty-fives...

"Quite possibly," Malcolm says. "As for Sophie Mills, two years in a sealed suitcase causes quite surprising changes in the human body. The process of decomposition is not halted, of course, but it is slowed."

Hart's not in the mood for another lesson on maggots – but at least Malcolm is warming up.

"Cases like Sophie's are what I signed up to this game for," he says. "A family needs answers when a loved one has been reduced to hand luggage. Two points of interest for you. One, it's impossible to say how she died from the remains we have, which makes me think the fatal injury was to her head. Two, it's not just her head that's missing. Her clavicle – collarbone – has been removed too. There's a crude incision around the left shoulder, not commensurate with the incision that was made to sever her neck. Like the head itself, it was possibly taken as a trophy of some sort."

"A trophy?"

"Bragging rights."

34

"That's the first search warrant she's turned down in a while," Hart says, sipping on his canteen coffee, even more awful than usual.

"Maybe she's a shooting buddy of Garstan's, too," Strover says.

"She has a point, I guess."

Hart was hoping that he would be outside Garstan's door by now, waving a search warrant under the psychiatrist's arrogant nose, but the magistrate had wanted more evidence. Instead, he's sitting in a car with Strover, outside a house on the edge of Shrivenham, waiting for Katya, Garstan's PA, to emerge. It's 7 a.m. and they're assuming she doesn't clock on for work in Pewsey, a forty-minute drive away, before 8 a.m.

The magistrate had dismissed their application as a fishing trip, just as Hart had feared. "One man's hearsay is not enough," she'd said, referring to Crispin, Milo's father, who had told them that Garstan kept illegal firearms, including a sawn-off shotgun. They needed more evidence, which is why Strover had tracked Katya down to a small semi in Shrivenham. It's a make-or-break escalation, based on an assumption that Katya is not happy with her employer. Her comments about Milo, that he was a "sweet boy" and that she had urged him not to continue seeing Garstan, have haunted Hart ever since. He was also intrigued by the way she had flinched at the sound of Garstan's gunfire.

"Go gently," Hart says. "If we frighten her, she'll alert Garstan."

One reason why they hadn't talked to her earlier. It's high risk. If Katya's loyalties are with Garstan, he'll have plenty of time to remove any firearms from his property.

"Bring her over to the car if you can," Hart adds. "And stick to innocent questions about Milo – say we just need a statement for the coroner's report – until you're sure she's onside." He looks up at the front of the house, where Katya is emerging. "You better get moving."

Hart watches Strover walk over to Katya as she's about to get into her own car. He's glad they arrived here early. She must start work in Pewsey at 8 a.m. Strover's good in these situations, blessed with a protean ability to morph into anyone. Right now, as the two women talk, Strover could be a friendly neighbour. Unlike Hart. He will always look like a detective. Even on a beach. Maybe it's the bucket hat and shades.

Katya glances around her, checking for curtain-twitchers. She seems anxious, crestfallen. *Come on, Strover, keep talking to her.* And for two minutes the two of them chat.

At one point, Strover rests a hand on Katya's shoulder. She looks over to Hart, glances at her watch, shakes her head. She's late for work. Time to dial up the charm. And then the two of them cross over the road and get into the back of the car.

"Katya's only got five minutes," Strover says.

"We'll be quick," Hart says, smiling at her. "I promise." She looks nervous.

"Are you recording this?" she asks.

Hart holds his hands up.

"She wants to talk off the record," Strover says. "No statement. Technically she's... meant to be back in Ukraine. Her paperwork is still being processed. I said we'd overlook that."

"Of course," Hart says. "Whatever you say is just between us."

"I think you had something to share about Milo," Strover says, glancing at Hart. They'll come to firearms later.

Katya straightens her skirt, looks out the car window.

"All I know is that Dr Rory..." she says, hesitating, "the treatment was different with Milo."

"You told him not to come back after his first session with Dr Garstan," Hart says. Strover throws him a look. Back off.

"Dr Rory, he helps people to live full lives," Katya continues, "by visualising what lies ahead for them. He is obsessed with seeing someone's future. I think it gives him a sense of control. Most of us do not know these things. Only present day and the past. With Milo..." She pauses. "He was very unhappy, of course, suicidal. But Dr Rory was fascinated by his fear of death. Which is why, I think, he tries something very different. An experiment. A very dangerous one. Too dangerous. Instead of telling him how to live the better life, he tells him when and where he is going to die. The exact time and place. Can you believe this?"

"7.30 a.m.," Hart says. "The windmill."

Katya nods.

"And Dr Rory, he used such a strange expression. He said he was 'boxing the compass'. I do not know what this English means."

It's a new one on Hart too. Reversing the polarity? Of what, though?

"Instead of running away from his fears, he tells Milo to run towards them. He explains to him that he can see his future very clearly: he will die in a few days' time, early in the morning. But if Milo can, how do you say, stare death in the eye…"

"Confront his anxieties about dying," Strover offers.

"Yes, if he can do this and survive, he will go on to live a happy and meaningful life. If we can cheat our own fate, he says, we can control anything."

"But he couldn't cheat his own fate," Hart says. "Couldn't box the compass."

"No."

"And he told you all this?" Strover asks.

She nods. "So I am thinking Dr Rory will be devastated by Milo's death, when he hears."

"But he wasn't?"

"No. Quite the opposite. He is amazed. Maybe I have this all wrong, but he sees it as a breakthrough. He worries that he can't actually predict the future, despite what he tells his clients. Tells the newspapers. But here is the evidence. He sees poor Milo's future, his death, and he dies, just as he predicted. It didn't make him sad. It made him powerful."

"Jesus," Hart says.

"But I can't tell this in any court," she says, turning to Strover for reassurance. "I can't testify against Dr Rory. In case…"

"In case what?" Hart asks.

"I don't want him to predict my own death."

Hart feels sick. "Has he ever threatened to do that?" he asks.

"Not yet. He might."

"I understand," Strover says, glancing across at Hart. "But you will carry on working for him?"

"I have no choice. I have a daughter. She is with her grandparents in Lviv. My husband died."

"In the war?"

"Mariupol."

"I'm sorry."

"Now I must leave."

Hart, still feeling nauseous, signals to Strover. They need to talk about guns before she goes.

"One other thing," Strover says. "The other day, we saw Dr Garstan clay-shooting."

"I hate it," she says. "Reminds me of the war." Hart was right about the flinching.

"Of course," Strover says. "I'm sorry."

"Does he have a lot of guns?" Hart asks.

Katya looks at Strover and then at Hart. "A lot, yes. He likes guns. Obsessed with them, you can say."

"Do you happen to know where he keeps them?" Strover asks.

"Why?"

Strover glances at Hart. It's now or never.

"We think he might not have the correct licences for them," Strover says.

"He doesn't," she says quickly. "I know he doesn't."

"How do you know?" Hart asks.

"Because he is always stressing about being found out. I ask him once about this. 'Why not get the correct licences if it makes you so nervous?' He says that some of the guns are illegal. The ones he took from patients. But I don't believe him."

"You don't believe that they are illegal?" Strover asks. "Or that he didn't take them from patients?"

"I don't believe they all belonged to patients. He loves to shoot them. He has guns with the short..."

"Barrel?" Hart offers, expectantly. It sounds like Garstan has more than one too. This is even better than he'd dared to hope.

"Yes. We call this *obriz* in Ukraine. Now I must go."

"Just one last thing," Strover says. "Where does he keep these guns?"

"There's a room, behind where he works. In the stable block. It's always locked. They are all kept in there. He keeps the key on him day and night."

35

Hart knows he's being heavy-handed. He could walk up to the front door and knock, talk politely with Garstan and ask to see the licences for his guns, but where would the satisfaction be in that? Garstan doesn't deserve politeness. There's also a risk he knows they are coming, even if it is 4.55 a.m. Although his instinct tells him he can trust Katya, after their meeting yesterday, she might have changed her mind, decided it was in her interests – and her daughter's – to show loyalty to her boss. Which means Garstan might have cleared out the guns or be waiting for them. Unlikely, but the possibility meets the risk threshold, which is why he has a team of ten Authorised Firearms Officers waiting in three SUVs two minutes away.

He and Strover are in the lay-by 300 yards down the road from Garstan's house – where, a few days earlier, they had ducked below the dashboard as Ward had driven past them. Ward is now safely more than 5,000 miles away in Sri Lanka. Hart had double-checked last night with his secretary. She'd even apologised, saying that her boss was having a proper holiday.

"I'm afraid he's turned his phone off and won't be checking emails," she'd said, unaware that her words were music to Hart's ears. "Doctor's orders." Maybe Hart isn't the only one to suffer from stress.

Strover had gone back to the magistrate with a summary of their talk with Katya. It had done the trick. She'd issued a search warrant for Garstan's house in Pewsey and told them to tread carefully. A recent armed search in Melksham had ended in tragedy, with one AFO dead and a second seriously injured. Another reason why Hart's not taking any chances.

"See what I mean about crime and beauty going hand in hand?" Hart says, looking around as dawn breaks on another July day. The fields are wrapped in gossamer-thin mist, the oaks behind them bathed in morning sunlight.

A voice cuts in on Hart's two-way radio. "Ready to go when you are, guv."

Hart glances at his watch and then down at Garstan's house. The main gate is open – a good sign. And they'll be using the big red key, aka the Enforcer, to batter down the front door. More overkill, but Hart can't deny he's partly doing this for Milo. And possibly for Sophie too. He might never be able to charge Garstan with their deaths – the evidence remains too circumstantial – but he can make charging him with firearms offences as unpleasant as possible. He tries to remain impartial as a detective, but Garstan's got under his skin. Is it because of the conversation he had about his own mother's untimely death? He should never have confided so much, betrayed his anxieties. Either way, he's angry, can't wait to wipe the smile off the psychiatrist's face.

"OK, let's go," Hart says. "We'll follow you in." A CSI team, currently parked up behind the AFOs, will wait for Hart to confirm that the guns have been secured and the site locked down, before coming in to conduct a forensic search of the stable block.

They've already been through the plans a number of times, yesterday and at 3 a.m. this morning. One unit of AFOs will peel off and search the stable block, while another will enter the main house. Garstan had some work done on the interior a year ago and the architect's floorplan was easy to access on the council's planning website. The new master bedroom is in the west wing. What they don't know is if Garstan has company. He's not married, has no children and doesn't appear to be in a relationship, but there's no telling. Thanks to Katya, they also know he has no dogs, which is a bonus. Just one elderly tortoise that roams free in the garden, which even Hart should be able to outrun.

One minute later, the SUVs screech through the gates into the courtyard, followed by Hart and Strover. Two AFO units, clad in black and wearing ballistic helmets, balaclavas and Kevlar vests, fan out to the main house and stable block, semi-automatic rifles pressed to their shoulders. Hart stands back from the front door with the first unit while Strover accompanies the second, with a brief to radio through to him as soon as Garstan's gun cupboard has been breached. If they can't get in with force, Strover will call through for Garstan's keys.

After three heavy swings of the Enforcer, the elegant front door falls in on its hinges, and the team pour into the house. Their aggressive shouts ring out in the early morning air as they search through the ground floor.

"Armed police! Armed police!"

Hart waits until the AFOs have moved upstairs before stepping into the hall. More shouts from above, including Garstan's voice.

"What the hell—"

"On the floor!" one of the AFOs screams. "Get down on the floor! Legs apart, hands above your head!"

For the first time, Hart wonders if he might be burning down the house to roast a pig. Ward will eventually see the bodycam footage and, as Strover says, he will go "mental". But that can wait. He just prays that Strover finds some guns.

He pauses at the bottom of the stairs. Come on Strover, dial it in. And then his heart misses a beat as he hears another voice: Katya's.

"Can I please put some clothes on?" she is saying.

Shit. They weren't expecting her to be sleeping over. Has she decided her loyalties lie with Garstan after all? Told him to ditch his unlicensed guns? Is that why Strover's taking so long to call?

And then his radio crackles into life.

"Sir, we've got them," Strover says. "At least ten. The legit stuff, including the Damascus and two Perazzis. And some… less legit. Looks like two boom sticks."

Thank God for that. One sawn-off shotgun would have been incriminating enough but two is serious, possibly suggesting an intent to supply. Hart walks upstairs to the landing, where Garstan is on the ground, hands cuffed behind his back. Katya is sitting on the edge of the bed in the master bedroom, wrapped in an oversized dressing gown. She looks up at him. A faint shake of her head and she turns away, but not before Hart notices a bruise on her left cheekbone. It's recent but not fresh. The front of her neck, too, has several older bruises. One of the AFOs, the only female on the team, stands near her. There should be more women here, but police firearms units have struggled to rid themselves of an ingrained culture of sexism. Another reason Hart hates guns.

"Get him up," Hart says.

He watches as Garstan, in striped boxer shorts and a white T-shirt, is lifted to his feet. His hair is dishevelled, nose bleeding. Ward won't like that. Remembering his bodycam, Hart pushes all thoughts of Sophie and Milo to one side and concentrates on the evidence in hand.

"That's gratitude for you," Garstan says, smirking. Is he going to break cover, tell the assembled AFOs that he helped to identify the human remains of a misper earlier in the week using psychic powers? Hart doubts it.

"I thought you would have seen us coming," Hart says, unable to resist. He's been looking forward to saying that for days. Visualising the moment…

"You have no idea who or what you're messing with here," Garstan says. "No bloody idea. Does Tarquin know about this?"

"If you mean DCS Ward, I'm afraid he's currently on the other side of the world, looking for the Buddha's long-lost tooth. But he'll be back in three weeks. No comms either, having a break from his phone." He leans in closer to Garstan to whisper in his ear. "Nothing that a little telepathic communication can't sort, of course, but watch out for all that static over the Indian Ocean, eh?"

Garstan shakes his head. "I'm talking about you, Silas. Your future."

"Quite promising, I'd have thought, after today's little haul. A promotion at the very least."

"Your health, Silas. I'm talking about your health. Your heart. Your mother. Fifty-seven, I think you said she was when she died."

Hart's had enough.

"Rory Garstan, I'm arresting you for the illegal possession of multiple firearms without a licence under Section 1 of the 1968 Firearms Act, and the possession of two prohibited weapons under Section 5 of the same Act. You do not have to say anything, but it may harm your defence if you do not mention, when questioned, something which you may later rely on in court. Anything you do say may be given in evidence."

Garstan snorts as he's led down the stairs. Outside in the courtyard, the CSI team, wearing white overalls, is already carrying guns and several boxes of ammunition out of the consulting room. Enough to equip a small army. Strover comes over with a satisfied smile as Garstan is taken towards a reinforced black van, which has just drawn up in the courtyard. Overkill again – the vehicle is usually used for transporting high-security prisoners – but Hart's happy to rub Garstan's bloody nose in it. Sophie's body had been beheaded, after all. No proof yet that it was Garstan, but for some reason it wouldn't surprise him.

"Good work, Strover," Hart says. "You had me worried there for a moment."

"Called as quickly as I could, sir. Garstan's gun cupboard was like Fort Knox."

Ironic, given that a secure place to store guns is a requirement of a firearms licence. An officer would have had to come out here and check it personally before the licence was issued.

"You've got three years, DI Silas Hart," Garstan shouts, as he's manhandled into the back of the van.

If anyone around here is getting three years – hopefully longer – it will be Garstan, but Hart holds his peace.

"Use them well," Garstan shouts again. "You're not going to outlive your mother. Never were. I felt it from the first time we met. Fifty-seven. Life is short."

Hart watches as the van drives off, his chest tightening. Fifty-seven's just a number, isn't it? And it's three years away. Plenty of time to get healthy. He'll cut out the bacon sarnies, ditch the late-night kebabs, take up running again, eat birdseed for breakfast, kale soup for lunch. Maybe a lettuce leaf or two for dinner. But all he can think of as he walks back to the house is his mother's empty stare as she lay dead on the sitting room floor.

36

"Do we just stick with the firearms offences or ask for an extension and try to pin the Sophie Mills murder on him?" Hart asks, as he walks into the custody suite at the back of Gablecross. Garstan was taken there after the early morning visit and they now have less than twenty-four hours to charge him.

"It was a good raid, sir," Strover says. "Two sawn-offs and seven shotguns without a licence. One of them looked like a Greener Sidelock – we're talking north of £100k."

"Not now, Strover." She'll be talking cars next. "Let's stick to charging Garstan with prohibited weapons, valuable or otherwise. Much as it pains me, the CPS won't buy anything else at this stage."

"What about Milo?"

"We can't prove a thing, particularly if Katya won't testify. Garstan tried an unusual therapy. The defence will argue it was just another way of helping a suicidal young man – deeply unorthodox, borderline unethical, but ultimately well-intentioned. He tried to get him to confront his fears head on. It didn't work, but it was worth a try."

"Exposure therapy," Strover says. "A friend had it once. Told to hold a furry tarantula to cure her arachnophobia."

"It was brutal, that's what it was," Hart says, knowing he needs to confront his own fears about dying. But Garstan's words struck a nerve.

"So we stick to the shorties," Hart says, keen to change the subject. "Ask him why he owns two of them. The CPS is happy there's enough already to charge him with possession of prohibited weapons, but they want to know if there's a case for intention to supply. It might affect bail. Are you ready?"

Again, Hart offers up a small prayer for the sawn-offs. Possessing standard shotguns, even seven of them, without the necessary licences, might have resulted in a fine and community service. But the law really doesn't like guns that have been customised to kill. Garstan is going down, Freemason or not.

Two minutes later, they are sitting opposite the psychiatrist in an interview room, formalities over, tape recorder running. Garstan is still looking a wreck, particularly beside his clean-shaven lawyer, who is well dressed in an expensive suit and has clearly told his client not to cooperate.

"Let's start with the shorties, shall we?" Hart says, turning from the lawyer to Garstan. "Are you aware, Dr Garstan, that a sawn-off side-by-side 12-gauge shotgun is a prohibited weapon under the 1968 Firearms Act?"

"No comment."

"Why did you have two of them in your possession?"

"No comment."

"Were you planning to supply them to someone?"

"No comment."

"Maybe there's an honourable reason for you owning the shotguns, which are, let's be honest here, the weapon of choice for organised crime groups. Perhaps they were handed over to you by particularly disturbed patients who felt they couldn't trust themselves to be in possession of such a dangerous weapon? In which case, you were doing society a favour and should be applauded. Was that it?"

"No comment."

Hart had been expecting as much and has a plan.

"Do you know how Sophie Mills was killed, Dr Garstan? You knew where she was buried, after all."

The question throws the psychiatrist, as Hart hoped it would. If he can't charge Garstan with Sophie's murder, he can at least make him sweat. Garstan glances at his lawyer.

"Is this relevant to the offences my client was arrested for?" the lawyer asks. "Sections 1 and 5 of the 1968 Firearms Act?"

"She was beheaded. Not nice. Let's hope it was after she was dead, eh?"

"This has nothing to do with the charges that have been put to my client," the lawyer insists.

"Maybe you are not aware, but your client helped us only this week to locate the whereabouts of Sophie's remains."

This time it's the lawyer who seems thrown. He glances at Garstan, who nods.

"I'll let him fill you in on how he knew her location," Hart adds. "A cynic might argue it was down to inside knowledge, but I've become quite the convert to remote viewing. Only this morning, I couldn't think where I'd left my car keys, but then I 'saw' them on the mantlepiece. Remarkable. But we're getting distracted. Ten other weapons were found in your gun cupboard, only three of which had licences. Would you like to explain why you hadn't applied for the necessary paperwork?"

"No comment."

"Perhaps you'd asked your PA, Katya, to apply for the licences and she had forgotten? In which case, she would be an accessory to the crime."

Another flash of concern crosses Garstan's face.

"It might even affect her ability to stay in the country," Hart continues. "Although I'm sure she's good at paperwork, has all the necessary documentation for living in the UK."

He can feel Strover's eyes on him too now. This wasn't in the script. He's got no intention of deporting Katya, of course, but if Garstan is sleeping with her, he might be sufficiently concerned to drop his "no comment" strategy. Or he might hang her out to dry. Either way, the new line of questioning covers their tracks, makes it less likely for Garstan to suspect that Katya has been helping them.

"Was it her fault the guns weren't licensed?" Hart asks. "As your PA, you would have reasonably expected her to sort the paperwork. Should we be bringing her in for questioning?"

"This has nothing to do with Katya," Garstan says. *Bingo*. Men are so predictable. Garstan's lawyer turns to whisper something to him.

"So what does it have to do with?" Hart asks. "Having all these guns in your possession?"

It's a long time before Garstan answers.

"When you first came to see me at my house, we talked about your mother's untimely death, your own health, your caring wife. Mel, I think you said she's called."

"Keep my wife out of this," Hart says, a sudden anger flaring up inside him. "She's got nothing to do with your illegal firearms."

Hart glares at Garstan and then his lawyer.

"I've never married," Garstan continues, "but it must be very comforting to have a loving wife at your side for those terrifying moments when you wake in the dead of night, heart racing, body soaked in sweat, knowing that you're going to die at the same age as your mother."

37

Garstan's lawyer shifts uneasily in his seat, glancing first at his client and then at Hart and Strover.

"Let's try again, shall we," Hart says, trying to ignore Garstan's words. "Perhaps you didn't hear my question."

He'd prepared himself for this moment, when Garstan would try to turn the tables, make things personal, put him on his couch again. But he wasn't expecting him to bring Mel into it.

"Why did you have so many unlicensed guns in your possession?"

"We all have to die at some point," Garstan continues, ignoring Hart's question. "Is it the knowing? Accepting that we are mortal? Or is it the knowing *when*?"

The lawyer clears his throat, as if to remind his client of his presence.

"It might have worked, you know," Hart says, determined

to block out Garstan's words, get the interview back on track. "Saying that the guns had been given to you by mentally unwell patients. A jury might just have bought that. Psychiatrists get such a bad rap these days when someone – a schizophrenic, say – is let out of hospital prematurely, only for them to go around shooting people the moment they are free."

Hart doesn't feel easy parroting such a tabloid narrative of mental illness. In truth, most schizophrenics are not violent – Conor was never violent when he was psychotic – but right now, needs must.

"Yet here you are, taking that possibility away, making the world a safer place," he continues. "Who gave you the seven unlicensed shotguns and two sawn-offs, Dr Garstan?"

Garstan sits back in his chair, looking relaxed for the first time in the interview.

"The longer I spend in your company, DI Silas Hart, head of Swindon CID, the clearer it becomes." He pauses. "The stronger I can feel it. Three years from now, just days after you've turned fifty-seven." He pauses. "Burnt orange. A number four. The 4th of December. It must be a Saturday – I haven't checked – but it's definitely an orange day."

Hart stares at Garstan. He knows he should ignore him, keep going with the interview, but his words have stopped him in his tracks. It's not that he suddenly believes that he'll die on 4 December in three years' time. It's that he knows himself too well, his overzealous midnight mind. He can already see himself counting down the days, the hours, working himself into a state of unhealthy agitation.

"And how do you know this?" Hart hears himself asking. He shouldn't be giving this charlatan the time of day, let alone engaging with his humbuggery. But he can't pretend his mother didn't die when she was fifty-seven, that he's always feared the same fate awaits him.

"All I can say is that it's the most extraordinary sense of certainty," Garstan says, "like slipping on a heavy winter coat that fits perfectly."

"I think we're done here," Hart says, gathering up his files and nodding at Strover.

"Do you wish to say or add to anything that has already been said?" Strover says, leaning across to the tape recorder on the table.

"Nothing more, except that everyone has a 'death day', just like we have a birthday," Garstan says. "A day that lies 'sly and unseen' in the calendar, as Thomas Hardy once wrote. You should learn to embrace yours, DI Hart, rather than deny it. Try to enjoy what little remains of your life."

Hart signals for Strover to terminate the interview.

"Wait," Garstan says, holding up a hand as if he's halting traffic.

The interview room falls silent, still, as if the very atoms of the air have ceased vibrating. Hart shifts in his seat, aware that he's lost control of the interview. It's so unlike him. He should step in, shut Garstan down, but the silence seems to stretch, forwards and backwards in time. He can feel Strover's eyes on him, the lawyer's too. They're both waiting for him to reassert his authority. But no words come.

"You really don't believe me, do you?" Garstan says, almost whispering.

"Believe what?" Hart asks, grateful for the power of speech again. For a moment he thought he'd been struck dumb.

"I'm not joking here, or being flippant, just because you've arrested me on trumped-up charges of gun licensing."

"They're not trumped up, trust me," Hart says, already feeling stronger, happy to be back on police ground again.

"I don't tell people lightly when I know they are going to die," Garstan continues. "If I'm honest, it's information that I often wish I didn't possess. It comes with enormous responsibility. But knowing your death day can be incredibly liberating, helping you to get the most out of your life. Would you continue with a boring job if you knew you only had a year to live? Of course not. You'd resign, cash in your life savings, travel the world, maybe even ask the person you've always fancied from afar if they would like to join you. I'm not revealing your death day as a threat. Some sort of petty revenge for what you've done here. It's just a memory from the future, one that I can see and others can't. Call it quantum entanglement, if you like."

"Quantum what?" Hart asks.

"It's when particles separated in space are linked at a subatomic level," Strover says. "Einstein called it 'spooky action at a distance'. But I wasn't aware that particles separated by time could also become entangled."

Hart can always count on Strover to weigh in with a bit of Einstein when required.

"Scientists are starting to realise that particles can be linked across time too," Garstan says, clearly thrown by Strover's interjection. "And in physics, as I'm sure you know, time isn't necessarily linear. Maybe our present brain can somehow be entangled with a version of itself in the future, allowing us to remember things that haven't yet happened."

Hart's had enough.

"Dr Garstan, this interview has now ended," he says, "1.03 p.m." He turns the recorder off himself.

"Let's just call it a gift," Garstan says, smiling, as Hart and Strover rise to their feet. "Much simpler than subatomic particles. And we haven't even talked yet about salience networks and the informational substrate of the universe."

"You can talk about what you like," Hart says, leaning down to fix Garstan in the eye. "We know what happened with Milo. Sophie too. And I don't need to believe in any of your bollockspeak quantum fuckery to know what lies ahead for you. I can see it now, sense it: a big fat number five. Five years, Garstan, you're going down for five years."

38

Warm spring rain fell on my face that night as I was wheeled out of my south London flat into the waiting ambulance. It wasn't a straightforward diagnosis – dissociative identity disorder – and I was so grateful for your timely intervention. I felt an enormous sense of relief too, not just that I was leaving my squalid flat behind, but that you and I were finally talking again.

I had no idea where I was taken at first. I'd been heavily sedated with a mix of atypical antipsychotics and benzodiazepines as part of my sectioning under the Mental Health Act. But I was in safe hands, and you kept me informed of what was happening every step of the way, one psychiatrist to another. Your planning was so thoughtful too. You'd arranged the necessary two doctors (one of whom had specialist experience with mental disorders) and an Approved Mental Health Professional. They were friends of yours, which made the whole process easier, so much less embarrassing for everyone.

My medication must have been marginally reduced after a couple of weeks, because I began to take in my surroundings: a small white room with a view through reinforced windows across flat farmland. In the distance, the dishwater greyness of the North Sea. According to the two young nurses who had been assigned to keep an eye on me, I was being kept in an isolation room reserved for special patients. I had a lot to thank you for.

As I lay there, day after day, conversations drifted through my drug-filled brain, voices carried in on the wind from far off places.

"This form of florid psychosis is often found in dissociative identity disorder," I heard you say at one point. "It's been troubling him for many years, ever since early childhood, in fact. We need to keep a close eye on his behaviour, monitor for discrete personality states. 'Alters' to you and me."

One of the nurses was very junior. I could sense when she was coming down the corridor: she had the flavour of sherbet, which fizzed on my tongue long before she arrived in the room. The other, more senior, was a scent rather than a taste: garden rose, like the Desdemona Dad planted after Mum had died. Almond blossom, cucumber. Again, I knew she was coming well before any perfume she was wearing (she wasn't) might have reached me.

It wasn't long before time had become meaningless, one day bleeding into the next, and I don't know how often you visited me. But I remember being so pleased when I woke one sunny morning to see you standing at the foot of my bed. (I sensed you were there before I opened my eyes.)

Desdemona was with you too.

"I hope you like your room," you said.

"Where am I?" I asked, my head full of fog.

"Where are we?" you said, looking around. "Norfolk. A secure psychiatric hospital. One of the best in the country. Private, of course."

My eyes widened in shock. I knew how expensive they were.

"It's OK," you said. "The American owners are friends. Mates' rates."

"Thank you," I said, blinking slowly. "For everything."

"You're my brother," you said.

"Are Mum and Dad OK?"

You paused before answering. "Mum and Dad are fine."

They must have been worried, though. "And Barka?"

"She's fine too."

You turned to Desdemona, who pulled out a clipboard and pen.

"We just need to run through some Section 132 formalities," she said. "It will only take a moment."

"No problem," I said.

"Do you understand why you are being treated here?"

"Because I'm not well," I said slowly. "And I'm indebted to my brother here for looking after me."

"You're currently being detained under Section 3 of the Mental Health Act," she continued, "which means you might be given treatment against your will. Any person who is compulsorily detained has the right to appeal against the decision to the Mental Health Tribunal."

"Or to the hospital managers," you added, "which might be easier."

Desdemona threw you a disapproving look.

"Sorry," you said, smiling.

"You may also be eligible for legal aid to pay for a solicitor to help you with this," Desdemona continued. "And you have the right to see an independent mental health advocate."

"I don't think there'll be any need for that," I said. "I really am very grateful to Rory."

After you'd gone, I sank back into the pillow, trying to piece together the timeline of my recent life, work out exactly what had happened. Mum and Dad would visit me soon. I needed to get better before they came. They would be so pleased to see the care you were taking, the love between their two sons. I would have been dead by now if it wasn't for you.

39

Present day

Hart and Strover pull over into the lay-by, 300 yards from Garstan's house in Pewsey. Snow is falling. Three years earlier, they had sat here as a hot summer's day had dawned, waiting to search Garstan's house with a team of pumped-up AFOs while Ward had been touring medieval cities in Sri Lanka. Now they are here again on a late winter's afternoon to see if Garstan has moved back into his old house after being released from Barontrent Prison just over a week ago. It looks promising – the gate is open, chimney smoke twisting upwards through thick flakes of snow – but Hart knows they should have got over here as soon as they'd heard yesterday that he was out. Something had made him delay the visit, deny that Garstan was a free man. It was back to his old "out of sight, out of mind" approach to life. Never a good idea. He needs to confront the man who once told him that he was going to die this coming Saturday.

"Someone's at home," Strover says.

Hart feels nervous, but he's angry too. If he's right, Garstan has sent two suicidal people his way, defaced his parents' grave and is deliberately targeting Conor. None of which he can prove yet, which is partly why they're here now. But their meeting with Malcolm, the pathologist, had confirmed his worst fears. Garstan is scaring people to death.

"The GMC's replied," Strover says, reading a new email.

"Please tell me he's been struck off."

"Far from it," Strover says, quoting from the message. "'Dr Rory Garstan was suspended for the duration of his prison sentence, but fitness to practise proceedings (FPP) were held shortly after he was sentenced.' Seems like he must have submitted evidence online. And get this: 'Possessing firearms that had been seized from potentially dangerous patients was ultimately considered well-intentioned, but he was naïve not to have handed them over immediately to the authorities.'"

"Naïve? How about cold-blooded and calculated?" Garstan's legal team had tried to mitigate the charges by pushing a public service defence, but the jury hadn't agreed, unlike the GMC, it seems. Unfortunately, the jury hadn't bought the prosecution's intention-to-supply argument either, much to Hart's dismay.

Strover continues to read from the email: "'In light of the current national shortage of psychiatrists and the ongoing crisis in our mental health provision, Dr Rory Garstan will be permitted to practise again on his release, under close supervision and following the usual rigorous checks. His therapeutic work in prison with fellow inmates has been noted. He has undertaken to comply with firearms legislation.'"

"Bit late now," Hart says. "Come on, let's welcome him back."

Strover drives down the road and turns in through Garstan's gates. They both notice the black Mercedes parked in the corner.

"Nice Merc," Strover says. "Same electric CLA that picked Garstan up from Barontrent. Sports edition."

"I'm more interested in her," Hart says, as Katya walks out to greet them. What the hell's she doing here? He'd assumed she would have left Garstan's employ – and bed – after her boss had been sent down. Returned to her daughter in Ukraine.

"This is a surprise," Hart says, stepping out of the car. Katya looks older, more troubled. "Is Dr Garstan at home, by any chance?"

"Of course," she says. "Are you here alone? Or…"

"It's OK, we haven't brought the cavalry this time," Hart says, as Strover steps out of the car too. "Just my colleague, DI Strover."

He'd felt sorry for Katya three years ago, when armed police officers had swarmed into the house. "You're still working for him, then?" Hart asks.

Katya glances around the courtyard before answering.

"I had to go back to Ukraine when Dr Rory was imprisoned. But I got a message, a few weeks ago, asking me if I would return and be his PA again. I need the money for my family, my daughter in Lviv. So here I am."

"Here you are," Hart says, smiling, wondering how she could possibly bear to work again for Garstan. Hadn't she been appalled by the way he'd treated Milo?

"Please, come in," she says, ushering them through the

front door and into the hall. It looks like the door has been replaced since the AFOs had forced entry with the big red key three years ago. Once inside, the first thing Hart notices is the artwork. Calmer pictures, landscapes and seascapes, have replaced the brash modern art. Cornish, perhaps. School of St Ives.

"I will find Dr Rory, tell him you are here," Katya says, showing them into a high-ceilinged sitting room. She seems very relaxed. Did Garstan know – sense – they were coming? Hart and Strover stamp snow off their shoes and follow her. "Please, can I take your coats?" she asks.

"It's OK, we won't be here long," Hart says, deciding to stay standing as Katya leaves them to go upstairs. They wait awkwardly for a minute or two and then Hart hears Katya talking, mentioning his own name and Strover's, as if she's briefing her boss. He can't imagine Garstan needs reminding of who they are. A moment later, the psychiatrist walks into the room.

40

"Welcome back," Garstan says, turning to each of them. "DI Hart, DS Strover. A more civilized time of day than your last visit. 5 a.m., I think it was. Would you like something to drink? Tea? Coffee maybe?"

Hart stares at Garstan, still annoyingly handsome. He's aged, though – prison does that to people – and looks thinner, gaunt around the eyes, his cheeks sunken. Dressed a little differently too. Like the paintings, his clothes seem softer than before: jeans and a fisherman's jumper, brown Blundstone boots. Maybe the prison system works after all.

"A tea, actually," Hart says. "Thanks." He needs something stronger, but it's too early for a drink.

"Me too," Strover says. "Both white, one sugar."

Garstan turns to Katya, who disappears off to the kitchen.

"Please, take a seat," Garstan says, gesturing to a deep

sofa. Even the furniture seems more comfortable than Hart remembers. "So how can I help?"

Hart looks at Garstan again. He doesn't feel any of the anger he was expecting. Where are the barbs? The digs about his impending death day? But then he remembers the blood pooling at the front desk.

"How does it feel to be out?" he begins.

Garstan pauses before answering, as if assessing Hart like a patient.

"Different. I was released a week ago, moved back here straight away."

"Your car was seen heading east on the M4 after leaving Barontrent," Hart says, cutting to the chase. There's no point in niceties.

"Katya picked me up. She's been very kind, came back from Ukraine to help me settle in. I'm not sure how long she can stay. She needed to collect some items for the house from IKEA in Reading. I wanted to make a fresh start, draw a line under the past. New furniture. New pictures too – I bought that one at the Jubilee auction rooms in Pewsey." He gestures at a stormy seascape above the fireplace. "Do you follow all prisoners when they are released?"

"No. And we didn't follow you. I'm not sure IKEA would be the first place I'd go if I'd been incarcerated for three years."

"Oh, I don't know. It's amazing what you miss inside. Their meatballs are very good. And you seem to be enjoying the sofa."

Hart sits up, conscious that he's sinking into the soft cushions.

"Actually, the thing I missed most was my matcha tea.

Katya kindly brought along a thermos when she met me at Barontrent."

"Are you going to be practising psychiatry again?" Hart asks.

He must try matcha one day. Anything's got to be better than the canteen coffee.

"I very much hope so, DI Hart. As soon as the GMC gives me the all-clear. The quicker life returns to normal, the better for my patients."

"But no shooting?"

Garstan smiles for the first time. "No shooting. The guns have fallen silent. I have learnt my lesson."

Hart will believe that when he sees it.

"I gather you volunteered while you were inside," he says. "Helping patients with their anxieties."

A brief flicker of concern on Garstan's face, like the shadow of a cloud passing over fields.

"That's right," he says, choosing his words carefully. "I did what I could. Under close supervision, of course, and in consultation with the medical team."

"But you only treated inmates who were frightened of dying."

Garstan hesitates before answering. Is he trying to calculate how much Hart knows?

"I specialise in anxiety disorders, that's true – specific phobias such as death anxiety – but I have always been happy to see anyone in need of help. And trust me, there are a lot of people in prison who require the services of a psychiatrist."

Hart will ask Strover to check again with her friend at Barontrent. They need more details about what exactly Garstan did inside.

"And you were released on temporary licence," he continues. "For a day. A week before your final release. You worked at a hostel on Fleming Way, I gather, helping the homeless with their mental health. To prepare you for life on the outside."

Another pause. "That's right."

"And can you tell me who you saw on that day? It was a Wednesday, 17 November."

"This might sound strange, DI Hart, ironic even, but I reacted rather badly after my day release. I spoke to the prison doctor on my return and was prescribed some anti-anxiety medication. Xanax, a fast-acting benzodiazepine that can cause anterograde amnesia – short-term memory gaps. Blackouts. It wasn't the first time I was given it. I'm afraid my memory of that day – indeed of a lot of my time in Barontrent – is consequently a little vague, but I hope I did some good."

Good? He had singled out Conor for his twisted death-take on therapy. Thank God he only saw him the once.

"So you didn't see my son, Conor?" Hart asks. "Give him an hourglass and tell him that he might not have long to live?"

"Not that I can remember. And I'm sorry if I said that."

Hart shakes his head. "How about Darren Eaves? Does the name mean anything to you?"

Garstan looks up at Katya as she comes back in with two mugs of tea.

"I'm afraid not," Garstan says. Hart's on shakier ground now. They have no evidence yet that Garstan met Darren in prison.

"He died in the Great Western Hospital yesterday,

right in front of me. 'Find DI Silas Hart if you want to side with the deniers.' That's what he said you told him to say."

Again, dodgy ground. Darren never actually mentioned Garstan by name.

"The deniers?" Garstan asks. He seems genuinely perplexed.

"Those who don't believe in 'death days'."

"I don't know anything about a Darren Eaves. I'm sorry."

"He was in Barontrent with you. Had a fear of dying. You played on those fears, told him you knew when he was going to die, down to the nearest minute, and when he was released, he died at the appointed time."

"As I say, I don't remember anyone at Barontrent called Darren Eaves," Garstan says, glancing again at Katya. "And, for the record, I would never tell anyone if I knew when they were going to die. It would be highly antagonising as well as unethical."

Garstan's good at bluffing, Hart grants him that. Three years earlier, he'd given him his exact death day. *Burnt orange. A number four. The 4th of December.*

"So you never told me that I'm going to die this Saturday?" Hart asks, forcing himself to fix Garstan in the eye, despite not wanting to know the answer.

"If I did say such a thing, I can only apologise," Garstan says, holding Hart's gaze. "I was a different person then. Angry about my arrest."

"But you do still claim to be able to see a patient's future?" Hart asks.

"If I've got to know them well, yes. As I say, I'm lucky enough to have a…"

"'Gift'. And you used it to locate the whereabouts of Sophie Mills, who had been missing for two years."

"That was five years ago," Katya says, interrupting.

"And you've only been in prison for three years," Hart continues. "For the illegal possession of prohibited firearms. You should still be locked up for the murder of Sophie. For beheading and dismembering her body."

"That's quite an allegation to make, DI Hart," Garstan says calmly. "One that I feel should only be made in the presence of a lawyer."

Hart's overdone it, pushed Garstan too far. The last thing he wants is a lawyer involved. The previous one was a pain in the arse. His defence had persuaded the judge that Garstan could only be questioned about the trumped-up firearms offences, something that's rankled ever since. Garstan needs to answer questions about Sophie. And Milo too. Strover glances in his direction, knows when to step in, turn down the heat.

"Going back to the hostel on Fleming Way – did you ever volunteer there in the years before you were arrested?" Strover asks. "This would have been five years ago."

"Not that I can remember."

"And you never saw Sophie Mills at the hostel?"

"Dr Rory helped to find Sophie's remains using remote viewing," Katya says, interrupting again.

"And I was thanked with a five-year prison sentence for firearms offences," Garstan adds. "I should have been out after two and a half years."

The Garstan of old has returned.

"What about Milo?" Strover continues. "Who you saw in a private capacity? You'd helped his mother in the past."

"Milo was a tragedy," Garstan says. For the first time, he seems genuinely moved, almost tearful. "I've been haunted by his death ever since."

"Why's that?" Hart asks.

"I should never have got involved."

Garstan's changed his tune. According to Katya, he was triumphant when Milo had died at the time he'd predicted.

"More tea?" he asks.

Hart and Strover shake their heads.

"We found a mobile that Milo had used to call you a few minutes before he died," Hart says.

He's been waiting three years to ask Garstan about the burner phone.

"It's not uncommon for a patient to call their psychiatrist in times of acute distress," Garstan says.

"You're always on call," Strover says, glancing at Hart.

"I try to be available to my patients twenty-four hours a day."

"Did you tell Milo he was going to die that morning?" Hart asks. "That it was his death day? Knowing that he had a deep fear of dying?"

"Again, I would never do that. Particularly if a patient was suffering from death anxiety."

Hart looks across at Katya, who turns away. Three years earlier she had told them that Milo had been the victim of an unethical experiment that had bordered on murder.

"And you didn't send me this," Hart says, pulling out his grim-reaper birthday card and handing it to him. It all feels rather pathetic now, like a child showing a defaced schoolbook to a teacher. "Or do this to my parents' grave?" He calls up an image on his phone and shows it to Garstan.

"Of course not," he says, handing back the phone and the card. "How utterly appalling. I would never do something like that."

And for the first time, Hart wonders if Garstan might just be telling the truth.

41

Katya is out in the courtyard when Hart and Strover walk over to their car. Garstan hovers at the front door. He glances at Katya, waves goodbye to them and disappears back inside the house.

"Thanks for the tea," Hart says, desperate to get something out of Katya, who walks over to the garage, beside the stable block, and picks up one of four crates of books that have been stacked next to a small side door. Has she come out here to talk to them?

"No problem," she says, walking back to put the crate down beside an old Nissan Micra. Hart hadn't noticed the car earlier.

"Did his reading habits change too while he was inside?" Hart says, as Katya fetches another crate from the garage.

"A lot about him has changed," Katya says, stacking the second one next to the first. "As you probably saw."

"Where are the books going?" Strover asks, picking one up and looking at its cover.

"A charity shop. Prospect Hospice in Marlborough."

"Do you want us to take them?" Strover asks. "We're heading that way and I know the shop well."

Hart's surprised by the offer, but then he remembers the connection. Strover's father had spent his last days at Prospect Hospice in Swindon too, where he had been well cared for, just like his own dad.

"You sure?" Katya says. "Otherwise I can drop them off on my way home."

"Are you back living in Shrivenham?" Strover asks, walking with Katya over to the garage to retrieve the last two crates. Hart notices that Strover waits until Katya sets off with her crate, before stepping inside the garage side door, which is ajar. A second later Strover re-emerges, picks up the last crate and walks over.

"I'm staying with a friend," Katya calls back to Strover. "In Avebury. Until I find somewhere to live again."

The three of them stand there, next to Katya's car. An uneasy silence descends on them. Is Katya prepared to talk? Shed some light on her boss's seemingly reformed ways?

"I must go back inside," she says, wary of their questions, perhaps.

"We never properly thanked you," Hart says, "for telling us about the guns without licences."

After Garstan's arrest, Katya had been called in for a formal interview, but she had only confirmed what she'd said earlier, that she didn't believe all the illegal weapons had been given to Garstan by patients. She couldn't shed any light on where he might have acquired them.

"I'd rather not talk about that," she says, glancing back at the house. "It was a long time ago. Dr Rory has come out of prison a better person."

"No regrets, then?" Hart asks. "Helping us to get him convicted?"

"Did I help?" She had been reluctant to testify in court, given her illegal status in the country, and Hart hadn't pushed for a witness summons.

"You told us about Milo," Hart says, "what Dr Garstan did to him."

"I must get on," she says. "Thank you for taking the books. Now I need to paint."

She points at a white wooden house sign, propped up against the far side of the stable block. The old writing has faded, but new letters have been outlined. Beside it, on the wooden stool, a paintbrush in a glass jar.

"Dr Rory's decided to change the house name – back to what it used to be called."

"Which was?"

"Palatine Hill."

"Are you a good painter?" Hart asks, thinking of his parents' neatly defaced headstone.

"I'm not Pablo Picasso, if that's what you mean, but I can do letters."

"And numbers."

"Numbers too," she says, puzzled. "Why not?"

Hart turns away. He's making connections that aren't there, joining the wrong dots. Strover opens up the back of their car and starts to carry the crates over. Katya helps to load them.

"Thanks," Strover says.

"Dr Rory is a good man," Katya says, before walking off to her paints.

Hart lifts the last crate into the back of the car, glancing again at the books that Garstan is throwing out. Most appear to be related to his job: *An Introduction to Physical Methods of Treatment in Psychiatry; Battle for the Mind; The Great Physiodynamic Therapies in Psychiatry: An Historical Reappraisal.* As he sifts through them, one catches his eye: a copy of *The Manchurian Candidate* by Richard Condon. He picks it up and reads the blurb out loud: "*Brainwashed during his time as a POW in Korea, Sgt Raymond Shaw is a living weapon, a sleeping assassin who will be triggered to kill by a secret hypnotic command.*"

"Did you see the film?" Hart asks, noticing that Strover's watching him.

"Which one? '62 or 2004?" Hart has forgotten that Strover's a film buff.

"The later one – I'm not that old."

"What about this one?" Strover asks, picking up another well-thumbed paperback. "*Scared to Death* by John Barker. Published in 1968."

"Sounds jolly," Hart says, trying to appear upbeat himself, but his legs have turned to lead.

Strover flips the book over and reads out the blurb, theatrically at first until its potential significance dawns. "*Thoughts can kill! A medical doctor's amazing, fully documented case histories of deaths caused by strange and terrifying psychic powers.*"

Hart tries to think of a joke, anything to defuse the anxiety that's now gripping him, but he can't find the words.

"You OK, sir?"

"Let's take these two books back to the office," Hart says, climbing into the passenger seat with the copies of *The Manchurian Candidate* and *Scared to Death* clutched to his chest. "I think I might need to sit down."

Strover gets into the car too and guns the ignition.

"Sure you're OK, sir?"

"I'm fine," Hart says, feeling terrible, even by his standards.

Is he suffering an attack of angina? His whole upper body has tightened, as if he's being squeezed. A bit like indigestion, only he's sweating too and feeling dizzy. He tries not to remember Malcolm's story of the angina patient who had died in front of the doctor. The discomfort starts to fade.

"What was in the garage?" he asks.

Strover glances at him.

"A silver Golf. With a cover on – odd inside a garage. And before you ask, I've got the numberplate."

They sit there in the car, engine running. Strover must sense that Hart is not himself, that he needs a minute to get a grip.

"Just tell me one thing, Strover," he says eventually, staring out across the gravel courtyard towards the house. "If it wasn't Garstan who defaced my parents' grave, then who the hell was it?"

42

"How was your day?" Mel asks, as they tuck into an Indian takeaway at their kitchen table. They'd both got in late from work and Hart had picked up a curry from Zaika in Marlborough on the way home.

"Strange," Hart says. "We visited Dr Garstan at his home in Pewsey."

"Had he been seeing Conor?"

"He said not. But—"

"But what?"

Hart's been dreading telling Mel all day.

"The date of his temporary release on licence – a week before he was out… it was the same day that Conor saw his life coach at the hostel on Fleming Way."

Mel puts her fork down, doesn't say anything for a while. Then she gets up, shaking her head in disbelief.

"I'm going to bed."

"It's OK, Mel, I've left a message with Conor – told him never to see him again."

But Conor's yet to call him back.

"Bit late for that," she says, slipping her plate in the dishwasher.

"He was different today," he says. "Dr Garstan. Chastened by three years as a guest of His Majesty. As if he'd—"

"As if he'd what? Seen the error of his ways? Give me a break, Silas, he's been in an overcrowded prison for three years, not on bloody bible camp. I don't want this guy anywhere near Conor," she adds, stomping out the kitchen.

Hart sits impassively at the table, listening to her run a bath upstairs. He can't blame her for being angry. Conor means the world to her, to them both. He picks at his chicken Chettinad, then at Mel's korma, but he's lost his appetite. He walks into the sitting room, still decked out with birthday streamers. They seem to be mocking him now: fifty-seven years old. Suddenly he feels overwhelmed with tiredness. Garstan's out, served his time for firearms offences, but Hart is still no closer to pinning the murder of Sophie Mills on him.

Mel is asleep when he finally goes upstairs, lying firmly on her side of the bed. He turns off his light, glancing at the clock: 11.56 p.m. In a few minutes, it will be Friday, 3 December, one day before Garstan had told him he was going to die. Total bollockchops, of course, but he has never been able to shake off Garstan's morbid prediction. The two deaths on his birthday didn't exactly help. And now his own apparent death day is almost here.

He lies on his back in the darkness, envying Mel's calm breathing as he thinks about his body, the niggles and pains jostling for his attention. He just needs to lose a stone, drop the snacking, run more regularly. Do all those things he vows every January to do. Before he knows it, his parkrun target of twenty-five minutes will soon become twenty-four, maybe even twenty-three. He smiles to himself. Who's he kidding? It will be fun to be out running with the family on Saturday, a relief after a difficult week. A chance to banish last night's dream.

"Sile!" Mel suddenly says, interrupting Hart's thoughts, but he's not listening. He's trying to jump-start Conor's heart with a defibrillator at the parkrun finish line.

"25.01," Conor says weakly, staring up at him. "I was just trying to help you, Da – so nearly there."

"Sile!" Mel says, louder this time. She turns on the bedside lamp and props herself up next to him.

"Oh, Christ," Hart says, a hand to his forehead. "Not again. I'm so sorry."

"You were dreaming," she says, resting a hand on his chest.

"And you know what they say about dreams," Garstan says. Hart spins round to his right, where Garstan is lying next to him on the bed.

"Sile!" Mel says again. And this time Hart does wake up.

"Shit. I can't do this anymore," he says, getting out of bed to walk over to the window. His heart is racing, his T-shirt drenched in sweat. "I can't run on Saturday." He can't bring himself to look back either, in case Garstan is still there.

"Come to bed," Mel says, walking over to Hart. She puts a hand on his shoulder, turns him around and holds him tightly. "It's OK, Sile," she says. "It's OK."

43

I might have been heavily medicated, but I was still aware of your kindness. And I wanted to repay it in any way I could. So when, one day, you asked if I could give my opinion on some of your other patients, I was only too happy to oblige. Not that I felt I could be of much help. My head was still a mess. But you sounded so compassionate when you talked about one patient in particular. Her name was S and it was heartwarming to see such empathy in you. And yes, surprising too, I couldn't deny it.

I sat up slowly and looked at the notes that you'd brought along, the words dancing on the page in a confusing jig. You'd asked for my meds to be reduced the day before, so at least I was a bit more compos mentis by the time you arrived.

"How do I help this woman, Finn?" you asked.

I read S's case notes as best as I could (her full name

had been redacted). From what I could tell, you were seeing her at a homeless hostel of some sort. I was pleased that you were balancing paid work with volunteering. It was too easy to get sucked into the private lane.

"It would appear she has an acute fear of imminent death," I said.

"So I need to convince her that she's not about to die," you said. "I could put her on SSRIs to dampen the existential angst, but wouldn't it be better if I could actually tell her that she wasn't going to die? Reassure her with a few hard facts about her future?"

You watched as I tried to scribble down some notes in shaky handwriting, desperate to order my thoughts. I was aware that I was misspelling words, but there was nothing I could do about it. I could barely hold the pencil you'd given me.

"That would be lying," I eventually said. "S is from a low sociomic background" – I was mispronouncing words too – "and often homeless, probably undernourished, prone to illness. Her life expancy is low."

You listened to what I said and walked away, looking out of the reinforced window at the flat landscape. I could sense your frustration.

"That's not what I'm after, Finn," you said, your back still to me. "How do you do it?"

"How do I do what?"

"How do you see someone's future?" You turned and looked at me from the foot of my bed. "How did you guess Dad's cards? Know when it was a plane and not a bottle? And why did Barka always wait by the window for you and not for me? How did that feel*?"*

Your voice was raised now, impassioned, and I felt sorry for you. Almost. Thanks to the meds, my emotional landscape was even flatter than the view outside. I also didn't know what you were talking about. It didn't make me feel *anything. I just knew.*

"I've been reading everything I can," you continued. "Ask me about quantum entanglement, circular notions of time, misfires in the medial temporal lobe, but none of it explains what you can do. And don't, please don't tell me it's just a bloody gift."

You paused and fell quiet.

"What if I can't tell her that she's going to live, Finn?" you said. "What if I told her she's going to die?"

44

Present day

Hart sits at his desk in the Parade Room, hoping for some good news as he nurses a cup of canteen coffee, his first and last of the day. He tries not to think of the night he had, his recurring parkrun dream. Mel had been kind over breakfast, but he could tell she was worried for him. He's worried too. He's never had a nightmare on repeat. He takes a deep breath and looks out the window. At least it's stopped snowing.

Strover had driven over to Barontrent at the crack of dawn, trying to establish more details about Garstan's stay, exactly which fellow inmates he had seen as an unofficial prison psychiatrist. Their visit to Pewsey yesterday has thrown him, not just his anxiety attack, but Garstan's apparent contrition.

Where had all the venom gone? The spite? Had prison really knocked it out of him? Three years ago, Garstan was railing at Hart, predicting that he would die on 4 December. Yesterday, he was offering him and Strover mugs of sweet tea and a cosy chat.

Hart picks up a copy of *Scared to Death* and flicks through it. At one point, the author, Dr John Barker, asks three clairvoyants in what circumstances, if any, they would tell their clients about the date and nature of their death.

One, a Mr King, says "never". Another, Katrina, agrees: "Death, never; illness, always." But Mir Bashir has no such qualms. "If a person is absolutely determined to know... then I would give him an approximation of the time of his probable death so that he could make arrangements for his dependents..." Very thoughtful. The difference with Hart is that he never asked Garstan for his own death date, never wanted to know.

"You alright, guv?" a uniform asks, walking past Hart's desk. "Look like you've seen a ghost."

"Never felt better," Hart manages to say.

He tosses the book away. Sooner or later, he will have to tell Ward what he's up to – more to the point, what he thinks Garstan is up to. Hart's relationship with Ward had gone from bad to worse when he had returned from Sri Lanka to discover that his shooting pal had been charged with firearms offences and was awaiting trial. Ward had punished him with months of door-to-door interviews on the Penhill estate, desperate to prove that Sophie Mills had been killed and dismembered by the mystery man at Angelo's nightclub. Surprise, surprise, they had never found him.

His phone rings. It's the CSM. Hart's been waiting for him to call back about the hourglasses and the nature of the red granules in particular.

"They're human," the CSM says. "'Cremains.'"

"What?"

"Ashes left over from a cremation. In this case, ground-up rather than cremated human bone, which is unusual. It's also been mixed with sand to enable a smoother flow. Some funeral directors offer cremains hourglasses – all part of the service. But they're not usually dyed blood red with cochineal, as far as I know. Or uncooked, as it were."

Hart exhales with a mixture of shock and satisfaction. According to Malcolm, the collarbone is one of the most frequently broken bones in the human body. Delicate, not very dense. Easily ground up, in other words. And Sophie's was missing.

He stares out onto the snowy car park. Despite the dreary view, he feels better already. The DNA results will take a while, but he's sure they'll be a match for Sophie Mills. It won't prove that Garstan killed her, but it makes it more likely.

Everything flows from Sophie's death five years ago, he's sure of it, and he'll never be able to rest until he can pin her murder on Garstan. Milo's suicide at the windmill two years later, and now the two men who died in front of him yesterday, all of whom had hourglasses. He just needs Forensics to prove that the ground-up bone belonged to Sophie.

Hart looks up as Strover walks into the Parade Room, seemingly buoyed by another trip to Barontrent.

"Why are you looking so bloody pleased with yourself?" Hart asks.

"Because I've just found out who Garstan's patients were – when he was moonlighting inside Barontrent."

45

Hart's never seen Strover so animated, moving from one foot to the other, as if treading on hot coals.

"Turns out Garstan recommended medication for some of his fellow inmates," Strover says, "but he obviously wasn't allowed to prescribe anything. It all had to be signed off by the prison doctor, who happens to be a young and efficient GP called Anwar Malik."

"I'm liking Anwar already," Hart says, glancing around the Parade Room.

"He wrote it all down, names included, before checking the prescriptions and signing off on them," Strover continues. "Even wrote up detailed patient notes, based on what Garstan had diagnosed and his own observations."

"Can we meet this guy?" Hart asks. "See his records?"

"He's waiting downstairs – interview room three."

No wonder Strover's buzzing. Hart follows Strover out

of the Parade Room.

"Some other news, too, sir," Strover says. "We have a DNA match for the man who shot himself at the front desk."

"And?" Once again, Hart finds himself dreading the answer.

"Si Kennington, twenty-three years old, homeless," Strover says. "He was released from Barontrent last week."

Hart tries to shut out an image of the young man's body, sprawled across the floor. Si Kennington. It feels only right to have a name for the person whose blood he'd wiped from his own face.

"And do we know if he was being seen by Garstan?" Hart asks.

"I haven't had a chance to check with Anwar yet," Strover says.

"How much have you told him about yesterday?"

"Just that Darren Eaves died in hospital, believing it was his death day, and that we think he might have been seen by Garstan when they were both in prison together."

Anwar looks world weary when they walk into the sparse interview room, as if he's just come off a night shift. He stands up to greet Hart with a nervous smile. Late thirties, thick, tidy beard and a stomach that's testing the lower buttons of his white shirt.

"Thanks for coming in," Hart says.

"No problem," Anwar says, waiting for Strover to close the door before he sits down and continues. "In my job, it's important that I can sleep at night, DI Hart. Which isn't always easy when every other patient is cheeking donkeys."

"I'm sorry?" Hart says, thinking he must have misheard the doctor.

"Hiding quetiapine in your mouth so you can trade it later," Strover explains. "Dr Malik's been describing to me his average day in a prison healthcare department. Makes our custody suite on a Saturday night seem like a picnic."

Hart was once told that prison GPs divide into two camps: doctors who can't get a job anywhere else and those who are genuinely committed to providing a decent service to people at their lowest point in life. Anwar seems like the latter.

"Quetiapine is an antipsychotic," he says, "and widely abused in prisons. Please don't get me started on pregabalin. Intended for epilepsy, anxiety and neuropathic pain, but given to prisoners with drug addictions and whatnot. I do my best to prescribe safely and responsibly, but it's not always easy. And my job was made tenfold more difficult when Dr Garstan was allowed to see prisoners. I was against it from the start, but what could I do? The healthcare department was short of shrinks and the prison governor authorised it."

"The governor?"

Hart glances at Strover and sits back, makes a mental note to ask around, check if the governor is a Freemason. A lot of them are. "As I say, we're grateful you've come in to see us today. Strover says you've kept detailed records."

"Which I'm *not* sharing with you, of course," he says, glancing at his notes on the table in front of him. He appears to be enjoying the clandestine vibe so much that Hart is almost expecting a wink. "It would get me struck off."

"We understand. For your peace of mind – to help you sleep at night – we could get a court order to see the inmates' medical records," Hart says. "And I have no doubt our request would meet the public interest threshold. But, as I say, we appreciate you coming here in person today to *not* share any records with us."

Anwar smiles again, happy that Hart's in on the game. "Your colleague here said it was important," he says, glancing at Strover. "And I didn't like Dr Garstan. There was a whiff of sulphur about him."

Hart fixes Anwar in the eye and then glances at the files. "Did Dr Garstan treat an inmate called Darren Eaves?"

A big question – the whole case against Garstan might depend on it – but Hart tries hard not to look bothered either way.

"Treated him for two months," Anwar says.

Long enough to fill Darren's mind with his witchery. If the implications weren't so grim, Hart should be punching the air by now, but all he feels is a sinking sense of inevitability. He thinks of Darren in the hospital, his manic behaviour, knowing that he was about to die. Mel tried so hard to bring him back, pumping his chest as if her own life had depended on it.

"Darren was suffering from thanatophobia," Anwar says, referring to his notes.

"Your fear of death, sir," Strover says to Hart, interrupting.

"Not mine," Hart says, suddenly annoyed, keen to distance himself from the condition. He has no intention of sharing Darren's fate.

"The phobia was originally diagnosed by Dr Garstan," Anwar says, clearly confused by the detectives' exchange. "He recommended that I put Darren onto sertraline, an SSRI used to treat depression and anxiety."

Hart closes his eyes. He knows all about SSRIs. "And you weren't happy about that?"

"Dr Garstan was too damn trigger-happy with the pills, even by prison standards. We give them away like candy, if I'm honest. Anything for a quiet life, that's what the screws always want. I was more worried about Dr Garstan's apparent use of hypnosis."

"Hypnosis? In what way?" Hart wasn't aware that Garstan was into swinging watches too.

"Please don't get me wrong, DI Hart, I've got nothing against hypnotherapy per se – it can be a gamechanger – but Garstan wasn't qualified to give it. I was concerned that by using it in combination with SSRIs, he might increase a patient's suggestibility."

"Make him more amenable to his ideas, you mean?" Hart asks.

Like killing themselves in front of him. Hart looks across at Strover, and then back at Anwar. Is everyone thinking the same as him? This is sounding increasingly like *The Manchurian Candidate*.

"I thought a course of cognitive behavioural therapy – CBT – might be better for Darren, but there was a long waiting list."

He and Mel had been forced to make similar choices for Conor.

"There was one other thing about Darren, which I'm also *not* sharing with you today," he says, with all the subtlety of an am-dram spy. "Darren's anxieties seem to have started from when his partner and baby died during childbirth – at the Great Western. He went downhill after that, fell into shoplifting, arson and eventually GBH."

Hart remembers the fear in Darren's eyes, like a caged animal. "You are aware that Darren died in hospital?" Hart adds, checking with Strover.

"I've just been acquainted with yesterday's events," he says, looking at Strover. "Truly remarkable. And most tragic."

"So you never heard Dr Garstan talk to Darren or anyone else about death days?"

Anwar shakes his head. "He saw patients one-to-one. In private. I didn't approve, he was meant to be under close supervision, but the governor..."

"Allowed it." Hart pauses. "Darren must have dreaded being back in the hospital, the poor man."

"This talk of a death day is interesting," Anwar says. "In Islam, we believe that when God made us from clay, he gave us a predetermined lifespan – a specified date and time when we will die. '*Then still you are in dispute,*' the Quran adds. For many of us, we don't want to believe this."

Hart's not alone, then.

"Dr Garstan was adamant he'd never treated anyone called Darren," Strover says to Anwar. "That's what he told us."

"Then I'm afraid Dr Garstan was lying." He checks his notes. "I can vouch – well I can't, not officially, of course – that Darren was his patient for eight weeks."

Hart shakes his head. It doesn't add up. He must have seen him.

"How about someone called Si Kennington?" he asks, again trying to sound casual.

"You see, I'm not really sharing any information with you today, am I?" Anwar says, laughing with relief as he sits back. "You know it all already."

"So Si Kennington was his patient too?" Strover asks.

"Of course. We all got to know Mr Si well."

Anwar checks his notes again.

"Dr Garstan saw him for six weeks," Anwar continues. "Put him on sertraline straight away for chronic suicidal ideation and existential anxiety. He was released last week. In my notes, I say that I was worried the sertraline might heighten suicidal ideation – you may have heard about it in the news, the risks of younger people taking the drug willy nilly. I also added a note about the dangers of 'emotional blunting', 'impact on moral judgement' and 'heightened suggestibility'." Anwar checks the files again. "Although that one is in parentheses with a question mark."

Strover glances at Hart, who nods.

"I'm afraid Si Kennington died yesterday," Strover says. "Here at the station."

"Are you serious?" Anwar asks, looking from Strover to Hart. He shakes his head and studies his notes again, clearly crestfallen.

"He shot himself at our station front desk," Hart says. He knows he's being too blunt, but he needs to hear himself say the words.

"I said he should never have been put on sertraline," Anwar says, standing up, clearly troubled, running a hand through his thinning hair. "Too young, too damn risky. That is also a tragedy."

"Both these people thought they were going to die when they did," Hart says. "They told me in as many words."

There's no need to tell the GP that they had specifically asked to see Hart, knew Mel's name too.

"There are eight more people on Dr Garstan's patient

list," Anwar says, looking through his notes again. He pauses and shakes his head, on the verge of tears. "Mr Si shot himself?" He tuts and returns to his notes. "Seven he stopped seeing after one week. Turned out they only said they had acute anxiety disorders to get the medication. Happens all the time in prison. But one, Grant Trumore..."

"What about him?" Strover asks. Hart looks up too.

Anwar consults his notes again. "What we call a 'frequent flyer', came to the healthcare centre so often. Ex-Army. Served in Afghanistan as a sniper. Suffered PTSD after his second tour of Helmand in 2009, went off the rails, got divorced, drank too much scotch. Dr Garstan saw him for longer than anyone else. Six months – the last six months of his sentence. He was released on licence ten days ago."

"Do we know where Trumore is now?" Hart asks. Six months is a long time, long enough for Garstan to have indoctrinated him.

"I have his probation officer's number," Anwar says. "You can try ringing him now?"

Strover takes the number and steps outside the interview room to make the call.

"What do his medical notes say?" Hart asks.

"Similar pattern to the others. Sertraline to treat a general anxiety disorder."

"But no specific fear of death?"

"A different kind of fear," Anwar says, reading. "He came to Garstan suffering from 'Harm OCD', a subtype of Obsessive-Compulsive Disorder. It's a condition characterised by intrusive thoughts and impulses about inflicting harm on others and themselves. In his case, he was worried he might go around shooting people."

"And this bloke was released?" It's Hart's turn to shake his head in disbelief. Sometimes he thinks the system is well and truly broken.

"Garstan claimed to have cured him," Anwar continues. "But people like Trumore aren't cured in eight weeks, DI Hart. I made it very clear that I didn't want to sign him off."

"But he was still released?"

"Garstan managed to get the governor involved. A second opinion was sought – I almost resigned. Trumore was eventually released on condition that he continued to be seen by a psychiatrist."

"So we need to find out who's treating him now."

Again, it's clear that Garstan was screening for specific patients, with certain anxieties, and discarding anyone who wasn't suitable for his purposes. Trumore had a love of guns too, which was a bonus. No prizes for guessing what Garstan talked to him about.

A phone rings outside. A few seconds later, Strover steps back into the interview room.

"That was Trumore's Community Offender Manager in Bristol," Strover says, pausing. "He's gone AWOL."

46

Hart puts his coffee down and walks around to where Strover is sitting in the Parade Room.

"Good work with Anwar," Hart says. "If I had any birthday cake left, I'd give you a slice."

"Thank you, sir."

It turns out that Grant Trumore ended up working for an organised crime group operating out of Bristol. Served half of an eighteen-year sentence for multiple armed robberies in Wales. Hart knows that his disappearance is serious, particularly given his military background.

"What do we know about the Golf?" he asks, hoping to distract himself.

"I've run the plates through ANPR, searched the last ninety days," Strover says. "The Golf was bought and registered in Dr Rory Garstan's name, his old Pewsey address – ten days before he was released."

"Sometimes I wonder why they bother calling it prison," Hart says. "Was he ordering pizzas and piña coladas too?"

"Katya must have picked up the Golf. She's been put on both cars' insurance as a named driver," Strover adds, opening another computer window screen.

"So Garstan contacts Katya from prison, asking her to work for him again on his release. She duly collects him from jail – but in the Mercedes."

"Appearances matter. It's a cherry Merc."

"If you say so."

"ANPR does pick up the Golf locally several times in the week before Garstan is released," Strover says, scrolling through the data. "Presumably driven by Katya. And then, on the morning of Garstan's actual release, it's seen driving from Pewsey up to the M4, where it heads eastbound, coming off at midday for IKEA."

"Which makes no sense at all. Do we know who was driving?" Hart asks, pacing around his desk.

Strover shakes her head. Unfortunately, police ANPR only shows the numberplate, not the driver. Katya was about to pick Garstan up from Barontrent in the Mercedes, so it can't have been her.

"Any more sightings of the Golf?" Hart asks.

"Nothing until 1.30 p.m., when it rejoins the M4 and drives towards London. It then takes the M25 and heads north to Norwich."

Norwich? Not back to Wiltshire? Hart walks over to the window.

"Remind me when Garstan's Mercedes arrives at IKEA from Barontrent?" he asks.

Strover checks the screen again. Garstan had talked about

visiting the Swedish store, the need to buy some things for the house after his release from prison.

"1 p.m.," Strover says. "An hour after the Golf. Just in time for meatballs. It heads back towards Pewsey at 2 p.m."

IKEA still strikes Hart as the most unlikely place for anyone to celebrate their freedom. It's his idea of a nightmare, wandering around a warehouse full of flatpack divorce kits. His attempt to assemble the Nordli modular chest was the closest Mel has ever come to murdering him.

"So who the hell was in the Golf?" he asks again.

"Katya can't have driven both cars," Strover says.

Hart sits down at his desk. Two vehicles, both registered to Garstan, overlapping at IKEA for half an hour on the day of his release.

"We need to access IKEA's security cameras," he says. "See who was actually behind the wheel of these bloody cars."

"Guv, this just came for you," a junior uniform says, walking across the Parade Room with a small, padded package. "Post room asked me to give it to you personally. The courier said it was urgent."

Hart doesn't like the sound of it, or the look of the package, which has his name printed on a label. "Put it on the table," Hart says, gesturing at his desk. "Is your DNA on the PED?"

He only asks because the uniform looks so young. The Police Elimination Database is compulsory for all new recruits, used to rule out officers' own DNA from investigations.

"Yes, guv," the uniform says, watching Hart pull on a pair of blue forensic gloves.

"You can go now," Hart says, waiting for the uniform to leave his corner of the Parade Room. He doesn't like an audience.

"You think it's from Garstan?" Strover asks, as Hart opens the package in his gloves and carefully removes a small cardboard box. He slips open the lid to reveal a brass cartridge with a long, sleek bullet, measuring about 10 cm in total and set in a bed of cotton wool. He can see at once that there's an inscription on the casing. Lifting up the whole box, his hand shaking, he peers at the writing. It's a date: *4 December*. And a time: *9.09 a.m.*

"Call Forensics," he says, hoping no one can hear the fear in his voice. "It's from Grant Trumore."

47

"Haven't you caused enough damage around here already?" Ward asks, as Hart stands on the other side of his boss's desk. There's no question of being asked to sit down today.

"I've barely started," Hart says.

For the past three years, Ward has displayed an arctic froideur towards Hart, asking his CID colleagues for operational updates rather than him. Today, because he is so angry, Ward is actually talking to him, but Hart's not bothered. He's always known that one day he'll have what he needs to silence his boss for good. And that day has arrived. Twenty minutes earlier, soon after he'd opened the box with the inscribed cartridge, Hart had taken a call from Forensics about the ground-up bone in the hourglasses. The DNA matches Sophie Mills.

"You know, I rated you when you first became a detective," Ward says, sitting back in his chair, hands behind his head. "Told the Chief that you were one to watch. A future DCS."

"Thank you, sir," Hart says. "The last time I met the Chief Constable, it was to receive a personal commendation for arresting Garstan."

Ward stares out the window of his office. "'Thank you, sir'," he smirks, shaking his head. "You're not grateful, Silas. That's your problem. You've forgotten who your friends are."

"Talking of friends, Dr Garstan was freed last week."

"So I hear."

No doubt on the Freemason grapevine, a tip-off from the Barontrent governor.

"He's a changed man," Hart continues. "Dare I say it, even a little remorseful."

"You've been to see him?" For the first time, Hart's got Ward's attention.

"Yesterday afternoon. Had a few questions for him about Sophie Mills."

"I thought I told you to keep away from him," Ward says, standing up. "Haven't you ruined his career enough?"

"I understood that only applied when he was in prison."

"You're not going to drop this, are you?" Ward says, walking around his desk to stand in front of Hart.

"No sir," Hart says. "Think of me as the hound who has sniffed the fox."

Hart hopes Ward appreciates the hunting metaphor. The two men stare at each other, their faces inches apart. His boss's skin is beginning to show signs of his drinking, which has reportedly got out of hand in recent months. Filigree veins spreading across his nose like a river delta.

"Sophie Mills was killed by a man she met in Angelo's nightclub," Ward says, turning away.

"A man who we've never been able to trace."

"Who *you've* never been able to trace," Ward says, spinning around, his voice raised.

Hart closes his eyes, controlling his own emotions. It's so much easier when you're holding all the cards.

"Sir, when Sophie Mills' headless body was exhumed, three years ago, her clavicle was missing too."

"I remember. The trophy theory was utterly absurd. An animal could have taken it."

Despite no damage to the suitcase. Ward must know he's beaten.

"You may also remember that I investigated the apparent suicide of a young man in Wilton called Milo," Hart says. "He was a patient of Dr Garstan and we found an hourglass beside his body, up near the windmill."

"Another waste of valuable CSI resources."

He's not going to rise to Ward's bait. There's no need to.

"Two days ago, two people, both recently released from HMP Barontrent, died in unusual circumstances. They had been informal patients of Dr Garstan in Barontrent. And we found hourglasses beside both bodies."

Ward looks up at Hart.

"Your point? It might have been a prop, something Dr Garstan gave to all his patients. A reminder of our mortality."

"*Tempus fugit.*"

"Quite," Ward says, clearly surprised. Garstan's words. Hart might not have studied the classics, but he's got a good memory.

"The hourglasses contained ground-up human bone," he says.

"Bone?" Ward asks. "Do we know whose?"

"We do," he says, savouring the bombshell he's about to drop, the uneasy pause before the bay doors open. "Sophie Mills'," he says. "The DNA match has just come through."

Hart thought he might experience a sense of profound satisfaction at this point, but all he feels now, as the blood drains from Ward's face, is pity. Years of society networking – all those drinks with the royals and retired politicians who have made Wiltshire their home – have come to nothing. Ward should have spent more time being a detective than a social climber.

"Is there any actual evidence that Dr Garstan gave the hourglasses to these two men?" Ward manages to ask. "While he was inside?"

"Not yet. Just like there's no evidence that he gave an hourglass to Milo three years ago. But all three were his patients. And all three were, shall we say, suffering from similar anxieties about death. Thanatophobia."

"*Thanatos*, the ancient Greek for death. A minor but important deity, twin brother of Hypnos," Ward says, almost to himself.

Hart moves towards the door, signalling that the meeting is over. He hasn't got time for a classics lesson.

"I'm going to bring Garstan in again, formally interview him about the Sophie Mills case," he says.

"I seem to remember that last time we spoke to him, he told us where to find her body."

Hart opens the door and hesitates before leaving. "My point exactly."

48

Hart looks around the small CCTV control room at IKEA in Reading, nodding at the two security guards, one in his forties, the other barely out of shorts. The bank of screens along one wall is showing multiple views of the car park as well as the store's marketplace and self-scanning tills. It's as close as Hart wants to get.

"The last time I visited IKEA, I got so lost I came out with a beard," Hart says, hoping to break the ice – they've been made to feel more welcome raiding cannabis farms.

The two security guards ignore him.

"What's the most shoplifted item, then?" Hart continues, trying a different tack.

"You mean apart from pencils?" the younger guard asks, zooming in on a shopper at a self-scan till. "Ten million a year at the last count. And that's just in the UK."

"Tight skankers," his older colleague says, putting on a pair of headphones.

"They're free, aren't they?" Strover asks, reddening.

"Been lifting pencils again, Strover?" Hart says, smiling.

"Belfast had someone walk out with a bed and wardrobe a couple years back," the younger guard says. He spins in his swivel chair and slides across the floor to a separate pair of TV screens in the corner of the room. "My mates call me Sunny – how can I help?"

Hart raises his eyebrows at Strover. Sunny by name, sunny by nature. Unlike the glum numbskull in the corner. Mind you, who'd want to be a security guard? Miserable job, up there with traffic wardens.

"We need to run through the car park footage from midday to 2 p.m. on Wednesday 24 November," Strover says, moving over to stand next to Sunny.

"We can start with the ANPR?" he asks. "We clock everyone driving in and out the car park. It was popping off like crazy that day. First day of the festive menu."

"OK," Strover says, passing Sunny a sheet of paper with two numberplates written down: one for the Golf and one for the Mercedes that picked Garstan up from Barontrent.

Thirty seconds later, they are looking at a frozen image of the front of the Mercedes.

"Gotcha," Sunny says. "Nice German whip."

"All electric CLA," Strover says. "Sport edition."

Sunny glances up at Strover, who ignores him, peering closer at the screen. Hart leans in too. The image isn't great, but the driver of the Mercedes is clearly visible through the windscreen: Katya. Unlike police ANPR, privately owned cameras often show the whole vehicle, driver included.

"That's her," Strover says.

"With her boss in the back, presumably," Hart says. They have decided not to mention Katya or Garstan by name. It's unlikely either security guard has a connection with Barontrent, but you never know with screws and rent-a-cops. Hart glances at the older guard, who is nodding to music on his headphones as he tucks into a burger. He leans in even closer to the screen. The graininess of the image makes it difficult to be sure, but there's no obvious silhouette of a passenger in the back seat of the Mercedes.

"Are we done?" Sunny asks.

"Thanks," Strover says.

"We've got cameras on every floor, we can see where the Merc parked."

Hart and Strover watch as a series of frozen shots show the Mercedes driving past the entrance to the first and second floors of the multi-storey car park.

"Must have parked up on two," the guard says. "Time stamp 13.04. We can find the CCTV from that deck if you like? We keep footage for thirty days, so you're in luck."

"You drive?" Strover asks.

"Zimmer."

"Nice."

"E30 325i."

"Manual, I presume."

"Of course. '87."

Hart listens to their exchange, no idea what they're talking about, but he's impressed how Strover gets people onside.

"Can we just confirm the arrival of this one too?" Strover asks, pointing at the Golf's numberplate on the piece of paper.

"Your wish, my command," Sunny says, happier now to oblige a fellow petrolhead.

They are soon staring at a front-on image of the silver Golf. Hart and Strover exchange glances and look at the screen again.

"That can't be right," Hart says. "Can you zoom in? On the driver?"

Sunny enlarges the image. It's Garstan.

"And the time stamp's correct?" Strover asks. "12.05?"

"Sound as a pound," Sunny says.

"An hour before the Mercedes arrives with him from Barontrent," Hart says, shaking his head. He thinks back to the photos of when Garstan was released from prison: 11 a.m. "That's impossible."

"Unless Lando Norris was driving," Strover says.

"Leclerc's better – ruthless," Sunny says, calling up another image. "Your Golf leaves the car park ninety minutes later, at 13.32."

"Zoom in, please," Strover says.

"It's him again," Hart says, looking at a grainy shot of Garstan behind the wheel.

"Do we know where the Golf was parked?" Hart asks.

Sunny closes one window, opens another, enters the time. They are soon scrolling through still images again, as the Golf passes the entrance to the first and second floors, just like the Mercedes had done.

"Deck two, same as the Merc," Sunny says. "We can speed-scroll through the cameras from midday onwards if you like?"

"You're being very helpful," Strover says, smiling at Sunny. "Thank you."

Two minutes later, the mood is less positive.

"What are the chances of that, bro," Sunny says, turning to his colleague, who is tucking into a second Big Mac. "They both parked on two, but you see here" – they watch as a ceiling camera tracks the Golf passing below it – "the car then turns off into this blind spot. The only one on the whole deck."

"What are the chances, as you say," Hart repeats. But he knows it's got nothing to do with chance.

They all watch the Mercedes arrive on the second floor too and disappear into the same blind spot.

"Would you look at that?" Sunny says, kicking back his chair and glancing at Strover and Hart, who stay silent. "OK," Sunny adds, "I get it. Some kind of drug deal going down, innit?"

"Can we see the ANPR of the Mercedes leaving?" Strover asks, ignoring Sunny, whose voice has gone all streetwise, now he's talking about drugs. "Should be around 2 p.m."

They watch Sunny call up the earlier window and type in the Mercedes' numberplate again.

"Pop, pop," he says, pretending to shoot at the screen. "Maybe I should have joined the feds, bro?" he says, calling across to his colleague, who's still ignoring them. "You got to be more curious in life, man," Sunny says, turning away. "The only thing he's ever been interested in is his next Maccy D."

But Hart's not listening. The photo on the screen is of the Mercedes leaving IKEA, with Katya still at the wheel. Again, it's not obvious whether she has a passenger on board.

"Thanks," Strover says to Sunny, following Hart out of the room.

"Safes," Sunny says.

"That makes no bloody sense at all," Hart repeats

outside, as they walk across the road to the multi-storey car park. "Why would Garstan arrive in the Golf an hour *before* Katya arrives in the Mercedes from Barontrent?"

"And why would he then head up the M4 afterwards in the Golf?" Strover asks.

Hart shakes his head as they take the lift to the second floor and walk over to the blind spot where the two cars had parked.

"Maybe Katya picked him up from Barontrent in the Mercedes and—"

"And what?" Hart doesn't mean to cut Strover short, but he's rattled by what he's just seen in the control room. Garstan can't have been in two places at once.

"They might have met somewhere outside IKEA?" Strover suggests. "Garstan gets out the Mercedes after being picked up at Barontrent and switches to the Golf, which he drives on to IKEA."

"But why? And who drove the Golf over from Pewsey? And why did Garstan drive on to Norwich when he'd just been released from jail? Nothing against Norwich, but you'd want to celebrate your freedom at home, wouldn't you? Particularly after a visit to IKEA."

"My family might be from Norwich, sir."

"But they're not, are they Strover? They're from Bristol." Hart throws Strover a withering look. "I need you to go through Garstan's background, search for anything that could possibly link him to Norwich."

"Early lunch first?"

Hart looks at Strover, appalled.

"You're joking again, right?"

"Sixteen festive plant balls, on me. You'll love them, sir."

49

I can't remember how long it was before you visited again. A week? A month? It was so hard to tell. But the next time you came, something had changed – in both of us. Was my disorder getting worse? Or better? Mum and Dad had also started to fade, like ships in a sea mist.

"Your brother is here," Desdemona said one day.

I opened my eyes and stared at the ceiling.

"How are you feeling?" you asked.

"Confused," I said slowly.

"To be expected with your medication. As you know."

I turned to look at him.

"What's going on, Rory?"

"How do you mean?"

"Mum and Dad, they're dead, aren't they?"

You swallowed before answering, glancing at Desdemona. "They're dead, yes."

"Barka too?"

You nodded the faintest of assents. Over the coming weeks, I started to feel something again, the first flush of emotion, coursing through my veins like flood water. A raw, existential rage. You seemed altered too, visiting me more frequently and, yes, with less empathy in your eyes. The moment I exhibited any signs of anger, my meds were dialled up. I just had to shout or rip off my clothes, and the control-and-restraint team would appear with straps and a small plastic beaker, a needle if I objected.

"You killed Barka, didn't you?" I shouted one day. "Drowned her in the stream."

Another time, I was sunk by a profound grief for Mum and Dad.

"They tried so hard to love you, but you wouldn't let them. Why didn't you help with the funeral? Dad died of a broken heart, you know that?"

It was then that electroconvulsive "therapy" was introduced. The first time it happened, I couldn't believe that you had sanctioned it.

"What's going on?" I asked, when an ECT machine was wheeled into my room one morning.

"It's for your benefit," you said. "You're getting the very best treatment here, Finn. Trust me. The very best."

The best? I knew what 110 bloody volts passing through the temporal lobe of the brain could do to people. Not just from the films – Dad used to say that One Flew Over The Cuckoo's Nest *had set psychiatry back fifty years – but from my attachment during foundation training, when we learnt that ECT used to be administered without a muscle relaxant or sedative. Fractured vertebrae and dislocated jaws were not uncommon. The treatment has changed since the 1940s, of course, become more modified and remains a life-saver for some, but it still causes substantial memory deficits.*

I cried out when an anaesthetist filed into my room after you, followed by the airway and crash trolleys. "Get the fuck out of here! All of you!"

I shouted even louder when I was strapped down to the bed. The needle soon followed, but not before I'd felt the electrodes on my salty temples.

"ECT can help reduce the most extreme treatment-resistant comorbidities," I heard you say to your team, maybe thinking that I was already sedated. "Where all else has failed, I've seen it work wonders with major depressive disorders, severe suicidal ideation."

And then there were the days when an anaesthetist wasn't present. Those were the worst, when it was just you and Desdemona. I knew that I was being punished. No anaesthetic, no muscle relaxant, just a rubber bite block in my mouth. ECT "in the raw", as a corrective, like it used to be administered at Broadmoor in the 1950s. I didn't want to think about it too much, but I knew, in those moments before the grand mal seizure was triggered, that my back would soon be flexing like a line-caught fish.

And you did something else, didn't you? Pushed the boundaries. Sometimes my neck was strangely sore after these sessions, and I knew what had happened: you had temporarily deprived me of oxygen – acute intermittent hypoxia. Psychiatrists used to pinch patients' noses in the early days to intensify the effects of ECT. But you must have compressed my windpipe. It happened a number of times and on each occasion I would come round not knowing who or where I was, an existential crisis far worse than before.

"How are you feeling, Finn?" Desdemona would ask after the latest round of ECT.

"Like my skull has been split in two with a battle axe," I wanted to say. But I was too groggy to speak, too disorientated by a headache that lasted for days.

For weeks I was kept in what was once called a sopor. I was not asleep, exactly – in some ways, that would have been preferable – but in a twilight state of drug-induced confusion. I tried to resist, taking advantage of small moments of clarity when my meds dropped, but the struggle to anchor my sense of self was proving too much.

The only retaliation I could think of was to become non-verbal. At first it was deliberate, but it quickly became a habit. Who were they to know if it was real or not? I'd seen enough non-verbal patients in my time to know how it presented.

Word must have reached you of my silent protest, because one day Desdemona said you were coming, your first visit in a while. And despite the mist swirling around my synapses, I was beginning to work out your game. I didn't know what it was yet, not exactly, but I knew there would come a day when I would understand what you were doing – be well enough to write everything down – and you would pay for it. And that time felt closer, like a rising tide in the dead of night.

50

Present day

"I thought I told you specifically not to see him," Hart says on the phone, looking out at the snow, which has started to fall again. He's walked away from their vehicle in the IKEA car park, leaving Strover to make some calls and find out more about Garstan. He should be doing the same, but Conor has just posted a message on the family WhatsApp group (Mel, Hart, Conor and now Jess): *I'm not about to die – it's official.* He must have seen Garstan again.

"I'm twenty-seven, Dad, not a child anymore. The sooner you and Mum get your head around that, the better for everyone."

Hart takes a deep breath. Conor's right. He and Mel both still treat him like he's a teenager, but that's only because of what happened, the choices he made and those he didn't, like reacting so adversely to skunk that he had to be sectioned.

"Where did you meet him?" he asks.

"Same place."

The hostel on Fleming Way. His WhatsApp message sounded upbeat, but he doesn't trust Garstan an inch. He'd pleaded Xanax-induced amnesia when they'd asked him about the hostel, but Hart's sure he visited it on the day he was released on licence – the date tallied with when Conor volunteered there. And now he's visited again.

"What did he say?"

"That I've got a long life ahead of me, have nothing to worry about."

"And did he do this with a crystal ball?"

"Dad, he's a well-known psychiatrist and life coach."

"He tell you that too?"

"As it happens, he did, yeah. And that he also used to practise in Harley Street."

"And you got a name this time."

"Dr Rory Garstan. Even gave me his card. I've kept it, just for you."

Hart closes his eyes. "Did he also tell you that he'd recently come out of prison?"

"He did, actually. Said there'd been an unfortunate misunderstanding about gun licences."

"And I don't suppose you told him who you were? That it was your old man who'd put him behind bars?"

A long silence. "No, I didn't. Was it you? Who arrested him?"

"Three years ago, Conor. And I don't think he's very happy with me, to put it mildly, which is why I explicitly told you to stay away from him."

Another silence.

"He seemed more sensitive this time, if that makes any sense?"

"Sensitive?"

"Less combative. A few weeks back, when I first met him, he talked about death days, shit like that. It was lit but, you know, heavy."

"Not this time, though?"

"He just listened – heard me. 'Tuned in'."

"Well, I'm glad you're not about to die."

"Me too. Maybe you should see him as well if you're worried. Mum says you're becoming a right massive hypo."

"I've got to run," Hart says, glancing back at Strover. "Speak later."

Hart hangs up and walks over to their car. Right massive hypo? Him?

"We need to go," Strover says with an urgency that he's come to recognise.

"I was talking to Conor," Hart says. It's not an excuse, but he knows Strover understands, that he only speaks to his son in police time when it's important.

"Everything OK?" Strover asks, as they drive off down the car park ramp.

"All good. You've got something?"

"Remember Rory's older brother?"

"Another shrink, wasn't he?"

Hart recalls they'd briefly looked into the brother three years ago, when they were preparing for Rory's arrest, but information had been scarce. In the event, the CPS had more than enough on Rory and his weapons. And the defence team hadn't bothered to call the older brother as a character witness.

"Used to work in a place called Hellesdon," Strover says. "An NHS psych unit outside Norwich."

"Their Dad was a shrink too, wasn't he?"

"Harley Street, apparently. I've been doing some more digging. Rory was asked about Finn once, in some obscure psychiatry publication a couple of years back. Just said that he and his brother were very different people. Reading between the lines, Rory was the flash one, Finn was quieter, more reserved. And it seems like Finn fell off the grid years ago. Certainly kept his head down when we banged his younger brother up."

"Where is he now?"

"We don't know. Hasn't practised for a long time."

"Hellesdon, the hospital in Norwich where he worked – have you contacted them?"

"They won't say much over the phone. Just confirmed that he used to work there."

"Then we better get up to Norwich, hadn't we?"

The bean-counters will mutter about travel costs and the benefits of Zoom, but Hart's always preferred face-to-face interviews.

"That's where we're heading now, sir."

51

Strover parks up in front of the old reception of Hellesdon Hospital, on the north-western edge of Norwich. The journey from Reading was meant to have taken more than three hours, but Strover had blue-lit most of the way. The imposing building before them now – red-brick, late Victorian – was once the centrepiece of the Norwich Borough Asylum, which had opened here in 1880. To their right, a water tower, its brickwork inscribed with a cross; to their left, small, low-level outbuildings, like army barracks, dotted along a tree-lined avenue.

For the past ten minutes, they've been cruising around the sprawling hospital site, a strange mix of green spaces (snow-white, today), derelict buildings covered in graffiti and a sleek, newly built medical facility on the lower part of the estate.

"We can drive around some more, sir," Strover says.

"All good. Just wanted to see what this sort of place must have been like once."

"Freaks me out, if I'm honest."

Strover seems fine with gore, less good with mental trauma.

"It's all going to be housing in a few years, this building included, but with a nod to the past," Hart says, gesturing at the old reception. He found these sorts of places frightening too, when Conor was first taken ill. Less so now. "Victorian asylums were quite compassionate in their own way, before they became overcrowded."

"If you say so, sir."

"Had their own farms, bakeries, slaughterhouses, you name it. Patients would often stay here for the rest of their lives."

They step out of the car and head off towards the Glaven Ward, where a Dr Yasir Khan has agreed to speak to them. On the way, they pass more dilapidated buildings, one of them fire-damaged, another with its windows smashed in.

"A few years back, a former patient broke into one of the old doctors' houses and squatted in it for a while," Hart says. He'd read up on the place while Strover was driving. "Patients come back to camp in the grounds too, apparently."

"Maybe they feel safe here," Strover says.

Two minutes later, they are sitting opposite Dr Khan, a consultant in acute inpatient psychiatry. He looks tired and overworked, his tie loose, jacket hanging untidily off the back of his chair. Nervous too, glancing from them to the door, the window.

"How can I help?" he says. "I'm afraid I don't have much time."

"Six years ago, you worked with Dr Finn Garstan, is that right?" Strover asks, getting straight to the point.

Dr Khan nods and seems to relax a little.

"We only overlapped for a few months. I'd just arrived, as a junior registrar."

"Do you know why he left?"

"He became unwell."

"And he never returned?"

"No," Dr Khan says, shaking his head. He glances at the door again before continuing. Hart can see why patients might confide in this man. Despite his evident tiredness, he has an attentive manner, his eyes focussed and kind.

"He had a breakdown," he says. "Not so uncommon for psychiatrists. A hazard of our job. I sometimes wonder if mental illness is contagious."

A light laugh.

"And you have no idea where Finn Garstan might be now?"

"I know where he went, but I don't know if he's still there. I sincerely hope not."

"And where would that be?" Hart asks, sitting forward. The interview's just got interesting.

Dr Khan leans forward in his chair too, tidies the pens on his desk.

"At first I thought he would be treated here, but he was admitted to a private mental health facility near the coast. A small unit outside Holt – the Randle Retreat. American owned. Someone said he knew the management."

"And you don't know if he's there now?"

"I barely knew him, DI Hart. It's a long-term care facility but, as I say, I hope he's not still their patient."

"Because?"

"They do things differently, that's all. It's a business at the end of the day. People stay much longer than they should. A bit like this place once – people could be locked away for life. Put it this way: I would never refer someone to the Randle."

Hart lets Dr Khan's words hang in the air, hoping he might say more, but he stays silent.

"I appreciate it was a long time ago, but can you remember anything else about Finn Garstan?"

Dr Khan sits back and smiles wryly.

"I'm not sure how much you know about psychiatry, DI Hart, but we don't often get to 'cure' patients, as such. What we can do is manage their symptoms and, if we're lucky, help them to live happy and meaningful lives. They're the cases that make this job worthwhile. If I'm honest, I'm not sure Finn had many moments when he felt good about his work. I may be wrong, but he struck me as someone who thought he had been hard done by in life. We all complain about being overstretched, but he… it was something else with him, more fundamental. He seemed resentful about his lot. Consumed with a self-destructive bitterness, as it finally proved."

"Did he have a partner?" Hart asks. "Any family?"

"I don't know about a partner – he was a very private man – but he has a twin brother, of course. Dr Rory Garstan."

"A twin?" Hart asks, sitting up, glancing across at Strover.

"I thought Finn was the older brother?" Strover asks.

"By a few minutes, but trust me, it mattered. I remember him once remarking – rather snidely – how well his 'baby' brother was doing in Harley Street. Sadly, I think they were estranged. Not uncommon with identical twins. The struggle to establish individual identities, the constant competition and comparisons."

Hart's mind is racing, trying to compute the implications, how the revelation plays into what they'd seen on IKEA's CCTV screens, the movements of the Golf and Mercedes. They should have known.

"Rory never mentioned his brother was a twin," Strover says, as if reading his thoughts.

"I'm not sure it's that well known, to be honest," Dr Khan says.

If he's hoping to make Hart feel better, he's failed.

"I think he was also involved in Finn's initial admission and care at the Randle, but don't hold me to that. Before he went to prison, of course," Dr Khan adds, smiling for the first time in their chat.

Hart senses Dr Khan is not entirely upset that Rory was sent down.

"Did you know him?" he asks.

"Only by reputation. Who didn't?" Dr Khan pauses. "I think it's fair to say that Finn felt overshadowed by his younger brother's success, even though there were rumours – just rumours, you understand – that Rory had also suffered a breakdown of sorts. As I say, it happens all too often in our line of work."

"You've been very helpful," Hart says, standing up, wondering if Dr Khan has battled with his own demons too. He's also struggling to understand why Rory Garstan would have been involved in his twin brother's care if they were estranged.

"And now I'm feeling bad about Finn," Dr Khan says. "Not knowing what happened to him when he left here.

But we were like passing ships. Please let me know if you find out anything," he adds, handing Hart his card.

Once back outside, Hart and Strover head towards their car in the early darkness.

"Jesus, twins," Hart says. "We should have known this three years ago, when we were sending Rory down."

"There was nothing in the files about them being twins. Just that one reference to an older brother, which didn't seem that important."

"It's OK, Strover. Let's get to Holt."

It's only forty minutes away. Less, with Strover behind the wheel.

"You think Finn might still be at the Randle?"

"It would make sense," Hart says. "Explain why Rory drove up here on the first day he was released from Barontrent. Particularly if he had been involved in his original admission."

"But why would he have cared for him if they didn't get on?"

"That's bothering me too. They were still brothers, I suppose."

"And who was looking after Finn while Rory was in prison?"

"DI Hart?" a voice says behind them.

They both spin round to see Dr Khan approaching.

"I'm sorry, there's one other thing."

Again, Dr Khan looks around him, as if to check no one is listening.

"Go on," Hart says.

"After Finn had been signed off from work, there was some talk in the department."

"What sort of talk?"

He shifts uncomfortably from foot to foot.

"Of malingering. Most mental disorders have well-defined symptomology." He pauses. "Dissociative identity disorder, the condition Finn apparently presented with, is notoriously difficult to diagnose. Its symptoms overlap with other conditions, such as depression, anxiety, PTSD and so on. As a psychiatrist, Finn would have known that. Let's just say some of his colleagues felt there were inconsistencies. The presentation was atypical."

"You mean he might have been faking his own breakdown?" Hart asks.

"Quite possibly."

52

Two psych units in the same day. Hart is beginning to feel like a psychiatrist on tour. Move over Ray Davies and the Kinks, it's Silas Hart and the Shrinks. (A shame Strover's too young to be a dedicated follower of fashion.) They park up outside the Randle Retreat, a modern, curved glass-and-steel building, low-slung and unobtrusive in the flat saltmarsh landscape, somewhere between Holt and the North Sea. Unfortunately, the light is fading, no chance to enjoy the view. It's bitterly cold too, an easterly wind blasting in off the sea.

Hart had called ahead and a Dr Jennings is waiting for them in reception, happy to talk about Finn Garstan.

"Welcome to the Randle," Dr Jennings says.

"Sorry we're early."

The roads were empty and Strover had been in Lewis Hamilton mode.

"No problem, do come in," Dr Jennings says.

Hart is immediately reminded of Jonathan, the kind psychiatrist who had turned Conor's life around. The likeness – open face, sincere smile – is so strong that he's tempted to ask if he knows him.

"You're here about Dr Finn Garstan," Dr Jennings says, taking them through to a private room off the low-lit, main reception. His welcoming manner is at odds with the deserted atmosphere of the Randle, which strikes Hart as less peaceful retreat and more futuristic morgue, like a communal area for deep-space travel: sparse, functional, polar white. He presumes everyone must be sedated.

"How long's he been with you?" Hart asks.

"Six years, I'm afraid, which I personally see as a catastrophic failure of care. It should never have happened – I'm still trying to establish who signed off on his most recent annual reviews. He was with us far too long."

"*Was* with you?" Hart asks, glancing at Strover.

"I discharged him three weeks ago. It was a risk but… I'm not at liberty to discuss private medical records, of course. Let's just say that Finn had struggled for years with issues of identity. More recently, he'd finally accepted who he was."

"Were those issues of identity related to him being an identical twin?"

"Quite possibly. There is some evidence that monozygotic – identical – twins are more prone to dissociative experiences. He'd also had a lot of trauma as a child, but we really shouldn't be talking like this. The point is that…"

Hart is surprised by the sudden emotion in the psychiatrist's voice.

"He was brought back in last week," he continues. "Had a relapse. I'm afraid it happens. Maybe we'd tapered his medication too quickly. He'd become quite violent, insisting that he was not 'Finn' – a delusion of identity that we thought he'd put behind him."

The fear of Conor having a relapse haunts Hart and Mel every day.

"So, he is here now?" Hart asks.

"Back with us again, yes. And against his will, sadly."

"Sectioned? Were there sufficient clinical grounds to do that?"

"Yes and no. Psychiatry is a very polarised profession, DI Hart. I won't bore you with the details, but let's just say I'm a firm believer that medication – sustained sedation in Finn's case – isn't the answer to everything. Of course it's essential at times of acute crisis. But as a form of long-term treatment?"

Dr Jennings is reminding Hart more and more of Jonathan. Hart's not a big believer in long-term medication either. It certainly hadn't helped Conor.

"But as his consultant psychiatrist, you were involved?"

Dr Jennings glances at the glass panel in the door.

"I should have been. But it was his brother who brought him back in. I think your paths may have crossed. The Harley Street psychiatrist, Dr Rory Garstan. He'd personally overseen Finn's care here in the early years."

Hart is stunned and looks across at Strover, who seems equally shocked.

"But Rory was in jail," Hart says. "We put him there."

"He was until nine days ago," Dr Jennings says. "He returned Finn to us on the same day he was released from prison."

Hart looks at Strover again and then at Dr Jennings.

"Last Wednesday? The 24th?"

Dr Jennings nods. So they were right about the Golf at IKEA, which had left for Norwich with Rory Garstan apparently at the wheel. But why had he changed cars?

"Did Rory have the authority to section him?" Hart asks. "He was only just out of jail, not yet been cleared by the GMC to practise again."

Dr Jennings looks again at the door.

"There were a lot of things that troubled me about Finn's readmission, DI Hart. He was formally detained for twenty-eight days under Section 2 of the MHA, but let's just say that the doctors who signed off on it were acting in the hospital's interests rather than Finn's. I'm in the process of compiling an official complaint to the CQC. I looked into a Hospital Manager's Review too, but it's a joke here. Which is why I'm currently working out my notice – I've resigned over the matter."

A man of principle. The Randle sounds like a nightmare. Not surprising, given Britain's in the grip of a mental health pandemic. Complaints against psych units – NHS and private – are higher than ever, amid reports of systemic failures in safety, staffing and care. Thank God Conor's not in an institution anymore.

"Do you know where Finn went?" he asks. "When he was initially released from here, three weeks ago?"

"Back to the family home, he said. In Pewsey. I dropped him off myself, at Sheringham, our local train station. That's the irony. He wanted to get the home ready for Rory's release from prison."

"But Rory wasn't so pleased to see him out of hospital and brought him straight back here?" Hart asks.

"I'm sorry, I've already said more than I should. There are people here – the Randle's American owners – who weren't exactly thrilled when I was appointed, but they had to do something to get the CQC off their back. It had just rated this place as 'inadequate'. They were even less pleased when I released Finn. He had been with us for a long time."

"Bills always paid?" Hart asks.

Dr Jennings nods.

"A good customer, in other words."

Dr Jennings' eyes are on the door again.

"This place could be busier. And our fees are considerable. Few people can afford them."

"But the Garstans could."

Another resigned nod.

"Six years of them. Rory had to sell his flat in London, apparently. I think he eventually struck a deal with the owners, but Finn was a very useful revenue stream."

"Can we see him?" Hart asks. "Finn?"

"He's heavily sedated. Unfortunately."

"We'd still like to see him, if that's possible."

"Of course. I think you'll be quite surprised."

They follow Dr Jennings down a long white corridor, broken up by a series of secure fire doors. If the fees are high, Hart's not sure where the money's been spent. Certainly not on interior design. More likely on lining the owners' pockets. The LED lighting is harsh, CCTV cameras everywhere. In the distance, a cry of pain. He turns to Strover, who is looking resolutely ahead.

"This is his room," Dr Jennings says. "I'm afraid you can't go in. But you can see him. Through the glass."

Hart looks through the reinforced inspection window at

the top of the door. It reminds him of checking cells in the Gablecross custody suite. Finn seems to be asleep on a bed, head turned towards the door. Hart catches his breath as he takes in the sleeping figure, transfixed by the sight of him. He blinks hard and looks again, staring in disbelief as if he's just seen a magic trick. Head reeling, he steps aside for Strover, whose eyes also widen.

"The likeness is remarkable, isn't it?" Dr Jennings says. "Even for identical twins."

Hart moves up to the observation window again and looks at the sleeping figure. He is prepared to swear on his parents' defaced grave that the man in the bed is the same person he put away in prison.

"That's not Finn Garstan," he says.

53

"I get that identical twins are, well, identical, but that was Rory Garstan back there, as sure as eggs is eggs," Hart says, as they pull away from the Randle and begin the long car journey south to Wiltshire.

"It doesn't make any sense," Strover says.

Hart knows how Strover feels. All this talk of twins is doing his head in. It must have been even worse for Rory and Finn's parents.

"Let's go back to Rory's release from prison," he says. "Finn was calling the shots that day, not Rory. Finn arrived first at IKEA and drove straight up to the blind spot on the second deck of the car park."

"Katya does exactly the same in the Merc an hour later, having picked Rory up from Barontrent."

"So Katya's in on this too, working for Finn now. Rory's shocked to find that Finn's been released from the Randle, but instead of taking him back there..."

"Finn must somehow sedate Rory and get him re-admitted to the Randle in his place. Both had been incarcerated for years, one in prison, the other in a psych unit, but they still looked identical."

"When Rory is detained at the Randle, he protests violently, insisting that he isn't called Finn, which only makes his readmission clinically more straightforward."

"Because Rory was displaying all the symptoms of a patient with identity issues who's just had a relapse."

Hart shakes his head. Someone's thought this through.

"But why, Strover? Why was Rory in such a hurry to get his brother readmitted? And why was Finn so keen to swap himself out? To reverse the tables?"

Hart and Strover drive on through the late Friday evening traffic, cursing the roadworks as they run through different scenarios.

"Remember what Dr Khan said to us at the Hellesdon?" Hart asks. "There were rumours that Finn had faked his own breakdown. Why would he do that?"

"Maybe he wanted a break from his job and pulled a sicky?"

Hart glances at Strover, surprised. He can't remember his colleague ever calling in sick. He hasn't either.

"If that's the case," he says, "it backfired spectacularly, given he spent the next six years at the Randle. No one in their right mind would choose to fake a breakdown in order to be admitted to a place like that – however much they disliked their boss."

"Didn't Dr Khan also suggest that Rory was involved in Finn's initial sectioning?"

"But why would he do that? If they were estranged?"

Hart sits up, struck by a moment of clarity. He tries to keep calm, wary of scaring the thought away.

"We've been looking at this the wrong way round," he continues. "According to Dr Khan, it was Finn who had the grievance. He was the one who felt embittered and overlooked by his more successful brother." He pauses. "What if Finn did fake his own breakdown? Six years ago. And then got Rory, his identical twin brother, admitted to the Randle in his place?"

They both fall silent.

"Dr Khan said that Rory might also have had a breakdown of sorts," Strover says.

"Exactly. So not such a leap for Finn to fake his own and get Rory sectioned in his place."

"And take over Rory's life, the life he'd always envied..."

They both stare ahead, letting the implications sink in. Hart glances across at Strover, whose fingers have tightened on the steering wheel.

"So, for the last six years," Strover says, "when he was working in Harley Street, seeing celebrity clients, going on pheasant shoots with DCS Ward, helping us find Sophie Mills' body using remote viewing, that was Finn impersonating Rory."

"Living his brother's best life in London and Pewsey," Hart says, "while he kept the real Rory locked away as 'Finn' – as himself – in the Randle."

Finn could have accessed Rory's money too. It's not unheard of for identical twins to activate facial-recognition banking apps on their siblings' phones.

"Finn's plan only went wrong when we sent him down,

which eventually allowed the real Rory to be discharged from the Randle," Hart continues. "And this time it was his turn to get his twin brother re-admitted in his place."

"Re-admitted as 'Finn', of course, which was actually his real name, despite him insisting he was Rory," Strover says, pausing. "You've got to admit, there's a certain symmetry to it."

"Sweet revenge for all those years Rory spent at the Randle," Hart says.

Unfortunately, Finn had a plan for revenge too – against Hart, for locking him up three years ago. A plan that's still very much in play.

"You OK, sir?" Strover asks.

He nods, but he's not OK. Far from it. His thoughts keep returning to the engraved bullet that had been sent to him at work, the two men who had died in front of him, his parents' defaced gravestone, the prediction of his own death day: tomorrow.

54

Strover and Hart pull into the drive in Pewsey, just as they had done yesterday, and look across at the snow-covered house. They are beginning to know the place so well it feels like home from home. Almost. Nothing has changed, apart from the property's name, painted by Katya on a board now fixed to the side of the gate: *Palatine Hill*.

It's late – past 9 p.m. – and they are both tired after their round trip to Reading and Norfolk. But the journey was worth it. If they are right, the real Dr Rory Garstan will be at home. The Rory who spent six years at the Randle as 'Finn'. The Rory who has just had the real Finn re-admitted in his place.

"Looks like Katya is here too," Strover says, nodding at her car parked by the garage. It's a bonus. Neither of them had expected her to be working this late on a Friday night.

"They're definitely in this together," Hart says.

They step out of the car and approach the front door. Their plan is to challenge Rory up front – he'll be suspicious why they have returned so soon after yesterday's visit – but Hart doesn't want to scare the horses. He has so many questions, none more important than what Finn was up to in the years before he was imprisoned, his role in the deaths of two young people: Sophie and Milo. The twins might be estranged, but Hart suspects that Rory still knows more about his brother than anyone else. He also needs to ask him about his own death day…

It's Katya who opens the front door.

"Sorry to call so late," Hart says. "Mind if we come in?"

"Of course," she says, stepping aside. Hart reminds himself to tread gently, keep her onside.

"Two visits in two days," Garstan says, walking into the hall. "It must be important. Please, come through."

Rory and Katya are playing it straight. No sign of any confessions. Hart and Strover hadn't known that the brothers were twins when they'd visited yesterday. This time Hart is already looking for differences, trying not to stare at Garstan. The physical likeness is still uncanny. Maybe his physique is marginally fuller (Conor had put on weight when he was sectioned), but the only obvious thing he can spot is that Garstan is wearing a watch on his right wrist, suggesting that he is left-handed. As a left-hander himself, Hart normally notices such things, likes to clock who else is in the ten per cent club. And he's sure Finn had worn a watch on his left wrist when he was clay-pigeon shooting that day. It might be nothing, or they could be mirror-image twins.

Hart and Strover follow Garstan into the sitting room, Katya behind them. The thick velvet curtains are drawn, the lighting low, a log fire burning in the grand fireplace, where an open bottle of Côte de Beaune is warming.

"To what do I owe this pleasure?" Garstan says, gesturing for Hart and Strover to sit.

Normally, Hart likes to remain standing when he is about to accuse someone of a crime, but he reminds himself that he's here to build a case against Finn, not Rory.

"We've just come back from Norwich," Hart says, settling into an armchair. "Holt too."

Garstan, now also sitting down, remains impressively impassive.

"Did you see my poor brother?" he asks. "Unfortunately, he'd been released prematurely and had a relapse. I had to go up there, oversee his re-admission. On the very same day I came out of Barontrent, can you believe it?"

Hart stares at Garstan, admiring his chutzpah. Or have they got this wrong?

"We did see your brother, yes. At a distance."

"I fear he's still heavily sedated. It was all very sad. And quite unsettling. He was convinced his name was Rory."

"You're identical twins. It must get confusing – for everyone."

Garstan allows himself a smile.

"When we were younger, Finn got into a lot of trouble at school," he says. "And of course he always used to say, 'I think there's been a terrible mistake, sir. It wasn't me, it was my twin brother Rory.'"

"And you took the rap," Hart says. Just like he'd done for six years at the Randle.

"Every time. Having done nothing wrong. We share the same DNA too, of course, which has always worried me."

It worries Hart too, could make charging Finn more complicated.

"To my great regret, we were estranged for many years," Rory says.

The two men stare at each other in the flickering firelight. It's time to end the charade.

"Which makes it all the more curious that you oversaw his initial detainment six years ago," Hart says. "All the more unlikely. We also met one of Finn's former colleagues at Hellesdon. A Dr Khan."

"I admire your thoroughness, DI Hart." For the first time, Rory seems concerned, shifting in his chair. "Did he say anything of significance?"

"That breakdowns were a professional hazard of your job."

"He's not wrong there."

"How he thinks mental illness might be contagious."

"Not so sure about that."

"He was joking."

Hart pauses, glancing at Strover, who leans forward.

"He also told us how Finn had faked his own breakdown six years ago."

"He had you admitted in his place, didn't he?" Hart asks.

Katya rushes out into the hall.

"Kat, come back in, it's OK," Garstan calls out.

Katya sheepishly re-enters the room.

"So we know who you are, Rory," Hart says.

55

A deep silence falls on the room, broken only by the crackle of the fire and Katya's sobs.

"This has nothing to do with her," Rory says.

"It's OK," Hart says. "Katya's been very helpful in the past. When we were charging Finn with firearms offences."

"She's told me everything, what my brother did while I was sectioned, how he abused her. But this whole plan – meeting him at Barontrent and taking him to the Randle. That was my idea. I wanted to punish him for what he'd done to me. To Katya. Just for a few weeks. So he could understand the hell he put me through – for six years. Six years of my life that I'll never get back."

Hart holds up his hands. It's not for him to apologise, but he does need answers.

"How did you transfer Rory from Barontrent to the Randle?" he asks.

Rory stays silent. Hart looks over to Katya for an answer.

"I think I should call my solicitor," Rory says.

"It's OK, we're not here to press charges," Strover says. "Against either of you."

"Presumably you sedated him," Hart says. "When you picked him up from the prison gates? I mean, you're a psychiatrist, you know what to give someone."

"If you're not here to arrest us, why have you come?" Rory asks.

"So we understand exactly what to charge your brother with."

And to find out what Rory knows about death days, whether Hart should believe his brother's prediction that he will die tomorrow morning at 9.09 a.m. But that will have to wait.

"Kat told me that Finn had become obsessed with matcha tea before he was arrested," Rory says. "She brought a thermos with her when she picked him up at the prison gate."

"And it was spiked?"

Rory nods.

"Midazolam. I'm not a big fan of medication, as you may know, but it's good for emergency sedations."

"I spat in it too," Katya says.

Hart suppresses a smile.

"One other thing that's puzzling us," he says. "How did Finn manage to get you admitted in his place? Did he fake your breakdown too?"

Rory turns away, pressing his lips together.

"It was a long time ago," he says, wiping away a tear. "Six years, as you say. On the surface, my career in London was flourishing, but yes, I had a breakdown. A very real one – florid psychosis, visual and auditory hallucinations. Generalised amnesia. I'd recently lost my father, my marriage had ended, and I was taking on far too many clients." He pauses. "My approach to treating a patient could be personally exhausting. I invested a lot of time getting to know them, their past."

"And their future," Hart says, remembering Finn's words when they had sat in this very room three years ago. "Clinical intuition, I think that's what your brother called it."

"Is that what he said?"

For the first time, Hart detects real animosity in Rory's voice.

"So yes, I had a breakdown. And my brother came to visit me at my flat in London, found me in pieces, saw his opportunity. I realise now that he'd been watching me fall apart, waiting to strike – like a leopard in the long grass."

"And had you admitted to the Randle in his place."

"I was presenting with acute dissociative identity disorder. Not so difficult to get me sectioned."

It's good to hear Rory confirm what Hart and Strover had been wrestling with in the car.

"And you were kept there for six years? Until Dr Jennings discharged you?"

"A very enlightened psychiatrist. If only he'd arrived at the Randle sooner. I'd become aware that my brother had stopped visiting me, but I had no idea he was in prison, of course. When Dr Jennings began to reduce my meds, I realised I wasn't called Finn, but I didn't protest or explain that my real name was Rory, because I had to demonstrate that I was of sound mind and no longer suffering from dissociative identity disorder."

"The same condition that you then had Finn re-admitted with?"

Rory nods. "He insisted he was called Rory, which made his admission easier." He pauses. "I've broken the law, haven't I?"

"By impersonating someone else? Technically yes. But of course, at the time, Finn was also impersonating you. I have no idea how a jury might decide on something like that. But as my colleague here says, we're not here to arrest you or Katya. Not yet."

"Not yet?" Rory asks, glancing at Strover. "I thought you said..."

"We need your help," Hart says. "And if it's forthcoming, I'm sure the law will look more favourably on you impersonating someone in order to have them sectioned."

Put like that, they all know how serious the charge against Rory could be. But Hart's focus is to get Finn behind bars again. He looks across at Rory. It's obvious now why he had seemed hesitant at times yesterday, feigning amnesia, and why Katya had stepped in to answer some of their questions. She might have briefed him on the past six years, but he's still discovering all the damage that his brother has done in his name.

"I'm happy to help in any way I can," Rory says.

"Thank you. We're not just investigating what he did to you, which was very serious, of course. We think he was also responsible for several deaths, before we arrested him for firearms offences. A woman called Sophie and a young actor – Milo."

Rory casts his eyes downwards.

"Can you tell us anything more about them?" Hart asks, knowing that he hadn't been able to speak truthfully yesterday.

Rory glances at Katya.

"Some wine?" Rory asks.

"Just a small glass," Hart says. He knows he shouldn't, but it's a decent Burgundy. Rude not to. Strover declines.

"I was being kept in a state of drug-induced semi-consciousness," Rory says, as Katya tops up his own glass and pours one for Hart. Her hand is shaking. "But I was aware of Finn's visits. My meds were always dialled down the day before and we got into a routine of sorts. It was still a struggle to concentrate, but he'd bring along the notes of some of his patients and ask for my advice. I didn't want to help him, but I was punished with ECT if I failed to cooperate. And put back on max observation."

"Not much fun," Hart says, remembering Conor's experience of one-to-one 'specialling'.

"Traumatic. Sometimes, he'd bring in pieces of clothing that belonged to his patients. A silk scarf, perhaps. He wanted to know when the owner of the clothing was going to die. I wasn't a performing poodle, but I felt like one. Because we both knew that, if I was left alone for long enough with the scarf, I could start to sense the patient's lifespan. Once, when I was struggling to keep my eyes open, let alone tune into anyone, I remember he became very angry, said that the pashmina cardigan I was holding belonged to a 'famous fucking celebrity'."

Hart swirls around his wine and takes a sip, transfixed by Rory's words. Strover is too.

"And then, one day, Finn said that he was conducting an experiment. I was more frightened than usual and refused to cooperate. But when the ECT machine was wheeled into my room, I'm afraid my resistance crumbled – to my lasting shame. I just couldn't bear any more shocks, the disorientation that followed, the brutal erosion of my past."

"What sort of experiment was it?" Hart asks, glancing at Katya.

"A relatively simple one – and deeply troubling. He brought me a well-thumbed copy of *Hamlet*, complete with marginalia. It was more like a palimpsest – the notes were so detailed. He gave me a patient history too and a passport-sized photo of my 'target' – Milo. I read his case notes as best as my coshed brain would allow. I studied the photo as well, but it was the *Hamlet* that did it. As soon as I held the copy in my hands, rubbed its dry pages between my trembling fingers, I knew Milo's days were numbered. The feeling was unmistakeable."

"You had complete certainty at this point?" Hart asks, thinking back to how Finn had predicted his own death day with such conviction. *Three years from now, just days after you've turned fifty-seven.*

Rory nods.

"There is never any satisfaction, only a profound sadness. I looked at the photo of Milo again and begun to weep. He was so young, full of anxieties. But the danger to him, such a heavy sense of imminence... it felt strange, artificial. Manmade. I returned the copy of *Hamlet* and wrote down what I thought – I was non-verbal at the time. Finn knew I was holding something back, but oddly he didn't press me for more information. Which only confirmed my worst fears." Rory pauses. "He was trying to kill him."

"So Finn has no 'gift' at all?" Hart asks, trying to conceal his own sense of relief.

"Never has. It's always been a source of the greatest frustration to him, ever since we were young. The root of our enmity. And I'm afraid it led him to mimic my 'gift', for want of a better word—"

"Precognition?" Strover interrupts.

"If you want to call it that. He tried to imitate what I can do in the only way he could. The most perverse, evil way. If he couldn't see the future, he could at least shape it – tell someone what was going to happen to them and then personally make sure that it did."

Hart closes his eyes, his relief ebbing away. He tries not to think about his own death day tomorrow, Trumore, the cartridge, his recurring nightmare.

"Either through self-fulfilling prophecy or… I'm sorry, I'm finding this very difficult. I can't believe my own flesh and blood could do something so pernicious."

"Take your time," Strover says.

"Through self-fulfilling prophecy or by personal intervention."

"Was that the case with Sophie?" Hart asks.

"Sophie?"

"A homeless woman he met at a hostel in Swindon."

"OK," Rory says, gathering his thoughts. "Patient 'S'. It was a long time ago. My memory is not so good. Sophie was on drugs and had a deep-seated fear of dying."

"Thanatophobia," Hart says.

"Exactly."

Rory's eyes linger on Hart for a moment, surprised, perhaps, by his medical knowledge.

"He told Sophie that she was going to die," Rory says. "I never knew what happened to her, but I feared the worst."

Hart glances at his colleague.

"I'm afraid she was killed," Strover says. "We suspected your brother, but we could only arrest him for the possession of illegal weapons, including two sawn-off shotguns. I'm so sorry."

"Sophie's body was decapitated too," Hart says. He knows he's being blunt, but they need to know the facts, however gruesome. "We've never found her head."

Rory turns away, clearly shocked. Katya starts to sob.

"I knew Sophie was in grave danger," Rory says. "Where did this happen? When?"

"We think she died five years ago," Strover says, giving Hart a leave-this-to-me look.

"Two years later, we found her dismembered remains, on some scrubland near the Cricklade Road in Swindon," Hart adds. He can't help himself. "Your brother had told us where to look."

Rory appears lost in thought, his demeanour different. Distant.

"This is all so upsetting," he says. "How awful – for her family. And you say her head's never been found?"

A longer pause, as if he's in a trance.

"Might that be something you could help us with?" Strover asks.

Rory stares at Strover before he speaks.

"Maybe."

"In what way?"

Rory turns to gaze out the window.

"I've worried so much about his poor patients over the

years," he says. "Milo was one of the first cases I asked Katya about when I was discharged. I was devastated to hear he'd died."

"But not surprised?"

"I'd worked out by then what my brother was doing. Written it all out in my final days at the Randle. I addressed my words to him, hoping he'd read them one day, but they were really for my benefit, to understand the damage he'd caused, establish where it had all started. Over the years, he'd clearly refined his own so-called 'gift'."

"How do you mean?" Hart asks.

"Telling Sophie she was going to die and then killing her himself – if that's what he really did – was a very crude way to have 'predicted' her future. With Milo, his method had become more subtle. Having established that he suffered from profound anxieties about dying, Finn told him in no uncertain terms that he was going to die. And then the poor young man dropped dead – of sheer fear, it seems."

"And you have categorically never told a patient he was going to die?" Hart asks, thinking of *Scared to Death*, the book they'd taken away from here. "Told them their death day?"

"Of course not. And I never would. As I said yesterday, it would be clinically antagonising as well as profoundly unethical. An abuse of something sacred. Why do you ask?"

Hart's not thought of the gift of precognition as sacred before. He takes a deep breath and glances across at Strover, who gives him a nod of encouragement. They're here about Sophie and Milo, but they both know there's something else they need to discuss with Rory too.

His own death day.

56

"Before we put your brother away, three years ago, he told me when I was going to die," Hart begins, taking a deep draft of wine. "Tomorrow – 4 December."

Rory shakes his head in obvious disappointment. "He told you this? I'm so sorry."

Why's he apologising? Does he know something about his death day too?

"Finn was under arrest when he told me," Hart continues, trying to hold it together, stay professional. "Not a happy man. Angry with the police – with me. Two days ago, two men died in front of my eyes, warning of death days. Both had been unofficial patients of your brother while he was in Barontrent."

"Katya managed to discover that he'd been treating fellow prisoners, but we didn't know the details."

"Apparently they had both suffered from thanatophobia.

And then yesterday another former inmate with death issues, Grant Trumore, sends me a bullet with tomorrow's date engraved on the cartridge."

"This could be very serious," Rory says, now walking around the room, lost in thought. "May I ask something? Have you had any nightmares recently? About dying?"

Hart's palms begin to sweat. How does he know?

"Not about my own death exactly…" He pauses, reluctant to go down this road in front of Strover. He suddenly feels like he's on the couch.

"About what then?"

"The parkrun. I know it sounds stupid, but I'm running it tomorrow morning, with the whole family." He glances across at Strover, who is a keen runner. He hasn't confessed about his personal target. Strover's even more rapid than Jess. "Trying to get under twenty-five minutes – impress the family, you know. Beat my son – the usual competitive dad nonsense."

"And this gives you nightmares?"

"Twice now," Hart says. "Horrific. Never experienced anything like them."

He can feel Strover shifting awkwardly.

"But you don't actually die in these dreams?" Rory asks.

"Other people do. Like my mother. My son. But why does any of this matter? They're just dreams, aren't they?"

Rory pauses in front of the fire, staring into the flames. And then he turns to face them.

"If one believes, just for a moment, that time is multidimensional, there are those who also believe that dreams allow us to access the past, present and future simultaneously. At a subconscious level."

"What if you believe that time only flows one way?" Hart asks. He's had enough of all this flummery. "Like in an hourglass."

"You can turn an hourglass upside down."

"J.W. Dunne, *An Experiment with Time*," Strover says.

"You've read it?" Rory's eyes light up.

"Our theology teacher gave it to us all when we were teenagers. Serialism, I think Dunne called it. Made a big impression on me at the time – for a while we all kept dream diaries under our pillows, tried to spot predictions – but I'm not sure his theories withstand serious scientific scrutiny. Confirmation bias and all that."

Rory turns away. For a moment he must have thought he had an ally.

"All I'm saying is if DI Hart here is having dreams about loved ones dying, it's an indication of how embedded the notion of death has become in his own subconscious. How seriously he is taking it, how his amygdala is processing the threat, whether it's fight-or-flight time. And that's problematic. His nervous system is fully charged, on edge, which isn't necessarily a good thing. It can make one particularly vulnerable to fears about death. At a neurological level."

"Wouldn't I have to believe in my death day to fear it?" Hart says, aware of a sudden uptick in his pulse. "And for the record, I don't."

He knows he's not convincing anyone, least of all Rory. It's like telling his GP how few units of alcohol he drinks in a week.

"Was there anything else engraved on the cartridge?" Rory asks. "A time, perhaps?"

Hart looks at Rory and then at Strover, fighting back a wave of nausea. For the first time, it feels like he's asking them for their help.

"9.09 a.m."

57

Strover draws up outside Hart's house in Marlborough just before midnight. They are still stunned by the Garstans, marvelling at the sheer brazenness of what both brothers have done.

"Rory wants to help us," Strover says. "With the Sophie Mills case."

"How?" Hart asks.

"I think he knows where her head might be."

"Knows? Or can 'see' it?"

"I'm not sure it exactly matters at this stage, does it, sir?"

Hart's too tired to argue the rationalist's corner, tell Strover that remote viewing is for the birds. They sit in silence, the air starting to cool. It's been a long day and they are both shattered.

"Good luck with the parkrun tomorrow, sir," Strover says, starting up the engine.

"I'm not sure I can face it, to be honest."

"Because of your dreams? The nightmares?"

"I haven't done the training."

He knows Strover doesn't believe him.

"I'll arrange for some uniforms to turn up," he says.

"Want me to sort?"

"Would you mind? I'm just worried, that's all. About putting my family at risk. We're all running it. I know the threat's not credible, that Garstan's just trying to scare me, but, you know..."

"I'll make sure some uniforms are there. Maybe get an ARV to drive past too, wave their Glocks about. You just need to relax, sir – go out there and try to enjoy it."

"You sound like Mel."

"She's right. Good night, sir."

"Good night."

And then, for the first time since they've worked together, Strover leans over and gives Hart a peck on the cheek.

Mel is asleep by the time Hart creeps upstairs to bed. He knows it's not the best preparation for a parkrun, but he'd poured himself a Talisker en route and sits down with it in the wingback armchair in their bedroom. Mel had bought and upholstered the chair for his last birthday. He takes a sip of whisky, enjoys the weight of the glass, swirling the liquid around. The glass used to belong to his parents.

He glances at his watch. 11.59 p.m. He could just stay in bed for the whole day tomorrow, play it safe, take no risks with the parkrun, which begins at 9 a.m. Tell Mel he's not feeling well. Pull a sicky for the first time in his life. But he knows he must be there. He's promised Conor and Jess. Mel, too. And it will be fun. A family outing. As Strover says, he just needs to enjoy it. He might not have trained enough to get under twenty-five minutes, but he's not going to die either. Finn's a fraud – he'd struggle to predict Christmas.

He looks at his watch again. Midnight. It's now 4 December – his official death day. At least Finn's safely under lock and key at the Randle, heavily sedated, not even aware of the date. What can he do from there? But he knows it's not Finn who's bothering him. It's Trumore, whereabouts still unknown. Forensics have been unable to find any DNA on the cartridge, but they have confirmed it was a standard 5.56 NATO round. Common enough, popular with the military – snipers such as Trumore.

Five minutes later, Hart's lying in bed beside Mel, trying to sleep. But he can't. He's scared. Not just about his death day, but the dreams that might chase him through the night. He can't face another parkrun nightmare. Not that he believes they are portents of the future, but he's never had a recurring dream before.

At 1 a.m., the shipping forecast over, the Shetland Isles braced for squally showers, he slips out of bed and sits in the armchair again, unable to sleep. Maybe he should pour himself another Talisker, forget about his twenty-five-minute target. He glances across at Mel. She's in a deep sleep now, peaceful, beautiful. Nimu, their cat, is curled up at her feet. He walks over to a chest of drawers, looks at some framed photos, straightens them. Their wedding day; Conor as a toddler; his parents. He picks up a photo of his mother, taken days before she died. Smiling, looking at the camera as she plumps up some dahlias in a vase. Did she have any sense of what was about to happen? Any inkling at all in the days and hours and minutes before she died?

Walking over to the window, he pulls back a slip of curtain and looks down onto the close. Maybe the weather will save him from the run. Thick snow is still lying on the ground and more is forecast over the weekend. But the Marlborough parkrun is a stubborn beast, unlikely to be cancelled because of a bit of bad weather. He knows nothing will stop Conor and Jess either. And if they go, he'll have to run too. He's about to get back into bed, try again to sleep, when his phone buzzes.

A text from Rory.

58

Hart scrapes ice off his car windscreen, worried he'll wake the neighbours, grateful he hadn't necked a second whisky. The nighttime air is bitterly cold, his breath clouding. He'd managed to change back into his clothes and leave the house without waking Mel. 1.15 a.m. is too late to be out driving, particularly with the roads so icy, but he'd replied to Rory's text, saying he would get over to Pewsey as soon as he could. He'd thought about ringing Strover too, but this is about him now.

He drives slowly through the darkness, thinking about the text message. Rory has found something in the cellar that he wanted him to see. Fifteen minutes later, he turns into Rory's drive. The psychiatrist is waiting at the door, dressed in a grey fisherman's sweater and cords. Hart had grabbed some old jeans and a beaten-up leather jacket. A pair of blue forensic gloves and evidence bags too.

"Thanks for coming over," Rory says, ushering Hart into the house. "You might want to keep your coat on. It's cold down there."

"Katya never mentioned this place had a cellar," Hart says.

"There's no reason why she would have known about it," Rory says.

"We didn't know either – when we searched this place three years ago."

In retrospect, a poor oversight. They'd been too focussed on the weapons haul in the stable block.

"Shall we?" Rory asks, gesturing at the open cellar door in the hall. A tall dresser has been moved to one side. Flush to the wall, it sits on its own rug, which might explain why there are no marks on the polished wooden floor where it had been moved. Still, Hart and his team should have noticed the hidden door.

Hart steals a look at Rory. It's 1.30 a.m. Nobody knows where he is and he's about to go down into an old cellar with someone who looks identical to a man capable of scaring people to death.

"Is there a problem?" Rory asks.

"Never liked cellars," Hart says, managing a smile. "After you."

He follows Rory down the rickety wooden steps into the cold, brick-lined cellar, holding onto a rope bannister. The damp space is poorly lit – one lightbulb hanging down from a solitary braided cable – and water has pooled at one end. A full wine rack runs along the far wall.

"Clarets, the lot of them," Rory says. "Finn's choice."

"And you prefer a good Burgundy," Hart says, thinking back to the bottle of Côte de Beaune by the fireside.

"You don't miss much, do you?" Rory says, as they stand in a shifting pool of light. He puts a hand up to the swaying lightbulb, which Hart had knocked on his way down. The shadows settle.

"Is that Finn's too?"

Hart turns on his phone torch and shines it at an old chest freezer. Never good. The lid's closed, rust blistering up one side. "Pheasant", "partridge" and "venison" have been written in faded marker pen on big white labels.

"I'm a vegetarian," Rory says.

"Did you ever come down here? Before your brother moved in?"

"Too cold and damp," Rory says.

"But your brother clearly did," he says, glancing again at the freezer. He then shines his torch further down the dark, narrow cellar. A steel cabinet fixed to one wall catches his eye.

"What the hell's that?" Hart asks, as he walks over, careful to avoid the pools of water.

"Another gun cupboard," Rory says.

Hart closes his eyes. This is far worse than he feared. "Do you have the key?"

"I found it upstairs," he says, holding it out in front of him. "Top of the dresser – where Dad kept all the keys."

"And have you opened it?" Hart asks, pulling on his forensic gloves. "Or touched it in any way?"

"I thought I shouldn't. That's why I texted you. But I did find these, just over there."

Rory points towards the far corner of the cellar as he holds out his other hand: two brass cartridges.

"OK," Hart says. They are the same as the one he was

sent. "If you see anything else like that, I'd be grateful if you didn't touch it."

"I'm sorry, I was forgetting."

In reality, it's not such a problem. Identical twins might share the same DNA, but their fingerprints are different. Hart takes the cartridges and slips them into an evidence bag. He tries not to think too hard about the implications, what their presence here means, the date and time on the cartridge that was sent to him. 9.09 a.m. Less than eight hours away now.

He slots in the key and unlocks the cabinet.

"Oh, Christ," Hart says, looking up at the small arsenal of weapons. One airgun and three high-powered assault rifles.

"Looks like there was another one here," Rory says, shining his own phone torch at the bottom of the dusty cabinet, where there is an outline of the bottom of a gun butt. It can't have been taken very long ago.

Hart's stomach tightens. Rory was quick to notice the missing gun. Is he telling him the whole story here?

"Has anyone had access to the house?" Hart asks. "Down here? While your brother was away."

"Not that I'm aware of. I've been here for the past three weeks."

"On your own?"

"Apart from Katya. Keeping a low profile until Finn was released from Barontrent and I'd got him into the Randle."

"And you say Katya doesn't know about this place?"

"I'm certain."

Hart's pretty sure too. Which leaves one other person: Grant Trumore. As a former sniper in Afghanistan, he would have known what to do with the rifle. Maybe even known how to break into the house undetected. Unless Rory had helped him…

"There's something else you should see," Rory says, cutting across Hart's thoughts.

Rory sets off down the long cellar, shining his torch torch back at Hart's feet to show him the way. He's got an increasingly bad feeling about all this and needs to call it in, get Forensics down here pronto.

The ceiling becomes lower as they approach the far end. And then the roof space opens up to reveal a small skylight, big enough to allow in the sun during the day. All Hart can see now is the clear Wiltshire night sky, a spill of stars. At his feet, some old paper shooting targets, rotten and faded. He picks one up. A bullet hole at the edge, nothing in the centre. He reaches for another and the hole is closer to the bullseye.

Rory taps Hart on the shoulder, making him jump. He wishes he wouldn't do that.

"Sorry, but you should see this," Rory says, directing his torch at the wall. He shines it on a small iron ring.

"What is it?" Hart asks, moving the ring up and down in his gloved hand.

It's cold and rusty, old too. In the distant past, perhaps, the cellar had been used for keeping livestock. The ring has the feel of a tether, a shackle. And then Hart sees something, about head height, above the ring. Too high for livestock. An accusing smudge of darkness, spread across the brickwork. Is it damp? He leans in and sniffs: a mossy wetness. Maybe some sort of oil? But it's an old stain, rusty brown, and he knows that the dispersal pattern, the way it dissipates at the edges, means only one thing.

Hart looks back down the long, narrow cellar, the gun cupboard, the paper targets at his feet, the shackle on the wall.

"He used this place as a firing range, didn't he?" he says.

"I think so."

"Practised with those," he adds, kicking at the targets. "But what about that?"

They both stare at the stain on the wall.

"When my brother and I were younger," Rory says, "Finn used to shoot a lot of things, out in the garden. Doves, squirrels, rabbits, the occasional muntjac. With his air rifle." He nods at the gun cabinet on the wall. "Later he got into serious game shooting. But he shot at me once too."

"At you?"

Rory tells Hart about the incident in the apple orchard.

"And you know what the really scary part was? He had his eyes closed when he pulled the trigger."

"Bloody hell."

"When I tried to challenge him later, he said that shooting someone like that made him an instrument of blind fate."

"Had he practised with his eyes shut?"

"Oh yes. He was obsessed with muscle memory, told me that the brain is good at sighting a target if it makes a sound. At least on the x-axis, left to right. The y-axis, up and down – that's a bit more hit and miss. People tend to shoot low if they are blindfolded."

"Not great if you've got an apple on your head."

"I was lucky." Rory pauses, glancing at the brickwork. "But I fear someone here was not so fortunate."

They both stare again at the wall, the dark stain.

"It was Sophie, wasn't it?" Rory asks.

"I fear so," Hart says. "Finn must have brought her here from Swindon, abducted her when she was walking over to her friend's house. Sedated her too, presumably. But probably not with matcha tea."

Below the belt, but Hart needs to keep some distance between them until he knows exactly what went on down here.

"For the record, I don't like matcha tea."

"But you knew your brother did."

"I didn't kill him, DI Hart," he says. "Didn't shoot him in a cellar. I just had him sectioned – for a few weeks."

"I know," Hart says. "But you're both psychiatrists, both know how to sedate someone without consent."

"Rapid tranquilisation is sometimes unavoidable for agitated patients. And you're quite right: Finn would have known what to give Sophie – intramuscularly. An injection. Midazolam, maybe something stronger."

"Do you think he meant to kill her?" Hart asks, trying not to think too hard how scared Sophie must have been, semi-drugged, as she was shackled to the wall in a freezing cold cellar. He can only hope the medication would have numbed the fear.

"Knowing Finn, he would have explained to her that it was down to fate, not to him. And then he would have asked her to place an apple on her head, just like he did with me."

"So she can't have been that heavily sedated," Hart asks. "If she had to balance an apple. She would have known what was about to happen to her."

"My brother is a sadist, DI Hart. Spent most of his childhood inflicting pain – mental and physical – on me, our parents, particularly Dad. Finn is fuelled by rage, envious that he doesn't possess my abilities. He had already told Sophie when she was going to die, preyed on her existential anxieties. Now it was crunch time: her death day. If she lived, she could walk away – her worst fears confronted. And if she died, well, that was her fate. And Finn could claim that he'd predicted the future."

"Dear God," Hart says.

"And knowing Finn, knowing his complete inability to see the future, he would have… aimed low."

Hart looks up at Rory, who has turned pale, his eyes closed.

"You OK?"

It's a while before he answers. "She's here," he says.

They both stand in silence, the temperature seeming to drop. If Hart was a religious man, now would be a good moment to offer up a prayer for Sophie, in this dark, damp cellar at 1.30 a.m., the ancient wall smeared with an innocent woman's blood. Instead, he bites his lip and reminds himself this is why he became a detective, to bring people like Finn to justice.

"He must have used a high-powered weapon, one of those," Hart says, as they walk back down the cellar, gesturing at the gun cabinet as they pass. He doesn't want to dwell on what Rory's just said. He'd rather stick to the procedural. "And then he took her body back to Swindon, in a suitcase, and buried her. Far away from here. And I suspect long after we'd finished searching the area too. Which means he must have kept her body down here for a while, a few months perhaps."

"The chest freezer," Rory says.

"It seems the most obvious place. I'm assuming you haven't used it? Being a vegetarian?"

Rory shakes his head as Hart walks over to the freezer. Manufacturers had to radically change their design in the 1960s after numerous deaths. Too many people – mainly young children – falling into them and unable to get out, dying of suffocation rather than the cold.

Hart slowly lifts up the lid. A wave of cold air sweeps up from the neatly wrapped joints of meat. Starting at one end, he stacks the pheasants to one side until he's reached the bottom of the freezer. Then he does the same with the venison, having first replaced all the pheasants. His hands are starting to freeze, despite the gloves.

"He certainly liked his game," Hart says, trying to sound relaxed, but his whole body has tensed up.

And then he sees it, sealed in bubble wrap, lying at the very bottom of the freezer. For a moment, he tries to dismiss it as an unusual cut of meat. The shape is so strange, the top split open like a Venus flytrap. Slowly, respectfully, he lifts it up to take a closer look, turning it in his hands. Apart from the catastrophic injury, the head is well preserved, suggesting that it must have been severed and frozen soon after Sophie was killed. He puts it back and closes the lid, his hands shaking with cold and fear.

"Thank you," he says quietly to Rory. "Thank you."

59

Hart watches Rory breathe life into the dying fire. He'd accepted his offer of a whisky – they both needed a drink after what they'd found in the cellar. He's already called the case in and CSI will be here any minute. Finally, he'll be able to charge Finn with Sophie's murder. With luck, CSI will find evidence of Grant Trumore too, whose biometrics are in the system thanks to his long stint in Barontrent.

Finn must have told Trumore about his secret gun cupboard when they were fellow inmates and he was purportedly treating him for "Harm OCD". How had Dr Anwar described it? *A condition characterised by intrusive thoughts and impulses about inflicting harm on others and themselves. In his case, he was worried he might go around shooting people.* Trumore had spent six months in Finn's so-called care. God knows what he'd said. Probably offered him money to finish the job. Either way,

Trumore now appears to be on the run with one of Finn's high-powered rifles.

"This place is going to get turned over by Forensics, I'm afraid," Hart says, as Rory sits back in the armchair opposite him. "I've told them not to blue-light it here."

"So the neighbours won't know? Thank you. I'm more concerned about the art. And Romulus here."

Hart watches as a black kitten skips up to Rory's chair for a stroke.

"I'll put in a special request," Hart says. He likes cats. Not so keen on the name, though. Didn't he kill his twin brother Remus?

They both watch Romulus attack Rory's hand, enjoying his attention. Rory had got him the day after he was discharged from the Randle.

"I'm so sorry about Sophie," Rory says.

"Me too. How did you know? That we'd find her head down there?"

It's a while before Rory answers.

"I'll leave that for others to decide. Perhaps I just understand my brother better than anyone. He's my twin, after all. Unfortunately. I could also sense her presence."

"I just wish we'd sensed her presence three years ago," Hart says.

Another silence.

"Are you OK?" Rory asks, glancing across at Hart.

"Fine, why?"

"I've got to be honest with you, DI Hart—"

"Silas, please."

It's past 2 a.m. and he's through with formalities.

"I'm worried about you, can sense how scared you are

about what might lie ahead today. Particularly after tonight. You must be on edge. I fear you have been ever since my brother first told you about these wretched death days."

"There's a man out there tonight with a high-powered rifle and a bullet with my name on it. I think I'm entitled to be a little scared, don't you?" Rory's right. He is on edge. And he doesn't like people pointing it out. "That's not some hokum bollocks about death days. It's a fact. Although, I'll admit, the death day thing doesn't help. Or don't you believe in them now?"

Hart sounds more angry than he means, but Rory must be used to people venting in front of him, expressing their darkest thoughts on his couch. The psychiatrist sits back, sips on his whisky.

"I think it's possible to foresee when someone's going to die, but I don't believe in telling them. That's the difference. Not unless it could avert, say, an accident."

"Wouldn't that rather invalidate your original prediction?"

"You're not the first to think so. Just ask Jonah, who prophesied that Nineveh would be destroyed in forty days. When God decided not to flatten the city, Jonah was furious, some say because he feared being branded a fool – a false prophet. But not all precognition is about prophecy – sometimes it can be a warning."

Hart's never been into religion, but it doesn't feel entirely inappropriate to be discussing the Old Testament in the early hours of his death day. 9.09 a.m. – seven hours away now. At times like this, he could do with a little faith. Damn Finn, damn his deadly portents.

"Jonah's prophecy was right," Rory says. "If the citizens

of Nineveh hadn't repented, their city would have been obliterated. But they chose to avert disaster because they had agency – free will." Rory pauses. "You have agency, too, Silas, even on your so-called death day."

Hart looks around the low-lit sitting room. Romulus has calmed down and is now posing like a miniature sphinx, staring into the flames of the fire.

"So what do you suggest I do? Stay in bed all day?"

"Tell me about this Grant Trumore."

"Former sniper in Afghanistan. Not used to missing his target. Your brother might have hypnotised him, for all I bloody know. Programmed him to kill me. Why else did he have a copy of *The Manchurian Candidate* on his shelves here? He spent enough time in jail with him – six bloody months." Hart looks away. "Sorry," he adds, waving a hand as if he's swatting a fly. "It's late."

Rory's a good listener. Something about his manner has made Hart open up tonight. He feels better already.

"It's OK," Rory says. "Finn's trying to get into your head and you mustn't let him. He's safely sedated in a bed in Norfolk."

"His game is still playing out here, though, isn't it?"

Hart's feeling agitated again, his pulse racing. He needs to calm down.

"From what you've told me, it seems that Sophie was the only person he physically killed. Shot her here in the cellar. Which was utterly unforgiveable, of course, but it was also high-risk and complicated, given he had to dispose of her body too. I know Finn and that would have frightened him. He might be a sadist, but he's also a coward. Everyone else? Milo, the two prisoners who died in front of you this week – he messed with their minds. Told them they were going to die, scared them to death. Much easier. No evidence. He's trying to do that to you too. And you just have to resist, not play his games. Believe me, I've endured a lifetime of his bullying. The only way you'll end up dying today is if you believe it's your death day."

"So I just go about my normal Saturday? Do the parkrun with my family? Never mind that there's a mad gunman on the loose. And even though the parkrun just happens to begin at 9 a.m. – nine minutes before I'm meant to die?"

Rory nods.

"Finn can't predict the future, Silas," he says. "You've got to trust me on this. He only chose the 4th of the month because it's unlucky for some. The Chinese and Japanese are both fearful of the number four, so much so that stress-induced cardiac arrests increase by thirteen per cent on the 4th of every month."

"That's not exactly making me feel better," Hart says.

"He's trying to scare you to death, that's all he can do. And it's pathetic. You need to forget about him. Live your life."

"So," Hart says, pausing. "Just for the record, you personally don't have any inkling, any funny feeling or foreboding that I'm going to die today? I mean you sensed correctly down there that Sophie's head was close by, so you've clearly got… a gift of some sort."

Hart's been wanting to ask him for a while now, but he has always resisted. Felt too embarrassed.

"I thought you didn't believe in precognition?"

"I don't," Hart says hastily. "But, you know, I take all the information I can, wherever it's from. I'm the sort of person who looks both ways before I cross a one-way street."

"Did Finn appear in your dream?"

"My dream? He did, yes. Ran alongside me."

Hart remembers how he thought he was hearing voices when Garstan had started to speak.

"Then maybe I'll come along too today. Run with you. That way, on one level, your dream will have been true, but he won't actually be there. His friendly identical twin will be instead. It might help to take the sting out of things." Rory smiles. "Negate the danger."

Hart doesn't like the logic, the assumption that his dream might prove to be true. At whatever level. He looks out the window. Two CSI vans are turning into the drive, followed by a patrol car and another plain vehicle – theirs. Earlier, he'd messaged Strover as a courtesy, to keep his colleague in the loop.

"Here comes the cavalry," Rory says.

"Your house is about to become a crime scene. I apologise again for what might happen."

Five minutes later, Hart is in the hall with Strover, watching CSI officers in white oversuits file through the front door and down into the cellar, carrying floodlights and boxes of heavy equipment. At Hart's request, Rory had left the dresser to one side and the door open.

"There was no need for you to come," Hart says to Strover.

"Had any sleep, sir?" his colleague asks.

He shakes his head. "How about you?"

"Three hours, more than enough."

Hart expands on what he'd briefly written in his text, tells Strover about the grim discovery in the cellar, how they should have searched the main house three years ago.

"At least no one's to blame for missing Sophie when we searched the scrubland first time around."

It's good of Strover to say so. Hart's always been bothered that his team had not found the suitcase, but Sophie's headless body had yet to be buried there.

"Swindon's more than thirty miles from here," Strover adds. "Presumably Finn thought it would incriminate someone local when Sophie was eventually found."

"Which it very nearly did, thanks to Ward's batshit theory of a fantasy man in Angelo's."

"And without a head, Finn had calculated there was no evidence that she'd been shot, which might have implicated him. Still high risk to tell us her whereabouts."

"He was desperate for people to believe he had a 'gift' – like his brother."

Once Forensics have finished setting up all their equipment, Hart and Strover go down to the basement, where he briefs the CSM on his own theory that Sophie Mills was shot dead in the cellar and kept in the chest freezer before being dismembered and moved, except for her head, to Swindon at a later date.

"I need Sophie's DNA from the far wall as well – and proof that Grant Trumore came here and took a gun. Oh yes, and look for traces of apple."

60

Hart stands next to Mel, Conor and Jess as one of the parkrun volunteers asks how far people have come today. Two runners are from Cardiff, one from Glasgow, but they are trumped by someone from Sydney. A loud, welcoming cheer rises up from the crowd, bodies steaming in the cold winter air. Another cheer for someone volunteering at their 100th parkrun. Hart scans his fellow runners: no sign of Rory.

More than 150 people have braved a misty December day to run two testing laps, several with yapping dogs straining on their leads, one with a pram. They're all mad, him included. Mel's wearing a bobble hat and gloves. He's sporting baggy trackies and a fleece. Conor and Jess have stripped down to their running shorts and vests. Nutjobs, the pair of them.

"Alright, Da? Ready for the big one?" Conor asks, putting an arm round Hart's shoulders.

Hart manages a smile. He must volunteer himself one of these days. They do a great job. And he likes the idea of shouting words of encouragement to passing runners as they reach the top of the long, painful hill beside the golf course, rather than struggling up it himself.

"You've got this," Jess says. "There are pacesetters today."

"I might need a pacemaker after this."

Hart's only half joking. Ever since he arrived, ten minutes ago, his body has felt heavy with dread, his soul weighed down by an existential anxiety that's off the scale, even by his own recent high standards. It might just be the lack of sleep – he got back from Pewsey at 6 a.m. and managed two hours – but a part of his brain, a very tired part, thinks that it's the beginning of the end: the first signs of one of Malcolm's autonomic storms that will soon sweep through his sympathetic nervous system and fell him forever. If only Rory was here. His presence would be reassuring.

At 5 a.m. this morning, while Hart was still chatting to the psychiatrist in the sitting room, the CSM had come up from the cellar to say that they'd identified a single fingerprint on the gun cabinet key that matched Trumore's. It was the sole print they'd found, suggesting he'd tried to be careful. And it confirmed Hart's worst fears: the former sniper was not only out there somewhere, having breached his licence conditions, but was now in possession of a high-powered assault rifle.

Hart had requested an immediate wanted/missing flag on the Police National Computer database, as well as an all-ports alert. He hadn't told Mel, just as he hadn't told her that he'd been out for most of the night. She was a deep sleeper and hadn't heard him leave for Pewsey or return at dawn. He didn't want to worry her. All he said over porridge was that Strover had dropped him off at midnight after a successful trip to Norfolk; Rory Garstan has an evil identical twin called Finn; and Strover's innocent kiss on his cheek, as unexpected as it was welcome, was like a daughter's. (The one they'd never had, but he didn't say that, of course, or that Strover would object to being gendered as a daughter.)

He glances around the common, checking the horizon, a cluster of trees by the car park, their boughs reaching up like gnarled fingers into the mist. No sign of Rory. At Strover's request, two uniforms are now standing on the roadside, near their parked patrol car. Another pair of officers is mingling with some onlookers by the car park. Strover, still at the house in Pewsey, had also spoken with a mate in the Armed Response Unit. An ARV is due to drive by in a couple of minutes, cruise the common for half an hour. Hart owes Strover big time. He couldn't face telling colleagues that he was requesting armed back-up because of a bad dream.

"You alright, Sile?" Mel says now, clapping her hands together in the cold. "You look crackered."

"Long day yesterday," he says.

"It's the weekend now," she says. "And if you're really good, we might all go for a bacon sarnie at the golf club afterwards."

"Did someone just say bacon?" Conor asks, jumping up and down in the cold. Jess gives him a playful hug. They're like a pair of puppies. Hart knows he should be happy, never seen Conor in a better place. But he can barely raise a smile. He glances around the crowd again as the cheery volunteer runs through the final checklist. One of the young uniforms by the road raises a hand of acknowledgement. Hart turns away and scans the assembled runners. Still no sign of Rory. Or Trumore.

"What's with all your colleagues?" Mel says, as Conor and Jess mess about, pretending to warm up. "Come to cheer you on?"

"Must be an exercise or something," Hart says, trying to make light of the police presence. But Mel knows him too well and shakes her head in disbelief.

"You're not serious," she says. "Tell me you didn't ask them to be here because of your nightmares."

It's no good. He can't deny it any longer.

"Strover asked, just as a precaution."

"Against what, Sile?" Mel says. "A prediction by some jumped-up shrink three years ago that you were going to die today?" She looks across at the assembled uniforms again. "Just don't tell the taxpayer – they might want their money back."

"I was sent a cartridge at the office with today's date engraved on it," Hart says. "A time too: 9.09 a.m." He glances at his watch. "Eleven minutes from now."

He didn't want to tell Mel, but he realises that she needs to know, calculate for herself the risk of being here.

"You what?"

"From one of Garstan's former patients. A gun's missing from his house too. So yes, it's just a precaution, as I say, and you really don't have to be here, or Conor or Jess. But I can't let this man win – can't let him get into my head."

"You should have told me, Sile."

"Well I'm telling you now. And it's nothing, Garstan's twin

just trying to scare me, but an Armed Response Vehicle will be driving by in a minute – another precaution. We don't have to be here, any of us – you, Conor, Jess, me – but I know how much everyone's been looking forward to it. As a family."

"Just a precaution," Mel says, sounding more serious.

"Just a precaution. Garstan's playing games. Messing with my mind. And I won't allow him. But if you want to go, I understand, totally get it."

"If you think it's safe to be here, then we'll stay too," Mel says, jogging on the spot.

Before Hart can reply, a parkrun volunteer asks if there are any under-11s running today. A few hands go up and she explains the rules.

"She says I mustn't leave your side, Da," Conor says, grinning at him.

"I think that's for people even more childish than you," Hart says. He needs to lighten up.

Preliminaries over, they make their way over to the start line with the other runners.

"Just forget about your time, Sile," Mel says. "And, you know, the other thing."

"Forget about his time?" Conor says, grinning. "It's twenty-five or die today. Isn't that right, Da? And what other thing? Lot of feds here, aren't there?"

But Hart isn't listening. He's looking towards the golf course at the far end of the common. No golfers have braved the bad weather, but he thinks he sees a figure in the mist-shrouded trees, where the footpath follows the road towards Rockley. Maybe not. He used to set off for runs down there, across to Fyfield Down, when Conor was young and had rugby training on the common on Sundays.

His phone starts to vibrate in his fleece pocket. Turning away from Mel, he glances at the screen. It's Strover.

"I've got to take this," he says.

"But we're about to start," Mel protests.

"Strover?" Hart says, one finger in his other ear. Dogs are barking all around him now. "Where are you?"

"Still at the house with Rory. Sorry to bother you, sir, but I thought you should know."

"Know what? Keep it quick. I'm about to break the land-speed record."

"Rory's just been called by the Randle. His brother Finn managed to get himself discharged early this morning. 5 a.m. They're not quite sure how or why."

Hart feels his chest tighten.

"Do they know where he is now?"

"I've asked Norfolk police to put out an alert."

"Jesus. Get it flagged on the PNC too. I'll call in twenty-five minutes. Maybe sooner."

Some chance. He puts his phone away just as everyone surges towards the start line.

"Here," Mel says, passing him an earphone. They've agreed to share playlists, providing Hart can have Thin Lizzy's "The Rocker" for the opening kilometre. After that it's over to her choice, usually Billy Joel. Maybe she's chosen something else for today. The guitar chords have started, powerful, distorted. Hart glances at his watch. 9 a.m. on the nose.

"Three, two, one..."

61

9.05 a.m.

It's at the 1 km mark – five minutes in, bang on schedule – that the pain begins in Hart's chest, growing worse as he slogs up the long hill at the far side of the common. The snow-wet grass doesn't help, nor does the sight of Conor in front of him, pulling further ahead. Hart's been here before, but this time he tells himself it's not a dream.

A fit father and his annoyingly young son overtake him. Seven, maybe eight years old?

"Alright?" the dad says.

"Saving myself for the second lap," Hart says, trying to remain calm.

And then he hears a familiar voice behind him. Or is it in his head?

"I thought I'd join you."

He spins round to see Rory – at least he assumes it's

Rory – running up beside him.

Hart tries in vain to focus on the runners ahead. As subtly as he can, he glances across at Garstan. He's not wearing a watch on either wrist. He looks at his own.

9.06 a.m.

"This is Dr Garstan," Hart says to Mel, not taking any chances.

"Rory, please," Garstan says, smiling at Mel.

"Nice to meet you," Mel says, but she looks anything but happy, glaring at Hart with wide, questioning eyes as the three of them run on together.

"I thought you were going to miss the start," Hart says. "Thanks for coming."

"Apologies, I was held up."

They run on in silence. Hart doesn't know what to say, wonders if he's being paranoid. Rory had offered last night to come on the run, after all, to "negate the danger", as he'd put it. So he should assume it's him, be pleased that he's here. It certainly *looks* like Rory, but Finn had left the Randle early this morning. It's possible, just possible, that he could be here now, if he'd driven like Strover, but he wouldn't be in a fit state to run 5K, surely? Not after being so recently sedated, even if his medication had been tapered before his release. The man running beside him looks positively relaxed in a dark-blue Nike tracksuit and Saucony shoes.

"Your brother's been discharged," Hart says, as the 25-minute pacesetter overtakes them. Today's no longer about times. He takes out his headphone, suddenly feeling the need to draw on all his senses. "5 a.m. this morning."

"That's exactly why I'm able to be here with you today,"

Garstan says, smiling. "Dr Jennings doesn't like to keep people sedated for ever."

What the hell's that supposed to mean? He should just pull over now, tell Mel to stop too. Go home and spend the rest of the day in bed, as he'd planned. Clear his head of all these bloody shrinks.

"And it's definitely you?" Hart asks. "I mean, stupid question, I know, but this is exactly what happened in my fucking dream. Why should I believe it's you?"

Mel suddenly calls out. "Conor, you OK?"

Up ahead, their son is on the ground, rolling over.

"Conor!" Hart shouts, accelerating towards him. This can't be happening again, not for real. But he knows he's not dreaming.

9.07 a.m.

"I'm fine," Conor says, getting back to his feet and rejoining the run, slightly embarrassed. He raises a hand above him. "Just slipped over."

Jess, further ahead, slows down to check on him and they run off together.

Hart breathes a sigh of relief.

"You're not dreaming, it's OK," Garstan says, back at his side again.

9.08 a.m.

For the next thirty seconds, they run on in silence, side by side, the three of them. Hart can feel Mel's frostiness from here. This isn't what they'd planned. It was meant to be a fun family event, but not for the first time in their married life, his work has come crashing in to ruin everything.

"Conor's doing well," Garstan says, just as he'd done in his nightmare. "I didn't tell you last night, but I dropped in at the hostel on Fleming Way earlier this week, reassured him that he wasn't about to die."

"Thanks for that," Hart says, his mind racing.

"You said that my brother had met him there when he was on day release from Barontrent, threatened to reveal his death day."

"He told Conor that he might not have long to live. Not great for anyone to hear, particularly someone as mentally fragile as him."

"Well I put that lie to bed – I can't believe how much harm my brother has done in my absence. Conor's an impressive young man – you should be very proud of him. Both of you."

Mel glances across at Hart. She seems less frosty now, but he still wonders if he's dreaming. And then, at the top of the hill, as they follow the path round to the left, he spots him again, this time more clearly. A figure in what looks like a black biker jacket, partially hidden behind one of the trees between the road and the golf course. And the unmistakeable profile of a barrel, complete with compressor. He must be at least 100 yards away and if Hart hadn't been looking in his direction, he wouldn't have spotted him. He glances at his watch again, barely able to breathe.

9.09 a.m.

A moment later, Garstan, to his right, accelerates and cuts across Hart's path, placing himself between him and the man in the trees. The shot that follows is not loud, more of a sharp crack, but the effect is instant, knocking Garstan backwards to the ground. Mel screams as blood blossoms across Garstan's tracksuit top. And then everyone else is screaming too, running in all directions, away from Hart, who has crouched down beside Garstan's body. He rips off his own fleece and presses it against the gunshot wound to stem the flow of blood.

"Let me take over," Mel says, by his side now.

"You should get away from here," Hart says. "Get Conor and Jess out of this place too. None of you should have come. I'm so sorry."

But Mel is insistent. He moves aside, glancing across at the trees where the shot had come from. He sees a figure jump on a motorbike, parked on the side of the road, and roar off towards Rockley. Pulling out his phone, he calls for an ambulance and backup, giving details of the bike and its direction.

"Grant Trumore," Hart repeats. "Ex-military, armed and dangerous." And then he gestures to the two uniforms on the road and points after Trumore. They jump into their patrol vehicle and speed off after him, followed a moment later by an ARV, which must have just turned up. A bit bloody late. Two more uniforms come running over from the car park.

"Check his pulse," Mel says.

Hart pulls up Garstan's sleeve, noticing a faint patch of paler skin on his right wrist. Is it a tan mark, from his watch? Enough to prove that he's left-handed? That he's Rory?

"Nothing," Hart says, as he feels in vain for a pulse. Garstan knew what was going to happen and stepped in to save him.

"What the fuck just happened?"

Hart looks up to see Conor with Jess, who is crying.

"Someone's been shot," Hart says, glancing at Garstan.

"I can see that."

Someone very brave, but now's not the time to explain that this man just took a bullet intended for him. He'll tell them later. Mel has started to give CPR, her hands wet with blood – he tries to banish an image of his mother – and then she glances across at him, resignation in her eyes.

"Keep going," he says.

"Where's that bloody ambulance?" she asks, as she continues to pump his chest. And then they hear the sound of a siren, coming up the hill from Marlborough.

Garstan's eyes are open, but Hart's not sure if there's any life behind them.

"Thank you," he hears himself whispering. "Whoever you are."

62

Hart turns into the house in Pewsey for what he hopes will be the last time. CSI officers are still crawling all over the property – he's asked them to search every inch – and a uniform is stood guard outside the front door. Mel had gone in the ambulance with Garstan, who was somehow still alive. Her CPR has given him a fighting chance. Hart, running on adrenaline, had stayed until Forensics turned up and the entire common had been sealed off. Because of his personal involvement, a colleague has been appointed Senior Investigating Officer. Ward had threatened to turn up too, which is why Hart had headed back over to Pewsey. He'll return to Marlborough shortly, give a more detailed statement to his colleagues, help where he can. And talk to Ward.

Strover comes out of the house as he parks up. He's already explained over the phone about Garstan, but he wants to give a fuller debrief on the parkrun, more for his own benefit, he suspects. He's so tired, he's struggling to distinguish between dream and reality, his nightmares and what just happened on the common. At least Conor is OK – shaken but physically fine. His fall had scared Hart far more than the sight of Trumore with a high-powered rifle aimed at him.

"What a bloody morning," he says, looking across at the house. He acknowledges the uniform. "They've just caught Trumore," he adds. "Up near Wootton Bassett." A colleague had told him on the drive over from Marlborough.

"He didn't get far."

"The chopper was already up, apparently."

Hart can't deny he's relieved Trumore has been caught. The colleague also said that he had a strange, glazed look about him when he was arrested, which didn't sound good. Maybe that's why he didn't have the presence of mind to take a second shot, once he realised that he'd hit the wrong target. He hadn't been programmed for a controlled pair. His thoughts are disturbed by Malcolm, who walks over to him in his forensic overalls.

"Couldn't resist coming over," he says, pulling off his blue of gloves. "For Sophie's sake."

Hart's strangely reassured to see the pathologist – providing he doesn't want to talk cricket.

"I'm assuming she was killed by a single shot from a powerful rifle?" Hart asks.

"Absolutely. Extensive comminuted skull fractures, typical of high-energy trauma. What's called a Kronlein shot."

"Which is?" Hart asks, not sure he wants to know the answer.

"First identified by Swiss surgeon Rudolf Kronlein in 1899, it's usually fired from close range, but it can be achieved at distance if the bullet velocity is more than 800 metres per second."

"What sort of weapon?"

"A Kronlein's possible from up to 35 metres with a standard 5.56 NATO round, so in this case an assault rifle or carbine. One of those guns in his cellar war chest would have done it. If you want chapter and verse, muzzle gases cause the entire skull to explode. Complete evisceration of the brain, I'm afraid. It would have been messy down there."

"Thanks for that," Hart says, as Malcolm strides over to talk to the CSM. It would explain the stain on the wall, how hard it would have been for Finn to remove all traces of blood and brain matter from the brickwork.

"You OK, sir?" Strover asks.

"Why does everyone keep asking me if I'm OK? I'm fine. In the circumstances. Just fine. Thank you for asking, though." He doesn't mean to snap at Strover. "Sorry."

"We were all just saying how lucky it was – at least for you, sir – that Rory actually made it to the parkrun," Strover says, pausing. "At one point, he wasn't sure he could be there."

"How do you mean?" Hart asks, trying to ignore a sudden sinking feeling. Maybe Rory hadn't made it?

"After you left here this morning, he said he would try to join you, but he had things to do in Marlborough first. Thought it was touch and go."

"Oh, he made it alright."

Hadn't he? Just as more seeds of doubt take root in his

tired, fertile mind, a silver Golf pulls in through the gates and parks up. They both stare at the driver in disbelief.

"So who the hell's that?" Strover asks, as Garstan steps out of the car in a navy Nike tracksuit and Saucony running shoes.

"What the—" Hart's not the fainting sort, but for a moment he thinks he might pass out.

"I've just heard what happened," Garstan says, walking over to them. "Am I glad to see you alive."

Hart tries to speak, but no words come. Strover is speechless too.

"It seems my brother had a conscience after all," Garstan says. "Got himself discharged from the Randle this morning – just in time to take the bullet. I'm so relieved – and surprised, to be honest. I never thought he had it in him. He must have had second thoughts, knew he had to stop Trumore, but didn't know how. That man was on a mission. Hypnotised, I gather. Sorry I couldn't get to the common in time. When I finally turned up, the whole place had been sealed off by the police."

Hart still can't speak. How does he know that Trumore had been hypnotised? He looks at Garstan's wrists, searching in vain for a watch. And then he stares into his eyes, deep into his soul, looking for a clue, anything, that might identify him. Because Hart is sure – as eggs is eggs again – that the man standing in front of them is Finn. Call it intuition. Maybe even a gift. The brazenness of turning up here is entirely in keeping with the man who was prepared to section his own brother and steal his life for six years.

He glances at Strover, whose eyes have widened in support. And then he calls over the uniform.

"Dr Finn Garstan," Hart begins. "You are under arrest for suspicion of the murder of Sophie Mills and for aiding and abetting grievous bodily harm. You do not have to say anything. But it may harm your defence if you do not mention, when questioned, something which you later rely on in court. Anything you do say may be given in evidence."

He nods at the uniform, who steps forward, pulling out a pair of handcuffs.

"What the hell are you playing at?" Garstan says, as the uniform secures his wrists behind his back.

"I'm not playing at anything," Hart says. "I'm assuming you calculated you'd be a wanted man from the moment you left the Randle this morning. And your only chance of escape – of freedom – was to impersonate your brother. Again."

"You've got this so wrong," Garstan says, shaking his head.

Hart ignores him. For the first time in days, he actually has some clarity.

"You were always planning to turn up at the parkrun today, weren't you? 4 December, my death day, to watch Trumore take the shot," he continues. "To witness your so-called prediction come true. It was a gamble, but three years ago, when you made the prediction, I had started to attend parkruns, first in Lydiard Park, now in Marlborough. My woeful results all on the internet. It was something to work with. A middle-aged, overweight man with advanced hypochondria and a mother who died at fifty-seven takes up running. And 9.09 a.m. was a pretty safe bet – I'd be out running somewhere, given parkruns always start at 9 a.m., worried about my health, my age. Sniper Alley – literally in this case. But you turned up too late today, didn't you? Hadn't anticipated your brother would get you sectioned in return. Hadn't anticipated his supreme act of selflessness, either. Not a human quality you're familiar with. So you started to spin your narrative again. Only this time, Finn, nobody's bloody buying into it, least of all me."

Garstan's been listening to every word, despite himself, and the colour has drained from his face. He's beginning to look pale, ashen, but Hart's not finished yet.

"Tell me," he says. "Those hourglasses. The ones filled with the ground-up collarbone of Sophie Mills that you gave to your victims. Sorry, patients. Clients. Milo, Darren, Si, even my own son Conor – how dare you? What was that all about? A symbol of their mortality? Of your power over life and death? Or just a nod to your Freemason friends?"

"Be very careful, DI Hart," Garstan says, looking more unwell by the second. "You have no idea who you're dealing with here."

"Is that right? I'm not sure DCS Ward can help you now."

Garstan looks away. Is he finally beaten? He turns to face them again, but this time he's lost for words. And then he begins to lose his balance too, swaying so much that the uniform steps forward to steady him. Something's not right. Is it remorse? Guilt? Unlikely. An autonomic storm?

"You OK?" Strover asks, looking at Garstan.

Hart's mobile starts to ring. It's Mel.

"How is he?" Hart asks, watching as Strover and the uniform struggle to keep Finn upright.

"That's why I'm calling. Rory's just gone into cardiac arrest again. Not looking good."

At least Rory's at the hospital now. Mel's done more than her fair share of chest compressions in recent days.

"Where are you?" she asks.

"Pewsey. At his house. With Rory's twin brother." He glances up at Garstan, who has now slumped to the gravel. "I'm going to have to call you back."

Hart hangs up as Strover and the uniform lay Garstan out on the ground. Strover takes off her jacket and props it underneath his head.

"Call an ambulance," Hart says to the uniform, "and remove those cuffs."

It's clear that Garstan is now very unwell. No big surprise, given he was in a psychiatric unit only a few hours earlier. Hart kneels down beside him, trying not to think that this is the second time today he's attended to a dying psychiatrist. Strover leans in close and puts an ear to his chest.

"Anything?" Hart asks.

"Nothing."

"You or me?" Hart asks, but Strover has already started to compress Garstan's chest.

Hart's about to leave his colleague to it, when he takes Garstan's left arm and gently pulls back his tracksuit sleeve. He's wearing a watch.

"Keep it going, Strover," he says, walking back over to the crowd of CSI officers that has gathered in the doorway.

"That's your man," he says to the CSM. "Lying right there. The one who shot Sophie Mills in the cellar. Dr Finn Garstan."

"We've found some traces of apple, on the wall," the CSM says, as they both continue to watch Strover perform CPR on the gravel. It's a surreal sight. For a moment Hart wonders whether he's dreaming again, but then Mel rings him back.

"He's gone, we've lost him," she says. Hart can hear the emotion in her voice as he watches Strover pump away.

"Say a prayer for him," he says, biting his own lip. "He saved my life."

"You need to tell me everything," Mel says. "Including why you've suddenly got religion. And promise me you'll never, ever keep me in the dark like that again."

"I promise."

"What's happening over there anyway?" she asks. "I can hear voices."

"Rory's twin brother has just had a cardiac arrest too. Strover's currently performing CPR in front of me as we speak. An ambulance is on its way."

"Bloody hell, Sile."

He can already hear a siren in the distance, but it's too late. They all know that. Strover stops for a second, listens to his chest, and begins pumping again.

"I think we might have lost him here too," Hart says.

"That's so weird," Mel says, lost in thought.

Hart doesn't want to go there, not now. He's too tired, been exposed to too much dipshittery in recent weeks. The fact that Rory and Finn Garstan appear to have died at the same time is pure coincidence. Nothing to do with psychological resonance. Nothing at all.

There's little the ambulance crew can do when they arrive. Despite Strover's valiant efforts, Finn Garstan is dead. Strover and Hart watch as the crew lift his body carefully onto a trolley.

"Thanks," Hart says to Strover, as the ambulance drives

off without a flashing light. "Not sure I would have tried quite so hard."

"At least he was finally arrested for Sophie's murder," Strover says, breathing heavily from the exertion. "If only for a few minutes."

"And this time not even Ward could save him."

63

Half an hour later, Hart and Strover are back on Marlborough Common. The mist has cleared, but it's even colder than it was this morning. A wind is whipping in from the north, flapping relentlessly at the crime scene tape. Ward is talking to a group of CSI officers and Hart knows he can't put off his boss any longer.

"Silas, Strover," Ward says, coming over to greet them both.

"Afternoon, sir," Strover says. Hart settles for a discreet nod.

"I owe you an apology, Silas," he says, looking around him, less to admire the view than to check that no one else is within earshot. Apologies from Ward are rarer than pothole-free roads in Swindon. "Seems like you were right all along about Dr Finn Garstan – I knew him as Rory, of course."

Even now, he's trying to make excuses.

"I'm not sure there was ever any real proof that he'd murdered Sophie," Hart says, opting for tact. Strover glances at him, clearly surprised by his diplomatic tone. "Not until today."

"But this whole business with his patients in prison, the man who died at the station desk, at the hospital. Horrific. I'm so sorry. You've been pursuing that angle for a while, I gather."

Hart looks across at his CID colleagues chatting with a pair of uniforms, near the start of the parkrun.

"I was going to come to you once we had built a watertight case against him," he says. "Didn't want to waste your precious time. But we were overtaken by events."

"I understand it could have been a lot worse – for you," Ward says. "Needless to say, we're all mighty relieved. Sorry for the real Rory Garstan, of course, a tragedy, but delighted that you're still with us."

As if he cares.

"We're also looking into a possible connection between the governor at HMP Barontrent and Finn Garstan," Hart adds.

"What sort of connection?" Ward asks, showing the first signs of concern.

"Seems like they both might have been Freemasons." Hart takes a breath and starts to walk off. "'*Audi, vide, tace*,' as they say," he calls over his shoulder.

"*Audi, vide, tace* indeed," he hears Ward repeat behind him, unable to disguise the stunned surprise in his voice.

"What was all that about?" Strover asks, catching up with him as they stride out across the common. Hart is keen to revisit where Rory was shot and Trumore's firing point. He already knows that HR will be dragging him off to trauma therapy next week. This is his own way of processing what happened.

"Oh, I was just reminding Ward of one of the Freemasons' favourite Latin mottos," Hart says, trying to sound casual. He'd been memorising the phrase all week. 'Hear, see, be silent.' One thing we won't be doing, Strover."

They walk on, approaching the tree from where Trumore had fired, now part of the crime scene and sealed off with tape. CSI officers are still working at the site, will be for a while.

"You OK, guv?" the CSM asks, coming up to them.

"All good," Hart replies.

"I thought you'd like to know," he says, holding up a plastic evidence bag. "We found another one of these, at the foot of the tree he took the shot from."

Hart takes the bag and looks at it. An hourglass, just like the others. He hands it back, shaking his head.

"Thanks."

It must have helped Garstan's victims to keep focussed on the task in hand, remind them of the sands of time. He and Strover set off again, back down the slope where, a few hours earlier, he thought he would be running a personal best.

"Next week, sir," Strover says, reading his thoughts. "Might even join you. They'll need a good turnout, after all that's happened."

Hart's not sure he can face another parkrun, but Strover's right. It will be good for the community, for him, his family.

"Can I ask you a question, sir?" Strover says, as they near their car.

"Of course."

"Do you now believe in precognition?"

"That sand in an hourglass can flow both ways? The only thing I believe in is that we're all going to croak one day."

"But you were told three years ago that you were going to die today and, well, you very nearly did, sir."

"But I didn't, did I? That's the point. And if I had, I think it would have been premeditated murder rather than precognition, don't you? Just like it was intuition rather than a premonition that made Rory step in front of me. As a twin, he understood the evil his brother was capable of."

He doesn't want to think about the two brothers dying within seconds of each other, not today. Weird, as Mel says. Tragic too. He liked Rory, very much, still can't quite believe that he died to save him. It will take time to process.

"How about your dream, sir? The one about the parkrun. It also very nearly came true."

It's been troubling Hart too, the accuracy of his recurring nightmare.

"I think those dreams reflected my fears, not my future."

They stop by the car. Hart looks around the common, the high chalk hills of the Marlborough Downs beyond. He's pleased they moved here, wants now to get home, spend the weekend with Mel and Conor and Jess, try to explain what happened at 9.09 a.m., apologise for ruining their day, for not warning them. For putting them in such danger.

"Here's the thing, Strover," he says, turning his collar up against a sudden gust of bitter wind. "You and I – you know what our job is, here in beautiful Wiltshire? It's to deal in criminal cases, not crystal balls."

Acknowledgements

Many thanks to my superlative agent, Will Francis, and his team at Janklow and Nesbit; and to Bethan Jones, my excellent editor, Anouska Levy and everyone at Head of Zeus. My early readers, Libby, Cameron, Alex Tait, Nita and Peter Mitchell-Heggs, and JP Sheerin, who all provided invaluable, expert feedback (precognition, mushrooms, motives, medical knowledge and storytelling); Andrew Rumsey for sharing his Jonah wisdom; Stephen Gooder for bike chat; Andy Beale for oxygen levels and takotsubo syndrome; Jonathan Rigby for the maths; Simon Fowler for prisoner location advice; The Royal Literary Fund and Marlborough LitFest for their ongoing support; and the late Canon Harold Blair, for introducing me, as a teenager, to *An Experiment with Time* by J.W. Dunne (A & C Black, 1927). *Scared to Death: An Examination of Fear, its Cause and Effects*, by J.C. Barker (Frederick Muller, 1968) and *The Premonitions Bureau* by Sam Knight (Faber & Faber, 2022) were also essential reading during my research. I recommend them both. As I do the Marlborough parkrun – and parkruns everywhere. The volunteers do an amazing job. (At the time of writing, 25 minutes still eludes me...) Finally, special thanks to my wonderful wife Hilary, my first and best reader, for her patience, humour and love; and to our daughter Maya, and sons Felix and Jago, for their eternal optimism and encouragement.

About the Author

J.S. Monroe is the author of six psychological thrillers, including *Find Me*, an international bestseller that's been translated into 14 languages. Writing under Jon Stock, his own name, he is also the author of five espionage novels, including *Dead Spy Running*, which was optioned by Warner Bros, and *The Sleep Room*, a non-fiction book about the controversial psychiatrist Dr William Sargant. Jon worked as a foreign correspondent in Delhi and was Weekend editor of the *Daily Telegraph* in London before becoming a full-time author in 2015. He lives in Wiltshire with his wife, Hilary Stock, a fine art photographer, and is currently a Royal Literary Fund Bridge Fellow, as well as a vice chair of Marlborough LitFest.

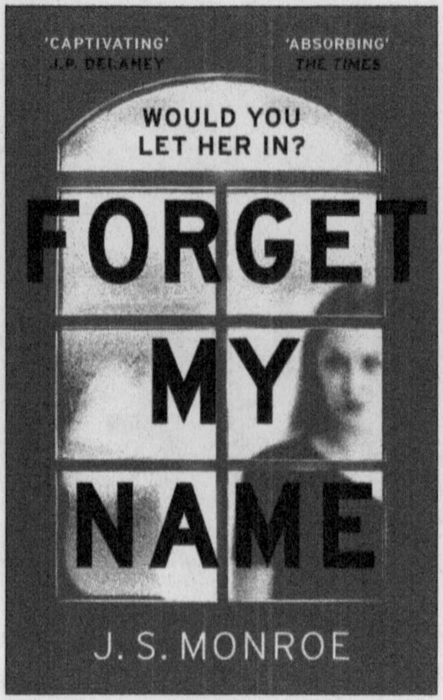

'An absorbing novel full of unpredictable twists'

THE TIMES

'A book that will send chills down your spine'

SUNDAY EXPRESS

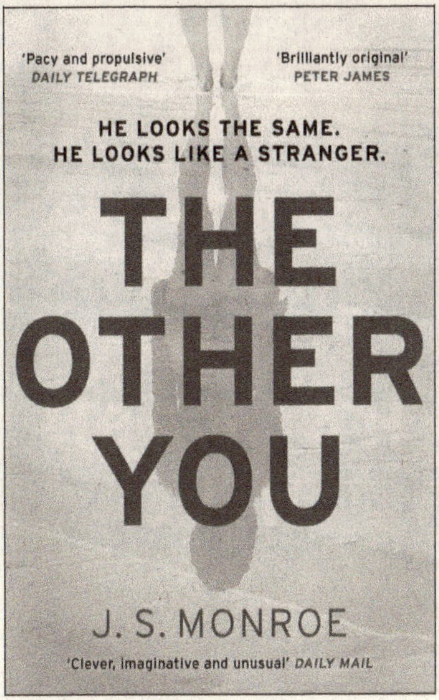

'You won't be able to turn the pages fast enough'

HEAT

'Kept me guessing to the very end'

PETER JAMES

'Not so much a twist but a seismic shifting of the ground under your feet'

ROSAMUND LUPTON

'An impressive twisty tale'

INDEPENDENT

'Highly recommended'

MICK HERRON

'*The Secret History* meets *The Capture*'

JP DELANEY